Dream of Me
Book 1, The Dream Makers Series
Quinn Loftis

Published by Quinn Loftis Books LLC

W0007301

Dedication

For Bo. Thank you for making all my dreams
come true.

Acknowledgments

For everyone who has believed in me, stuck by
me, encouraged me, helped me and listened to all
my worries that this book wouldn't be good
enough. I truly hope I prove myself wrong. Thank
you truly from the deepest part of my heart for
reading my books. I can't imagine a greater
compliment than to know you took your time to sit
down and immerse yourself in the world and
characters I tried so very hard to make enjoyable. I
hope I meet and exceed your expectations, and if I
do not I promise to try even harder on the next
book.

"In the evening, while the children are seated at the table or in their little chairs, he comes up the stairs very softly, for he walks in his socks, then he opens the doors without the slightest noise, and throws a small quantity of very fine dust in their eyes, just enough to prevent them from keeping them open, so they do not see him. Then he creeps behind them, and blows softly upon their necks, till their heads begin to droop. [...] Under each arm he carries an umbrella; one of them, with pictures on the inside, he spreads over the good children, and then they dream the most beautiful stories the whole night." ~ Hans Christian Anderson

Dair was pretty sure that if ever an angel had an equal on earth, Sarah Serenity Tillman was it. He watched her as she carried boxes, helped organize each booth for the sale, and brought plates of food to everyone after having taken it upon herself to order and pay, though no one realized she had, for the pizza. She appeared tireless. After five hours of helping three churches put together a large fundraising craft fair/bake sale, Serenity still had a smile on her face. She was asked the same question by every elderly lady with purple hair in the county, and with each one she patted their arm, smiled warmly, and answered with just as much patience as she had the very first time. Dair was just waiting for the moment when she finally threw her hands in the air and said to hell with it, the way most would have. But as he watched her get into her car waving at the pastor's wife and telling her she would be back at 6:00 a.m. to help tomorrow, he realized that Serenity was not *most* people. She was something else and he wanted to know more. Not just because she was his next assignment but because she was different and he wanted to know why.

The next day, she did just as she said she would. She was the first one at the building to help with the fundraiser. After lunch she told a lady named Pearl, apparently the person in charge of the entire event, that she needed to leave. She apologized profusely and then explained that she had volunteered to help her aunt decorate the library for Christmas, to get the Angel tree organized, and to wrap the gift boxes for the presents they were sending overseas to the soldiers still stationed there.

"I truly am sorry, Mrs. Pearl," Serenity said sweetly. "I didn't realize I had overbooked myself."

"You go on, honey," Pearl waved her off. "You've done more than enough. I think we can handle it from here. Thank you for everything."

"It wasn't a problem. I'm glad I could help."

Dair had watched as she decorated the library, made posters for the canned food drive and Angel tree, and then wrapped twenty small boxes that people could take and fill with things to send the soldiers. The entire time she talked happily with her aunt, Darla, who might be the only person as angelic as Serenity. They sang Christmas hymns and told stories of memories from the previous year's Angel tree event. Not once did she complain that her feet hurt, or that she was tired, or that she had had to smile so much in the past two days that she was sure her face would split in half. Her kindness was contagious, Dair noticed, because people smiled when they saw her coming. They went out of their way to wave at her or stop and talk to her, and he could tell that they genuinely liked Serenity.

He could have finished this job days ago, but he continued to observe her daily life for a week. The only time that Serenity ever allowed her weariness, worries, or any emotion other than care and kindness, to show was in the privacy of her room and only to her cat, Mr. Whitherby. It was in those times when the house was quiet and still that she would pour out her heart to her faithful, but cantankerous, feline sounding board. It was also during those times that Dair truly got to know and begin to understand Serenity Tillman.

He had been weaving the dream every night for the past four nights, while silently watching her during the day. And still after four days he had yet to get the entirety of the dream into her mind. It was on that particular night that he felt the burden of his position for the first time in a very, very long time. He listened to her talking to Mr. Whitherby, and his soul shrank at the frustration and hint of fear he heard there.

"I've never been afraid to go to sleep before, Mr. Whitherby," she told the large cat that lay in her lap flicking his tail as he purred under her attentive petting. Her hands stroked down his back over and over in a methodical rhythm. "It's not necessarily that the dream is scary. It's just that it is not what is supposed to happen; it's not what I want for my life. I feel so selfish for wanting out, especially when I've allowed others in this town to rely on me." She paused and took a deep breath letting out a long sigh. "I've already told Mrs. Brown that I can't look after her dog on Tuesdays, and I've told the Humane Society that I won't be there every other Saturday anymore, and yesterday I called the afterschool program at the elementary school and told them I couldn't be a mentor any longer. Maybe I'm stopping all these things too soon, but I just want to have a clean break when it's time for me to leave. Is that selfish of me, Mr. Whitherby?"

No, that's human of you, Dair thought to himself. Didn't she see that she couldn't just take care of everyone else all the time? Didn't she know that eventually everyone else would drain every little drop from her without ever wondering if Sarah was being taken care of? There was no doubt that Serenity's Aunt Darla and Uncle Wayne loved her, and would do anything for her, but they couldn't meet all of her needs. They couldn't fill every void inside of her.

If Dair was honest with himself, he would admit that he wanted her with a passion he had never felt before. As the ocean's tide was drawn to the bank and helpless to deny the pull of the moon's call, so he was drawn to her. The human female had no idea he even existed, and yet he longed for her to see him, know him, and want him as he wanted her.

In that moment, as she stared at her cat and her weary eyes filled with tears, Dair realized that he wanted to be the one to meet those needs. He wanted to be the one to take care of her when she refused to take care of herself. But though she fascinated him, this Sarah Serenity Tillman, he had a job to do. And this fascination was one that he could not afford. It didn't matter that his feelings had grown beyond her being an assignment for the Sandman. She was human; he was something more than human. His kind were never to mix with the Creator's children, and yet Brudair could not deny his need to see her, be with her, and know more and more about her.

When she finally drifted off to sleep hours later, she wasn't aware of his presence. Instead she was lost in her dreams—dreams that he helped create. That was what he did. He was the Sandman, after all, and dreams were his specialty. His name, Brudair, was Scottish Gaelic that literally meant *dream*, though the messengers of the Creator often simply called him Dair. Humans had heard of him, of course, but they thought of him as a myth, like the tooth fairy. They even had stories about him and his job as the Sandman but they were way, *way* off. Oh, he did give dreams but not to everyone and not only to children as the human myth implied. No, his job was much more important than just making sure that children had pleasant dreams.

The Sandman's job was to go to the people designated to him by the Creator and influence their dreams for the Creator's plan. These people were not just everyday Joes. The people on the list were people who would influence the course of history, usually in some major way. They would save a life, lead a country, start or end a war, or perhaps find the cure to a deadly illness. They were game changers and it was Dair's job to help influence them to move in the direction the Creator wanted them to go. His dreams did not guarantee that the humans would follow because they had free will. They were able to make their own decisions about the direction of their lives. He could no more force them to do as his dreams suggest than he could turn himself into a human. There were times in his long existence that he wished he could just tell the humans he visited why they must go a certain direction in their lives, but that was not his place. And he didn't always know the full plan of the Creator.

So, since the beginning of time, he, the Sandman,

aka Brudair, had been casting dreams. His life was one of solitude, his only interactions being with the messengers of the Creator and inside the minds of the humans he visited. He had never been bothered by this existence—had never questioned the Creator's design for his role in the human world. Not until now. Not until her.

The very first night he had come to her, she had drawn him in by her gentle spirit. He had watched her interact with her family and seen the selfless way in which she helped them. Dair had seen her fret over her future because she didn't want to leave those she loved, even though she so desperately wanted to get out of the small town where she grew up. He had listened to her pour out her heart to her cat, who followed her around like a loyal dog. She shared all of the worries that she quietly bore. But it was the times that he had seen into her mind while she slept that she had become even more alluring. She was so very in tune with her thoughts, even while asleep, that he had had to be very subtle about his suggestions. She seemed to question her own dreams while slumbering. Questioning was rare, and also troublesome, because it often caused the human to wake up before the dream could take root. Serenity, as she liked to be called—he had learned from his completely unabashed spying—was making his job take longer than normal because he had yet to plant a full, complete dream in her mind.

She stirred, drawing his thoughts back to the present, and he found, as he stared down at her, that he didn't mind at all that his job was taking longer than normal. He wasn't ready to move on to the next human. Dair wanted—no, he needed—more time with her. He longed to know more about her, to hear her voice, and to watch her live selflessly, putting others' needs before her own. She baffled him because of her behavior. It wasn't normal for a human to think of others first. From his long, long time in the world he had seen how self-serving the human race could be, and Serenity truly was a diamond in the rough on that rock called earth.

"Sleep, Princess of Peace," he whispered to her. "Let go of all those burdens you bear and listen to the tale I weave." He took a step closer, and another, until he was standing right beside her. It was too close, and yet not close enough. He hummed as he entered her mind with his own and began to build the dream once again.

Dair tried to create the thoughts in such a way that she would believe they were created by her own subconscious. He gave her very subtle suggestions and for a few minutes he thought that perhaps she was finally going to accept that there was nothing strange about the dream she was having. But as she rolled over onto her back and pushed the hair from her face, he knew she was already beginning to wake. Her eyelids fluttered several times before finally rising, revealing startling sea green eyes. Her eyes seemed to meet his but he knew that couldn't be because she couldn't see him, not unless he truly wanted her to. She blew out a deep breath and rubbed the sleep from her eyes. Then, as she had done every night he had woken her up, Serenity reached for the notebook on her bedside table and began to write down her thoughts about the dream. The pages of the notebook crinkled as she flipped to the next empty page. Then the only sound in the room was the scratching of the pen as she wrote about the things he had planted in her mind.

"You're a determined one; I'll give you that," he told her, regardless of the fact that she couldn't hear him. Dair knew that she wouldn't be going back to sleep anytime soon so he took a seat in the chair at her desk and watched as she turn her head, deep in thought. As minutes turned into an hour, he considered that perhaps he should get some sort of hobby for times such as this when he was simply waiting. But then he thought that such a thing might distract him from Serenity.

"That's sort of the point, you stalker," he grumbled to himself. But, stalker or not, he didn't leave and he knew he wouldn't. Instead, he would sit there, watching and wishing that he could reveal himself to her. Dair knew that would never happen, but for once he allowed himself to dream. Though he did not require sleep, he submitted himself to day dreams filled with sea green eyes and a voice that spoke to the empty places inside of him.

"It can't be normal," Serenity said as she looked over at her faithful cat. She reached over and scratched him under his chin, much to his delight as she continued to talk to him. "I just can't believe that my mind is coming up with these ideas. There has to be another explanation." When she pulled her hand away from the feline, he stood and arched his back, stretching as only a cat could. Then he walked gracefully over to her only to then ungracefully plop himself onto her lap over the notebook in which she had been scribbling.

"Demanding much, Mr. Whitherby?" Serenity asked the male cat. He gave her a look that Dair could only interpret as *get over it*, and then he proceeded to lick his paws and clean his face. "Well, don't let me interrupt your bath while I try to figure out how on earth I'm having dreams that I think are telling me to stay in this small town—this town that I would practically give my right arm to get out of." Mr. Whitherby made a grunting noise that caused Serenity to smile which, in turn, caused Dair's breath to catch in his chest as he stared at her.

Serenity had a smile that could make a man want to move mountains for her. It was all innocence and joy wrapped up and surrounded by love. She was a girl who truly knew how to love without strings attached and that love came bursting through when she smiled.

"I want to make you smile like that," Dair told her. There was no response and his heart broke a little more, just as it had done each day he had returned. The life she represented was not for him and being near her only made him want it more. He needed to leave her, but as he listened to her laugh and saw the life that danced in her eyes, he didn't know if leaving was something he could do. The idea of never seeing her again, of not being able to be a part of her life, caused such pain that he didn't know how to cope. Dair was so unexperienced with the emotions running through him, there were times when they threatened to overwhelm him. The only thing keeping him grounded was Serenity's calm demeanor. As he finally stood to go, he walked over to her, leaned down, and pressed a kiss to the top of her head. It was the second time he dared to do it, and he found that he would endure many horrific things just for one real touch. For one touch that she could feel from him, and one that he could feel from her, he would face any punishment that would be sure to come his way.

"Goodnight, Sarah Serenity," he said gently as he

walked to the closed window and began to step through it as if it were open to the outside world. He looked back one more time at the girl who held him captive. "I wish you could dream of me. I would dream of you if I were capable of such a thing."

Chapter 1

"Indeed God speaks once, or twice, yet no one notices it. In a dream, in a vision of the night, when sound sleep falls on men while they slumber in their beds, then He opens the ears of men, and seals their instruction." Job 33:14-16

S erenity stared out of her window as she watched the sun begin to break over the horizon—the reminder that once again she hadn't been able to sleep past sunrise. The disturbing dream had started four nights ago. Well, *disturbing* wasn't really the right word. There was nothing disturbing about the actual content of the dream. There were no monsters or terrible falls or anything like that. Rather, in the dream, Serenity was nineteen, though how she knew that little fact she didn't have a clue, but she was sure of it. Despite being nineteen, she was *still* living in Yellville, Arkansas, the tiny town of 1,204 people nestled in the Ozark Mountains. This disturbed her greatly. It wasn't that she didn't *like* the town. It was just that she felt as though the rest of the world was moving on, growing, and changing while she stayed stuck in the little quaint town in the middle of nowhere. She was eighteen and only five months from graduating from high school. And regardless of the persistent dream, she had no intentions of staying. There was a part of her that felt so very guilty for leaving when she had so many responsibilities, most of which she had yet to relinquish. She was attempting to prepare not only herself but also those in the community for her departure.

Serenity had not come to the decision to leave easily. She hated to leave her Aunt Darla and Uncle Wayne. They had raised her since she was nine after her parent's death, and they had been nothing short of amazing. She worked a part time job to help them make ends meet because there weren't a whole lot of riches to be had in Yellville unless you came to it with your pockets already lined. Serenity didn't want to put them in a tight spot by leaving, but she also didn't think she could spend the rest of her life in the small town. She wanted to see the world, to experience things that she never would in the mountains of Arkansas. Her attention was drawn away from the golden rays of the morning sun when she felt Mr. Whitherby, her obnoxious albeit strangely comforting cat, winding himself around her legs. She looked down at him and couldn't help but smile at the huge fuzz ball.

"Another day in paradise, Mr. W," Serenity told him as she reached down and scratched behind his ears. He made a swipe for her hand when she pulled away but, being clawless, caused no harm. "I can't sit around and pamper you all day no matter how much attitude you give me. I've got things to do, people to see." Her cat plopped down on his haunches and stared up at her with an almost bored expression. She laughed. "Okay, so maybe there isn't really much to do, but I do have school and then work, so make yourself useful and go fix me some breakfast." Of course, he didn't do anything other than yawn and flop over on his side, making it perfectly clear just how unimportant her day was to him. Serenity shook her head at the defiant little beast and headed for the shower.

"Made your favorite," Aunt Darla said as Serenity

entered the eat-in kitchen—showered, clean and dressed—way too early if she did so say herself. "Cheese and ham croissants. Your uncle is already gone; he's going to help hunt down a mountain lion that is killing the Thompson's goats. They've planned to be out overnight and then go to Bill's house for supplies before they head out again." During the summer months, Wayne was a guide on the White river. But not just a guide, he was one of the best. Wealthy people from all over the world came to Cotter Trout dock to get to spend a few days on the river in hopes of catching *the big one* with Uncle Wayne. She'd been out with him a couple of times, and though some girls her age might think being on a fishing boat for hours on end would be boring and tedious, it was anything but with Uncle Wayne as the guide. He was one of those people that could make anyone feel at ease. His easy going attitude and ability to talk to just about anyone made him very likable. Not to mention he had a certain love of dirty jokes and was eager to share his material on new, unsuspecting victims. Serenity was beginning to believe he liked the shock factor as much as he liked delivering the punch line. During the winter months, when the fishing season slowed down, he did odd jobs. Sometimes he cut firewood or helped others with their goat or cattle herds. He stayed busy to be sure.

"So they're going to be out in the cold overnight?" Serenity asked.

"They gotta do whatever they can to kill whatever is killing off his goats. That's the Thompson's livelihood; every goat killed represents bills not paid," Darla told her. "I'm going to get dressed; don't leave without saying goodbye."

Serenity gave her a 'thumbs up' as she filled her

plate with the wonderful goodness that was her aunt's cooking, too focused on her food to turn and look up at her. She was amazed that they weren't all severely overweight because her aunt was a firm believer in feeding anyone and everyone as often as possible. Homemade food was her version of a hug and it didn't hurt that she was a fantastic cook. Twenty minutes later Darla reemerged dressed as cave woman.

"Story time today?" Serenity asked around a bite of croissant.

Darla nodded. "Favorite day of the week." She smiled warmly and Serenity loved knowing that her aunt enjoyed her job so much. She had worked multiple jobs most of her life, not having any time for herself. But since she had begun working at the Marion County Library, she had been able to quit her other jobs, and Serenity had seen a distinct change in her aunt's demeanor. Suddenly, she was bright and eager for the day because she truly enjoyed her job—not just because it was the only way she could get through the long days.

"What's the story today?"

Darla began washing the dishes left over from making breakfast as she spoke. "It's a book version of the Disney movie, *The Croods*. Have you seen that movie? It's so hilarious."

"No, I haven't seen that one, but I've heard it's good," Serenity admitted.

Darla turned and looked at her as she wiped her hands off with the dish towel. "You work too hard for someone your age, Sarah Serenity." Her aunt had a habit of calling her by her first and middle name. Serenity had decided it was a Southern thing. "Why don't you cut back on your hours at the vet clinic? I know you think we can't get by without the money that you contribute, but we'll be alright."

Serenity shook her head. "I don't want to cut back on my hours. I love working with the animals. There's no drama with animals and they love unconditionally."

"I imagine that college boy that just started working there isn't hard on the eyes either," Darla said with a grin.

"Please," she huffed. "I don't have time for the nonsense called boys."

The look Darla gave her told her that she didn't quite believe her. In truth, Serenity just hadn't found anyone that she would want to put the energy into that a relationship takes. Sure she noticed good looking guys, and Darla was right, Jackson, who had started working two months ago at the vet clinic where she worked, was definitely easy on the eyes. But other than that, he did nothing for her. She wasn't willing to give her heart to anyone who didn't make mountains move for her. She wanted the heart pounding, toe tingling, stomach dropping kind of attraction that took her breath away every time he walked into the room. Until that happened, she was not available for any type of relationship with the opposite sex.

"Okay well, have a good day and be safe." Darla gave her a quick hug before heading out.

"Have fun being a Crood," she hollered over her shoulder. Serenity glanced at her phone for the time and saw that she still had an hour to kill before she would need to leave for school. She let out a low sigh as she slumped down in her chair. She was tired. The lack of sleep caused by the dream was definitely beginning to catch up with her. But she didn't know how to make it go away. She'd never given much thought to dreams and whether or not they actually meant something or were simply the result of an unconscious mind being given free reign during slumber. Perhaps, it was time to do some research on dreams. She did know there were many religions that believed very firmly in the idea that dreams could be prophetic. Even in the Bible she read dreams had often been a message from God to his people. She'd been raised with a Christian background, and while she was still attempting to find where she stood in her own faith, she figured a book that had been around for a couple thousand years might have something important to say about the subject. She decided she would include it in her research along with some other sources. Unfortunately, she would have to wait until she could use the internet at the school or library because her aunt and uncle's house was far enough out that the only internet they could get was dial up. She snorted out a laugh as she considered her aunt doing the cave woman look and how appropriate it was considering the distance their house was from civilization. It often made her feel like they lived in the Stone Ages.

Serenity pulled into the parking lot of the high school and sat staring as her classmates filed into the school. The bitter cold of the December mountain air was enough to keep her from wanting to leave the comfy warmth of her car. She had five months until she graduated—five more months of teachers, high school drama, and terrible cafeteria food, though that was her own fault because she was too lazy to make her own lunch and unwilling to let her aunt make it for her. She was eighteen for cripes sake; it would make her feel like a bum if her aunt was making her lunches. Serenity rubbed her eyes, attempting to push away the drowsiness, still battling the sleepiness that threatened to overtake her. The warm air blowing from the car vents wasn't helping. Finally with a resigned sigh, she grabbed her book bag and climbed out into the frosty winter air. It stung her lungs and immediately did the job of waking her up. She knew she had better have her wits about her if she wanted to navigate the ice covered parking lot without ending up as the morning entertainment. It never failed that at least once or twice a week one of the students ended up on their backsides like an overturned turtle with their limbs flailing in the air as they skidded across the ice. Most took the good natured ribbing given by their classmates pretty well, laughing along with them. Frankly, when your tailbone hit that ice it was either laugh or cry because you instantly felt a distinct kind of pain, which was often accompanied by a string of curse words.

As she entered the building, having made an uneventful trek through the parking lot, Serenity headed for her locker nodding to several of her friends. She hadn't grown very close to any of them because her time had been so limited over the course of her high school career. As soon as she had learned to drive she had started working, volunteering, and helping as much as possible. Deep down she thought her desire to help others was her penance, a debt owed because of the death of her parents. She wondered if they had been taken from her so soon before their time because of something she'd done, or not done. Perhaps, God was punishing her for not being good enough, for not obeying more, or for not being the model daughter she could have been. Because of her lack of involvement at her school, she didn't have a best friend that went to her school. Her best friend had already graduated and was now twenty-two years old and working at the local tourist-attracting restaurant called The Fireside Restaurant and Mountain Store. Serenity had met Glorious Day, and yes that was really her name, one day at the library when Glory had been looking for books on Multiple Sclerosis. Her mother had been diagnosed with the devastating disease and Glory and her father were her caretakers. Glory and she had immediately hit it off despite the four year age difference. Since then they had hung out as often as possible and texted relentlessly. With Glory she had finally found someone she could be completely herself with. Glory accepted her no matter what. Serenity knew her aunt and uncle did as well but it was different with them. She felt like they had to love her because they were sort of her parents, and didn't parents have to love their children unconditionally? But Glory didn't have to, yet she did anyway. Although she loved Glory like a sister, she also desperately wanted to escape the fate that had been given to her best friend. Glory was stuck. She would live in Yellville probably for the rest of her life. The idea made Serenity feel trapped and if she thought about it too long, she would begin to feel like the walls were closing in around her. Serenity never mentioned it to Glory because she didn't want to hurt her, but every now and then she would see the sadness in her friend because she too knew that she wouldn't be going on any grand adventures. Glory didn't hold it against her mother. She loved her mom and was completely willing to help take care of her, but Serenity knew that it still wasn't enough to take the sting away from the lack of a future ahead of Glorious.

The rest of her day was as uneventful as her walk from her car to the front doors that morning. She didn't have much homework, which was a definite plus considering she was desperate to do some research on her dream. Her phone rang as she was climbing into her car, and she searched through her bag until she found it.

"How goes the wonderful world of waitressing?" she asked Glory.

"Let's just say that it's a good thing you chose the vet because, girl, you could not handle the excitement that goes on at the fire pit." Glory had nicknamed the restaurant *the fire pit* after the massive fire place that took up one whole wall of the dining area got out of hand one day after a waiter had dropped a grease filled bucket on it when he tripped on the leg of a chair. They had managed to get the fire out before it did too much damage, but from that day forward the Fireside Restaurant was deemed the fire pit.

"Let me guess," Serenity said as she considered the many scenarios that had previously happened to her friend. "One of the male tourists got handsy with you when you offered him some pie? Or perhaps Shelia finally fell out of one of those low cut tops she's always wearing while she was bending over after she conveniently *dropped* the silverware in front of the male customers?"

Glory laughed. "I think I've shared way too much with you about the goings-on of the pit if those are the things you think of first."

"Well, if it isn't one of those then it's hardly worth mentioning," Serenity teased.

"Then I guess I don't need to tell you that Tommy Peaping hit on Shelia, and she accidently spilled his water on his head."

Serenity let out a bark of laughter. "Awe man, poor

Tommy Peepers," she breathed out using the nick name that everyone in town had used for him for as long as she could remember. "When is he going to learn that girls like Sheila only go for a certain type of guy, and it isn't guys with names like Tommy Peaping?"

"Well, I don't feel sorry for him. What do I always say? The definition of insanity…"

"Yeah, yeah I know…doing the same thing over and over again and expecting different results," she finished for her.

"It's true. He keeps hitting on that hoochie thinking she's suddenly going to think he's the best thing since tampons but it isn't going to happen."

"Maybe he likes the abuse," Serenity pointed out.

"Maybe so. Whatever the reason, it keeps the customers entertained. You headed to the flea hospital?"

Serenity rolled her eyes at her friend's quirkiness. Serenity guessed she came up with nicknames for just about everything in an attempt to entertain herself. "Yep," she answered giving the 'p' a slight pop as she finished the word. "I'm going to try and get off a little early because I want to hit up the library before it closes."

"Why on earth would you hit up the library? They definitely don't have any money to be taken. If you're going to rob someplace, at least go for something worth your time, like the armored truck that goes to the bank each week."

"I'm not going to even ask why you have thought of something like that, Glory."

"Puuhlease, you're the one who said you were going to hit up the library," Glory pointed out.

"You must be exceptionally bored if you are

turning my statements into absurd scenarios," Serenity pointed out. "Why don't you come to the vet and help out. You'd get to meet Jackson."

"Hmm, tempting, because you know I completely appreciate the hotness of the opposite sex, and he seems to be the talk of the town since he moved here a few months ago. But, I just don't feel like attempting to put on the whole happy face, notice me, let me try to convince you *I'm the greatest girl you'll ever meet* front. It's exhausting."

"One of these days you're going to have to put yourself out there. You can't hide forever." Serenity had to admit that part of the reason she wanted Glory to find a man was because she was leaving, and she didn't want her best friend to be alone once she was gone.

"Okay, enough counseling for one conversation. Get your butt to work and try not to drool too much over your fellow flea lover."

"Bye, Glorious," Serenity chuckled when her friend growled at her for using her full name; she hated that.

Dair followed Serenity from her school to the veterinary clinic where she worked. Being who he was, and what he was, had its perks when it came to travel. He didn't need a car. Dair had the ability to will himself to the location he wanted. It was known as 'transporting' in the spiritual realm. As he continued on the path that her car was taking, he told himself it was because he wanted to keep her safe. If you asked him from what, well, he really couldn't tell you. He hadn't been informed of any immediate danger to Serenity, but there was always life itself. She could be in a wreck or be hurt by some crazy human, of which he knew plenty because he had been in some depraved minds over the decades. She was so fragile, so mortal, and she didn't even know it, or if she did she didn't pay any heed to it. *What do you expect her to do, Dair, surround herself in bubble wrap and never leave her house?* he asked himself. He supposed that option wasn't really feasible, but he wouldn't deny that the idea had its merit.

Dair trailed her into the clinic, unseen by anyone or anything, until the cat that was lying on the bench in the waiting area hissed at him. He had found that some animals were more sensitive to the spiritual world and could actually detect him, if not see him outright. Other animals' reactions were often just as unfriendly as the cat's because they sometimes felt that he was something that should not be there. He waved his hand in front of the feline's face and the animal quieted immediately and then drifted off to sleep. *Sleep dust indeed*, he chuckled to himself.

"Hey, Serenity." A deep voice drew Dair's attention from the sleeping cat. His eyes narrowed on the boy named Jackson. Dair had discovered something new about himself, which was a feat in and of itself considering how old he was. He had realized that jealousy was an emotion that he was not immune to. From the moment he saw the way Jackson looked at Serenity, a possessive—almost animalistic—need to claim her came over him. He didn't like the gleam in the human's eyes or the way he smiled at her or talked to her. Okay, so he didn't like that he breathed air in the same vicinity as Serenity. Perhaps, he was a tad out of control when it came to this new emotion of jealousy.

"Hey, Jackson." Serenity smiled at the boy and Dair ground his teeth together. "How is Mrs. Green's dog doing today?"

Jackson took a step closer to her and then leaned casually on the counter where the human owners checked in their animals. *Not a step further,* Dair thought and fought the desire to plant the words in the boy's head. He could only imagine the look on his face when he heard Dair's voice in his mind. And he found that he took a little too much pleasure in inducing fear in the male.

"Layla is doing better," Jackson answered. "She's even gone outside twice without having to be carried."

"That's great!" Serenity smiled. She was just too damn nice and naïve for her own good. Jackson's smile widened as he took in what Dair knew he was seeing— the sheer beauty of the woman before them. Dair could see the intent in Jackson's eyes before he even began to speak. *The fool was going to ask her out,* he thought. "Not today you're not," Dair said as he walked towards Jackson until he was just beside him. He leaned forward and allowed his invisibility to drop just enough that Jackson would hear his voice.

"You will only see Serenity as a friend. She is not for you. You will not ask her on a date," he whispered and allowed his power of influence to lace his words. It was underhanded, not to mention strictly forbidden for him to influence a human for selfish reasons, but this time the rules didn't seem to stop him. Dair watched as Jackson stiffened. Shock, and then fear, and then confusion, came over his face. Finally, he looked back at Serenity who was watching him with wide eyes and her head tilted slightly.

"Are you okay?" she asked him.

Jackson nodded. "I'm fine. . .just thought I heard something, but it must have been the dogs barking or something." Without another word he turned and hurried towards the back of the building where the kennels were located.

Dair should have felt remorseful over his interference, but as he watched Serenity hum as she cleaned the front part of the clinic, alone, without any males drooling after her, he couldn't bring himself to be the least bit repentant. He had told Jackson that she was not for the human and he had meant it. Serenity was meant for him, whether it was forbidden or not; he knew with absolute certainty she was his perfect counterpart. The idea of her with someone else did not bring Dair pleasant thoughts. In fact, the sort of thoughts it induced might be considered dangerous. As long as Jackson kept his hands, eyes, and desires to himself, he would be safe from the Sandman's wrath. But if he pursued Serenity, then Jackson just might find himself having the kind of night terrors that could cause a grown man to wet the bed.

Chapter 2

"To dream of aliens or UFOs means that you should be wary of new people. They may have your best interests at heart, but they may also want to probe you."

Serenity's eyes began to glaze over after a couple hours in front of the computer. She had left the vet clinic early, after two very strange hours of working with Jackson, and come straight to the library. When she had asked Jackson if he minded that she leave early, he almost seemed relieved to be rid of her. *Whatever,* she thought. It wasn't like she was interested in him. She had bigger things to worry about, like a recurring dream. But after two hours surfing the internet, she was coming up empty. Sure, she found plenty of website that claimed they could interpret her dream. All she had to do was type it in the box, and some little analyzer would spit out an explanation. But she felt like there had to be more to it than that. She felt that dreams were an incredibly personal thing, and she believed from what she had read in her Bible, that they were also sacred—used by God as a form of communication to His people. This alone made her believe that there was no way a computer could analyze her dream, much less give her anything close to an accurate interpretation.

"Closing time, kiddo," Aunt Darla called to her from the front desk of the library.

"Okay, I'm coming." She closed the internet

browser and gathered her things, feeling utterly discouraged and dreading going to sleep. She didn't want to revisit the dream again. She didn't want to face a future that was anything less than what she had planned for herself. The dream was the complete opposite of what she wanted—what she had already planned to do once she graduated.

Serenity walked out with her aunt and the other ladies that worked at the library and waved to them as they got in their cars.

"I'll see you at the house," Darla told her. Serenity noticed the weariness in her aunt's eyes and frowned. "Aunt Darla, is there anything I can do for you? Any way I can help at home or the library?"

Darla smiled at her and walked back to her giving her a tight hug. "You aren't supposed to be worrying about me; you're the teenager remember. You're supposed to be going to parties, crying over boys, and falling asleep in class because you stayed up way too late reading the latest teen romance novel."

"Oh, is that how a teenager acts? I didn't realize; I'll be sure and make those changes for you," Serenity teased.

Her aunt's face grew serious. "Thank you for asking, but really I'm fine. Just tired."

Serenity nodded and watched her aunt get in her car before she climbed into her own. Trusting that her aunt was being honest with her, she pushed away her concern and focused on the mystery that continued to plague her. The entire drive home her mind was sifting through the information she had read on the internet, hoping to find something that might help. But regardless of how many times she recited the information to herself, it didn't change the content of it, and the content was completely unhelpful to her.

Her evening consisted of a quick dinner with her aunt and then homework, a shower, teeth brushing, and finally the dreaded walk to her bed. Only a little over a week ago, she had seen her bed as a haven to escape into sleep from the worries and stress of the world, but now it was a prison. It held her captive, as the rest her body required forced her to relive the dream, and none of her attempts to change the dream had been effective. It was almost as if someone else was controlling it. She shivered at that thought as she pulled back the comforter and slipped beneath the cool sheets. That was a feeling she had always loved—the first moment of getting into bed when the sheets weren't yet warm from her body and the cool fabric eased the tension from tired muscles. Now it only caused her to shiver as she prepared herself to allow sleep to pull her under.

Serenity knew she was asleep, even as she was blinking her eyes open. She looked around her and, once again, she found herself sitting in the waiting room of her family doctor. There were a few other adults sitting in the room, and on the far side of the room, a young girl of about seven or eight years of age was standing, staring at the large aquarium that took up most of the wall. She had smooth, ebony skin and her hair was pulled back in a tight braid that hung down her back in a shiny rope. Serenity had the distinct impression that she needed to talk to the girl, but just like the other times in the dream, she resisted. Something about the child felt ominous, and Serenity didn't want to know what it was. All of a sudden the heads of everyone in the room snapped up and looked straight at her. She turned to her right to see that even Darla was staring at her. The only one not looking at her was the little girl.

"You must stay," they all said in unison. Serenity was sure that at any moment the music from Psycho would begin playing over the loud speaker instead of the local Christian radio station that the office usually piped in. "Your place is here. You are needed. The future depends on the path you will choose."

"Oh, for goodness sakes, are you trying to scare her half to death?" To Serenity's surprise, the girl was the one who had spoken. She had turned around and was looking up at the ceiling as if it would speak back. "For someone who has been doing this for as long as you have, you'd think you could be a little less creepy."

"Who are you talking to?" Serenity asked.

The girl's head lowered and kind hazel eyes met her own. She smiled at her and Serenity found herself smiling back.

"The Sandman, of course," the girl told her matter-of-fact like. She walked over to the seat on her left and sat down with her legs dangling freely in the air. "I'm Emma," the girl said as she held out her hand to Serenity.

Serenity took the offered hand and shook it, noting how much smaller it was than hers. "Nice to meet you, Emma; I'm Serenity."

"You don't have to do what they say—what he," she motioned up to the ceiling, "is trying to influence you to do."

"You mean the Sandman?" Serenity asked. Her interest had been peaked the moment Emma had mentioned the mythical character, and she wondered if the need to know if he was real made her just a bit loony.

Emma nodded. "Who do you think brings the dreams?"

"But how does he give dreams to everyone that is sleeping? How can he be all those places at once?"

Emma giggled and looked at her as if she'd just asked her what shape a yield sign was. Apparently, the girl deemed her question ridiculous. Finally, Emma let out a sigh as she shook her head with a grin on her face. Her obvious disappointment in Serenity's lack of knowledge appeared to be amusing the young girl.

"He doesn't give dreams to everyone, silly, that just how the story has been told. Mama says, 'Fairytales are just real stories that got told so many times that the facts get stretched like over strung taffy.' "

"Are you saying the Sandman is real?"

"Yep, he's as real as me. But he isn't human; he works for…," she pointed up with her finger and then whispered, "you know who."

"God?" Serenity asked.

Emma shrugged. "Dair calls him the Creator."

"Who is Dair and how can the Sandman work for God, or the Creator, or whatever?"

Again with the look. "Don't they teach you anything in that high school?" Emma asked.

"Sure, we studied mythology in our English class, but they didn't exactly tell us the myths are real," Serenity explained. "So," she prompted.

"Okay, I'll give you the quick version. The Sandman is Dair. . . that's well . . .wait okay; his real name is Brudair, but all the angels call him Dair for short. So Dair, known to the humans as the Sandman, is the Creator's deliverer. He is the one who brings the dreams to those that the Creator deems important. But Dair says that when he says important it means, *important*, like these people are going to change the course of history in some way. Like Solomon in the Bible, he had tons of dreams; do you know anything about the Bible? Because, if not, than that point is not going to make sense to you."

"I know enough to understand what you're saying. The God in the Bible spoke to lots of people in the Bible through dreams."

"Exactly," Emma agreed.

"Are God and the Creator one in the same?"

Another shrug. "I don't know. I'm only eight," she said it as if she hadn't just explained a mythological being with as much clarity as a college professor. "All I know is what Dair has told me, and he always refers to his boss as the Creator."

"Okay, unlike the myth, Dair," Serenity said the name as if it were a question, "doesn't bring dreams to children all over the world but only to people he is assigned to by this Creator."

"Now, you're catching on," Emma grinned, her white teeth standing out like beautiful pearls against her dark skin.

Serenity wasn't sure if she should be embarrassed by being praised by an eight-year-old or proud of herself for following along and not just telling the kid that there was no Sandman.

"Dair said his job is to make suggestions in a person's dream to help them decide to go in the direction that the Creator has planned for them. He said he can't force them to make the decision, but he can influence them so that the choice seems like it was theirs all along."

"Can I just ask—how did you get so smart and mature for an eight-year-old?" Serenity interrupted.

""My mama says, 'I have an old soul,' " Emma told her.

"Well, your mama's apparently done a pretty good job of raising you," Serenity told her.

"Well, duh," Emma said suddenly sounding very much like an eight-year-old. "I test at a college level in nearly all my subjects. Now can we get back to Dair because we don't have all the time in the world; we have to wake up eventually."

Serenity decided not to touch that comment with a ten foot pole. Though Emma had just implied that she was asleep and somehow a part of her dream, it was just too much to even consider.

"Please continue," she told the girl.

"Dair can't tell the people he's assigned to why they have to go a certain direction, and he said sometimes he doesn't fully know why. All he can do is give them a dream that will hopefully result in them doing the Creator's will."

"Wow," Serenity breathed out. "No pressure on the Sandman, huh?"

"Yeah, I wouldn't want his job. Imagine if he was assigned someone that was supposed to do something like cure cancer and they choose the wrong path."

Serenity didn't know if she believed a word of what Emma was saying, but for a moment she thought about the possibility that Dair was real and how difficult his existence would be. She wondered if he felt responsible when his charge chose incorrectly, and then something awful happened because of that choice. As Emma had said, she wouldn't want that job.

"My times up," Emma suddenly said as she stood. "Remember you don't have to do what the Sandman is trying to get you to. You do have a choice."

"But at what price?" Serenity asked.

Emma shrugged. "Could be world peace or the answer to global warming, although my mom says that's a crock."

Serenity laughed. Emma waved at her and then headed for the door of the clinic. Before the door had fully closed, Serenity was pulled from the dream and her eyes opened to the sunlight shining through her window. She sat up in bed as Emma's word echoed in her mind—*Could be world peace.* That was what the little girl said could be the price paid if someone picks the wrong path—if they don't follow their dream. Was the same true for her? If Serenity chose to leave Yellville, to follow her dreams, the consequences would not be something small. Because according to the eight-year-old in her dream, the Sandman only came to those who were going to influence history in a big way.

"The Sandman?" she huffed out as she let the moment of panic slip away. Was she really going to base her decision off of what a kid said in her dreams about a children's tale? Perhaps, the dream was just her subconscious way of dealing with the guilt she felt over leaving. Maybe some small part of her wanted to stay because she didn't want to leave Darla and Wayne to fend for themselves.

Blowing out a breath that caused her cheeks to puff out like a blowfish, she pushed the covers back and got out of bed. Serenity raised her arms up over her head and stretched the kinks out. For the first time in six days, she had slept through the entire night. She had finally just given into the dream and let it run its course.

Though she didn't feel completely rested, she wouldn't complain. At least the dark circles under her eyes were gone she noted as she walked past her dresser mirror toward the bathroom.

After showering, dressing, and taming her wild, long locks, she headed down for breakfast only to find a note next to gravy smothered biscuits. The note read: *Had to get to work early to put up the Christmas decorations. Eat your breakfast and have a great day! Love, Aunt Darla.*

"Like I have to be told to eat biscuits and gravy," she muttered under her breath as she began shoveling the gooey goodness into her mouth. As she ate, her mind revisited her conversation with Emma.

As the day wore on, the strange conversation refused to leave her mind. By the time the school bell rang signaling the end of the day, Serenity's head hurt from all the concentration she had given to the dream. She couldn't really bring herself to believe in a being such as the Sandman, not to mention the fact that his real name was Dair. What kind of a name was Dair, anyway? It sounded like, 'I *DARE* you to go jump off a bridge.' Maybe now that she had let the dream play out in its entirety, it would go away and she could finally move on. Surely that would be the case.

As she headed to work, she shoved the tiny voice that wanted her to give the whole Sandman some consideration into a mental box. *I'm eighteen years old for goodness sake,* she told herself. *I don't believe in mythical beings, especially not when I'm told about them by a kid in a dream. But what if that kid is a self-professed genius who spouts out knowledge as if she's a scholar and uses words that no eight-year-old should comprehend?* "No, Sarah Serenity," she said firmly and this time out loud. She pulled into the parking lot of the vet clinic and took several deep breaths. "There is no Sandman; there is no eight-year-old genius, and the world will not implode on itself if you leave Yellville." Saying it all out loud made her realize just how ridiculous it sounded. Sufficiently convinced of her sanity, she finally opened her car door and headed in for work. She didn't allow herself to think about the Dair character at all, okay no more than a few dozen times, and she didn't come up with bizarre scenarios for why she would need to stay in the small town—well, not more than fifteen, she was sure. And when her cell rang and she answered it knowing it was Glory on the other end, she did not immediately ask, "Do you know anything about the Sandman or an inhuman being named Brudair?" Yep, she had officially jumped off the deep end, head first, while her last shred of dignity peered down at her from the top of the cliff.

His patience was beginning to wear thin as he watched Serenity argue back and forth with herself about the possibility of his existence and the truth behind the things Emma had told her. His need for her to believe in him irritated him.

He had been shocked when the girl had taken over the dream. One of the things Dair was able to do when dealing with a particularly difficult human was to link others to the dream he created. This little trick had its own set of rules, however. The most important of these was that the linked individual had to be connected to the dream somehow. The subject had to somehow be involved in the decision his charge was supposed to make. He had no idea how Emma was involved with Serenity's fate considering they didn't even live in the same state, but he had hoped the girl would be able to sway her. Instead Emma might have done the complete opposite. She'd given birth to the concept of free will within the dream. She blatantly told Serenity that she could ignore the dream if she wanted to. He would have to have a visit with little Emma. As he thought about the talk he would have with the child, he found himself wishing that Serenity had the faith of one as young as Emma. It wasn't unusual for children to be able to see him. Not just any children, mind you, but those who were predisposed to seeing the world as more than what was visible to the naked eye. Children weren't hindered by the need to have facts and tangible evidence that something exists; they just believed because their faith was still innocent, unjaded by the world.

As Serenity left her job muttering under her breath, "not real, not real, not real," Dair decided it was time to take matters into his own hands where her belief was concerned. Tonight he would be paying Serenity's history teacher a visit.

As always, he followed Serenity home to ensure she arrived there safely. Dair had this need to keep her safe, to ensure that nothing would harm her. He had never felt protective of a human. Then again he had never before been so enamored with one.

As he waited in her room while she went about her evening activities, he felt a blast of heat engulf him. Dair let out a sigh. He had known it would happen eventually. He was breaking the rules now and that would not go unnoticed.

"Brudair," the deep voice from the messenger

angel filled the room. Dair turned from the pictures he had been examining that were stuck to a bulletin board on Serenity's wall and looked at the formidable male. He supposed he could understand why people often freaked out when they saw angels. They were big, and the radiance that was the Creator enveloped them, going with them wherever they went. They, of course, could tamp down that glory when need be but he imagined for humans it was very difficult to be in the same vicinity when their magnificence was on display.

"Hello, Raphael," Dair said to his old friend.

"You know why I'm here."

Dair nodded.

"You are not going to leave, are you?" Raphael asked. He had known Dair a very, very long time, and Dair knew it would be nearly impossible to try to lie to the angel.

"I cannot leave, not yet," he told him.

Raphael's eyes narrowed and he tilted his head, studying him. "You care for this human." It wasn't a question.

"She's different, unique, and I'm drawn to her."

The angel chuckled as he shook his head. In a very human-like manner he rubbed his forehead. "I never thought it would be you—the brooding loner who has kept to himself for centuries now—enamored with a mortal. You know it will not end well. There is a reason the Creator set up the boundaries between our kinds."

"I am not an angel, Raphael. Why should the rules be the same for me?" Dair asked, suddenly angry as the thought of the rules squeezed him like steel bands tightening around his chest. "Why should I not be allowed a mate, someone to care for and be cared for by? You were created to worship Him and to deliver

His messages, but that was not and is not my purpose. I am simply the dream maker, the Sandman, as the humans like to call me. I have walked this earth since the beginning of time with no real home. I don't belong in the celestial realm, nor do I belong in the human one."

"But you feel that you belong with her," Raphael finished for him.

Dair nodded as the fight was quickly drained from him like a balloon loosing air. "I have never felt as though I belong anywhere until Serenity."

"What if she does not accept you? What will you do then?"

"I will leave her and let her live her life without me." Even as he said the words he wondered if that were true. Could he leave her? Could he allow her to give her heart, body, and spirit to another?

Raphael was obviously thinking the same thing. "We do not feel as humans do, Dair. Our emotions run much, much deeper and stronger. It is one of the reasons the Creator has forbidden relationships with humans. They are finicky and impulsive, while we are steadfast and determined in our choices. They do not mate for life, or at least the vast majority of them do not. The longer you stay, the more difficult it will be for you to let go. She will never be able to feel the kind of love that you will feel for her; she is not capable of something that pure. If she ever tired of you and decided she did not love you, as they so often do, I do not think you would be able to let her leave you, not even for her own happiness."

Dair knew the things he said were true, except for one thing. "I don't believe that she is not capable of loving as I do. She is different, Raphael; her spirit is different."

"Perhaps, but are you so sure that you are willing to risk destroying her if that is not the case? Because your need of her—, your need to protect, to love, to possess, and to touch—will only smother her if what she wants is to be free of you."

Dair didn't want to hear anymore. He didn't want to think about Serenity rejecting him, though he didn't know when he had decided to try and win her heart. But he had. He wanted a chance to know her, to see if she could feel for him what he did for her. "I cannot leave just yet," he said again, when what he really wanted to do was roar at his friend that he knew that he and Serenity might not be able to overcome their differences. But he wasn't ready to admit that out loud.

Raphael nodded. "You know the Creator might send others."

"I know."

"So be it. Take care my friend," Raphael told him and then was gone, taking all of the heat with him and leaving Dair wrapped in the cold arms of uncertainty and despair.

"Good night, Aunt Darla." He heard Serenity's voice just before her bedroom door opened and, just like that, the feelings fled and were replaced with his need of her. He was so lost in watching her that it was nearly too late when he realized she was about to be undressed as she began changing into her night clothes. He turned around quickly just as she began to lift her shirt, feeling even more like a creepy stalker. He had to reveal himself to her. He couldn't just keep following her around and listening to her conversations without her knowledge. It was beginning to feel like a betrayal of her trust. When he no longer heard the rustling of clothes, he slowly turned his head back, prepared to quickly look away if she was still not dressed. But she was fully clothed and sitting on her bed. Her notebook, where all her notes on her dream were written, was sitting in her lap and she was thumbing through the pages. He figured now was as good a time as any to leave her for a short while and go have a chat with Mr. Sweeney, her history teacher. Of course, Mr. Sweeney would never be aware that it happened.

Dair stood staring at the middle age man who lay sleeping in his bed. What he was about to do was completely against the rules, but then he seemed to have decided to throw the rulebook out the window when it came to a certain lovely brunette. He began to weave a dream in his mind and push it into the mind of the human before him. When Mr. Sweeney woke up in the morning, he would suddenly have the urge to teach about folklore stemming from central and northern Europe with a particular focus on the legend of the Sandman. Perhaps, *that* would get Serenity's attention.

When he arrived back in her room, she was sound asleep. Her face was so peaceful and she looked so relaxed, he decided to forgo the dream that night. He would let her rest, but tomorrow all bets were off. He was going to stop being a spectator in her life. The time had come to find out if fighting the rules for her was worthwhile. And the only way he could answer that question was to find out if she was even capable of feeling something for him.

As he bent down over her and pressed a kiss to her temple, he whispered against her skin, "Tomorrow I will begin to make you mine, Sara Serenity."

"Tell me more about this dream," Glory said as she sat across from Serenity in one of the booths at the fire pit. She had called early that morning, demanding to have breakfast because she wanted to know more about the whole Sandman thing. Serenity hadn't meant to spill the beans, but her mind had been dwelling on it so much that it had just come pouring out of her. And she probably needed to talk with someone about it other than an eight-year-old girl who was actually in the dream. So she had forced herself from the warmth of her bed and met Glory before time for school. The only bonus was that she got an awesome breakfast out of the deal.

"I already told you the entire thing the other night," Serenity said. "I think I dreamed it because even though I want to leave this little town, I'm also scared to venture out into the wide world, and I must subconsciously be trying to find an excuse to stay."

"What about this Dair character? What's he all about?" Glory asked, ignoring what she had just said.

Serenity rolled her eyes and set her fork down on her plate. It was obvious that Glory wasn't going to give up. "The girl, Emma, said he is the basis of the myth about the Sandman," Serenity explained *again* to Glory everything the girl had said about Dair.

"He sounds mysterious," her best friend crooned.

"Give me a break, Glory. For all we know he's a short, fat, bald man like in the movie *The Rise of the Guardians*."

Glory shook her head. "No, I'm not getting that

vibe from your story. This guy sounds powerful in an *I'm so hot I scorch the ground when I walk* sort-of way."

Serenity choked on the drink of orange juice she had been taking. "Sometimes, you really worry me, Glory Day."

"You're the one having dreams supposedly sent by a mythical being that have to be explained to you by an eight year old genius."

"Good point," Serenity conceded. She glanced down at her phone and noticed that she had fifteen minutes to get to class. "I've got to go now, so you'll have to table any other questions you have."

Glory stood up with her and walked her to the door. "Do not worry. I will be sure to make a list."

Serenity shook her head with a small laugh. "You do that," she told her as she headed out to her car.

The muttering of words coming from Serenity's second period class caught her attention as she neared the door. It wasn't just the voices that had grabbed her attention, it was the subject matter. She had distinctly heard the word *Sandman* spoken by several different classmates. Her breath grew heavy in her chest as she entered her history class and read the notes on the board.

Topic for Friday, December 13, 2014. Central and Northern Europe folklore. Who was the Sandman, really? What are the origins of the myth?

Serenity was pretty sure her stomach no longer resided in her abdomen, but had somehow relocated itself somewhere in the vicinity of her feet. Meanwhile her heart had decided to take a trip up to her throat. Her mind was reeling. This could not be a coincidence. But how on earth could it be related to her dream? She stood dumbfounded with Emma's words echoing in her mind. *Yep, he's as real as me. But he isn't human.*

"Ms. Tillman are you planning on joining us today?" Mr. Sweeney's voice pulled her back from her slight panic attack.

"Oh. . .um. . .yes, sorry, I'll just." She pointed in the direction of her chair while heading that way. As she took her seat and looked up to the front of the room, she tried to calm her jittery nerves so she could listen—really listen to what Mr. Sweeney was about to teach. If it was only about the folklore that had always been told, regarding the Sandman giving children good dreams, then she was going to blow it off as coincidence. But if there was any information remotely different, then she would consider the possibility that this, Dair—Emma had spoken of—might actually be real. And maybe he could control things. What else could explain the change of subject matter—they were supposed to be studying The Black Plague this week.

"I know that the topic for today might seem a little off the wall," Mr. Sweeney began. "But I've learned through the years that when I get inspiration to teach something, then I should follow through. I woke up this morning after having a vivid dream last night, and the Sandman was a part of it. It made me curious to learn how this mythical figure came about and to see if there were any factual underpinnings to the story, much like with St. Nicholas and his relationship to Santa Clause. I did some quick research in the library this morning and found some interesting things." He sifted through a pile of books that were on his desk and finally chose one that was filled with sticky notes protruding from the pages. He flipped to a certain page and ran his finger down the page until he found what he was looking for. "Okay, here we are. Listen to this."

Serenity listened as Mr. Sweeny recited the legend that she, and everyone else, already knew. The Sandman sprinkled dust over children while they slept and gave them pleasant dreams—blah, blah, blah. *No new information there*, she thought. But then Mr. Sweeny paused as if gathering himself and said the magic word: BUT. That three letter word often was the catalyst into a change in direction of the information. Desperate for more information, she leaned forward in her desk as she focused on her history teacher.

"But, that is not the only published information we have about the Sandman. After much digging, I actually came across another story about him in a very, very old book. It actually seems strange that our library would have such a treasure, but I won't look a gift horse in the mouth. This book is a study on ancient texts written between the third and fifth centuries. Most of it was written by a tribe of people from Persia that studied the mystical and spiritual happenings in the world at that time. They took note of everything and anything they heard that seemed unnatural. They were so opened minded that they even listened when children spoke of things that couldn't be explained by anything other than the supernatural. They studied the supernatural, no matter the form—Jewish God, Greek gods, Egyptian gods, it didn't matter. This tribe recorded it all. Since they did not practice any particular form of worship, they simply were spectating, observing things that many chose to ignore. I'm going to read a particular entry from during their travels near Syria. *We have had several accounts from the children in this region. They say no one will believe them, but their stories are remarkably similar, despite the fact that the children all live miles and miles apart and would have no way to collaborate their stories. They each speak of a man who has come to them in the night after everyone else in the house is sleeping. Each child reports being awake when they meet this man. He calls himself the dream weaver. The children are not scared of him. Each of them says that the man told them that he was there to guide them to their fate. He told each of them that they were special and that not every child got to meet him. He said he only comes to those who would change the course of history. My companions and I have decided to test the story. We have written down the name of one of the children and, should we live long enough to see her grow into adulthood, we will see if she does indeed play such a vital role in the world. It might not give irrefutable evidence of this dream weaver's existence, but it would certainly give his apologists a strong argument. The name is as follows: Julia Aurelia Zenobia.*

"It is noted several pages later that Julia Aurelia Zenobia became the Queen of the Palmyrene Empire," Mr. Sweeny continued. "She led a famous revolt against the Roman Empire that prevented them from taking Palmyrene as part of their conquests. So it was apparent that this Julia truly was important in history.

Now, I ask you," he questioned, his eyes roaming the classroom, "Does that mean the Sandman, or Dream Weaver as he's apparently sometimes called, really exists? Perhaps, or perhaps not." Mr. Sweeney closed the book and held it in his lap as he took a seat on the end of his desk. "This is a great lesson in digging deeper. Oftentimes in history we have a tendency to accept secondhand accounts at face value, instead of seeking out the source. So though he wasn't called the Sandman during that time, it is obvious that these children were describing the same mythical figure the Europeans later spoke of."

Serenity was pretty sure that her jaw had gotten lower and lower as she listened to the story about the legend of the Sandman aka the Dream Weaver. It couldn't be a coincidence. Regardless, she knew one thing for sure, *this shiz just got real.*

Her feet moved on autopilot as she went about her duties at the vet clinic. She hardly spoke to Jackson, not that he noticed since he was constantly avoiding her. She had never wanted the day to be over as bad as she did that day. After the information vomit Mr. Sweeney had unknowingly dropped in her lap, she had decided it was time to confront this so called Sandman. If he was the one behind her dream, then, from what she understood, he would have to be there in her room with her. She shivered at the thought of someone watching her sleep. Trying to control her through her dreams was creepy enough, but if he was watching her drool, while she slept, well that was on a whole other level. By the time she left the clinic, she was so keyed up she felt like she had just drank ten sodas and chased them with energy drinks.

"Get it together, Sarah," she told herself as she pulled into her aunt and uncle's driveway. The first thing she noticed was that Wayne still hadn't returned from his hunting expedition. At least that was one less person she had to convince that she was okay. She imagined Darla would have a few concerns if Serenity continued to shift from foot to foot like a three-year-old needing to pee. She took several deep breaths before finally going inside.

"Hey, honey," Darla greeted as she looked up from the book she was reading. "How was your day?"

Play it cool. she told herself. "It was good," she nodded and then realized that her head was moving entirely too fast. She snapped it to a stop and then smiled at her aunt. She was pretty sure it was one of those wide smiles that made her look like she'd had her face lifted just a little too tightly. "I'm just going to, that is, I'm pretty tired so, busy day." She stumbled over her words because she was just so cool under pressure. She pointed in the direction of her room. "I'm going to lie down." *There, I made sense, surely she can't be suspicious of me now.*

"Are you sure everything is alright?" Darla's eyes zeroed in on her.

Well crap, Serenity growled at herself. "Yes, I'm just a little scattered because I've got a lot of homework and I'm worn out."

Darla watched her for a minute longer, making Serenity feel like she was some newly discovered bug under a microscope. She finally decided that Serenity was telling the truth. "Okay, then you better get on it. I'll bring dinner in to you in about an hour."

"Thanks, Aunt Darla," she called back, already moving before the 'okay' left her aunt's mouth.

Serenity closed her bedroom door and threw her backpack onto her bed as she let out a relieved sigh. Her cat climbed out from under her bed and let out a big yawn as he looked up at her. "Looks like you had a rough day," Serenity said dryly as she watched Mr. Whitherby wind himself in and out of her legs. Unable to focus on showing him the attention he usually demanded, she grabbed the notebook that contained her thoughts from the past week and snatched up the pen lying next to it. She wanted to get down everything she had learned in her history class. It was the first bit of possibly factual information she had on this Dair being, and she wanted to confront him about it, if he was indeed real and if he'd show himself to her. She shook her head and squeezed her eyes tightly closed.

"I'm going crazy. There is no other explanation for planning a conversation with an immortal being only known from folklore."

After having written everything she could remember from class, she set the notebook down, pushed her backpack from the bed, and laid down. Who knew doing research could be so exhausting? Serenity didn't intend to go to sleep; she just wanted to rest her eyes for a few minutes. How many times had those been famous last words.

Sometime later she woke to a dark room. She didn't remember turning off the light but then her aunt could have done it. There was something strange about the darkness that surrounded her. Like a blanket being wrapped around her shoulders, the darkness seemed to envelop her. She pushed herself up until she was sitting and blinked several times, attempting to get her eyes to adjust to the lack of light, but it was no use. She was about to stand up when a chill ran down her back. It was one of those feelings she got when she knew someone was staring at her, even though she couldn't see them. Serenity licked her lips nervously and swallowed down the lump that had developed in her throat before she spoke.

"Sandman." The word came out much more desperately than she had intended. It almost sounded as if she were calling out to a lover. She swallowed again and then said more firmly. "If you're there, please answer me. I sort of feel like an idiot talking into the dark." Her words were met with silence, but still she felt the presence of something or someone. Good thing she wasn't easily dissuaded. Unless of course she was indeed talking to an empty room, then perhaps it was less of a good thing and more of a need to get your brain checked out thing. "Please answer me, Brudair; are you here?"

"Yes." A deep, rich voice threatened to lull her to sleep with one tiny word. She shook herself, pushing away the drowsiness.

"Can I see you?" she asked and felt her heart beat speed up at the prospect of finally seeing the object of her obsession for the past few days.

"I haven't decided if that is a good idea or not."

Okay, so perhaps she didn't need to ask him any more questions because his voice was doing tingly things to her. *Not okay, Sarah, not okay,* she silently reprimanded herself. "Why are you still here if you've already shown me the dream meant to influence me?"

No answer.

"Why haven't you moved on to someone else?"

Again no answer.

Getting frustrated, Serenity ground her teeth together as she spoke. "Why are you here?" Perhaps, that came out a little more rudely than she intended, but she wanted answers.

The deep voice finally rumbled "I am here because I want you."

Whoa, did not see that coming.

Chapter 3

"To see the moon in your dreams means you will soon be confronted with an unstoppable force, object, or personality that will have an immediate and irresistible pull on your life."

Dair had not meant to be so blunt with her. He knew that his words had come through in a near growl because of how possessive he felt towards her, and he imagined that she was probably terrified of him. He had followed her, as usual, all day, and several times he caught her talking to herself about how she was going to confront him and ask him to reveal himself to her. All day he had thought about what he would do once the sun finally set and the moon took over. Up until the moment she had spoken his name, his true name, Brudair, he hadn't known if he would answer her. But then she had said his name. Hearing it in her angelic voice caused his stomach to tighten and his hands to twitch with the need to hold her. Silence permeated the room as he waited to see how she would respond to his declaration. He was expecting her to tell him to leave and never come back, but, as usual, Serenity surprised him.

"I'm not really sure what that means," she admitted. "Is this like a want like a man wants a woman or is this like a want because I'm a shiny new toy?"

Dair thought about how to answer her. She was indeed shiny and new, but not in the way she was implying. She was those things because of her differences from the rest of the world. To him, she shined like the brightest beacon in a world of muted greys. And though those things are what drew him to her, they weren't the only reason he wanted her.

"You are new to me, but not for the reasons you believe. I have been around for a very long time, Serenity. I have come across all sorts of people in all walks of life. I've seen the good in them, and the bad. In all that time, I have never come across a human that drew me the way you do. Your selflessness is a breath of fresh air. You listen to people and not just listen but you hear them and you care about what they have to say. You're so good, so pure, and unjaded. Even though tragedy has touched your life, you have not let it rule you." He paused then, thinking of how he should tell her about his other wants without coming across like some strange pervert. She was quiet and though she could not see him, he could see her just fine. He was, after all, the dream weaver and the night was his domain. Her eyes were wide and her plump lips were pressed firmly together as though she was trying not to blurt something out.

"As for the first want you mentioned, I want to be honest with you and want you to know right from the start what you might be getting into so I will be blunt. Yes, I want you as a man wants a woman. I am attracted to you on more levels than I knew even existed. Your interior beauty captivates me, and your exterior beauty calls to the primal part of me that wants to claim you as a mate. I want to know what your skin feels like and how your hair smells just after a shower. I want to see you smile because of something I have said. I want." He paused and let out a painful groan. "I want things I shouldn't want and things that I am forbidden from having. Those things all have to do with you, Sarah Serenity Tillman. I want you for my own and I want to be yours."

Dair could hear her rapid breathing and see the quick rise and fall of her chest. She didn't say anything for a very long time, but simply stared into the darkness. He didn't know if that was better than her telling him he was a lunatic and to get out, but waiting for her response was still difficult. Just when he was considering the idea that maybe she had gone into shock, she cleared her throat.

"Okay, so that is a lot of information to process. And frankly it's a tad, okay more than a tad, ridiculous and weird. . .and. . .and creepy and just so not normal."

"I think I understood what you meant back at ridiculous," he said coolly. He wasn't upset or hurt by her words. Dair was actually amused by her frankness.

"Well, you got to say your peace and, brother, let me tell you, you said enough. Therefore, I get to say my peace."

"I do not want to be your brother." The idea of being related to her had his stomach churning uncomfortably.

"It's just an expression." Serenity took several breaths and rubbed her hands up and down her thighs. "Basically, I'm trying not to flip out."

"I would never hurt you," he told her suddenly. For some reason he felt the need to mention that.

"I'm thinking that if you wanted to hurt me, it would have happened by now," she said still rubbing her hands up and down her legs. He wanted to comfort her, to reassure her that everything would be alright, but he had not earned that right——yet.

"I think I need some time," she nodded her head.

"Yes, time would be good. Can you just maybe not come into my room and give me freaky dreams for a few days, maybe a week, and let me think about the heavy stuff you have just dropped on my head?"

A week! His throat constricted and his heart pounded as he thought about being separated from her for that length of time. Somehow, if it was what she needed in order to come to terms with him, he would have to give her that time.

"Very well," he finally, though rather reluctantly, agreed.

"Can I see you now?" she asked him again and the eagerness in her voice nearly had him giving in to her request.

"I think I should wait to show myself to you after you have thought about the things I have shared. If, at the end of a week's time, you want to consider us a possibility, then I will show myself to you. But if you decide that there is no place for me in your life, it would be better if you did not see me. It would be easier for your mind to push away the fact that we spoke and return me back to the myth you believed me to be." As her shoulders dropped forward and the eagerness faded from her eyes, he realized just how difficult it was going to be not to give this woman everything she asked for.

"Okay, so I guess I'll talk to you again in a week?"

"You will," he confirmed. "Goodnight, Princess of Peace," he said in a near whisper. And before he could change his mind and pull the darkness away revealing himself to her, he transported from her room. He ended up across the street behind a large tree staring back at her house with a near instinctual need to go back to her and to be by her side so he could protect her and shelter her. Dair had laid his cards on the table, as the humans say, and now all he could do was wait to see if Serenity would play or fold. He still didn't know what he would do if she told him she wasn't interested in knowing him better. Raphael had made an extremely valid point about him and how strong his feelings were. Could he walk away from her? He didn't know the answer to that question.

As he watched a soft light come on in the window of Serenity's room, he wondered if she was sitting on her bed with her notebook in her lap. She was probably scribbling down their conversation furiously so as not to forget anything. It settled something inside of him to realize that he knew her well enough to know what she would be doing after such an intense talk. After about twenty minutes, the light finally went out, and for the first time in his existence, Dair found that he didn't know what to do with himself. He didn't have a home, so to speak, to go to because he spent all of his time finding his next assignment. Then he spent all of his time with his charge until his required task had been fulfilled. He considered staying close to her, but he didn't want to go against her wishes.

"Perhaps, you should go to the next human you are supposed to dream weave while she thinks on the things you have said."

Raphael's voice behind him didn't startle him, but he was surprised that the angel had stuck around.

"Did you hear everything?" Dair asked him as he turned away from Serenity's house and faced the celestial being.

"I heard enough," he admitted. "I am not telling you to move on, Dair. I am simply saying that you could still be doing your duties while the human makes her choice."

Dair knew Raphael was right. A sharp pain radiated through his chest as he considered leaving the small town and Serenity. He didn't want to be away from her, definitely not as far as his duties might take him which could be anywhere in the world.

"I will even accompany you," Raphael said with a twitch of his lips that suggested at a smile. "It will be like old times."

"Except you won't be delivering messages and scaring people with your overwhelming countenance," Dair pointed out.

"Hmm," Raphael nodded. "That does make things a little less exciting, but somehow I think we will manage."

With one last look at Serenity's window, Dair let out a resigned sigh. He turned back to his old friend. "First stop is a small village in Africa."

Raphael frowned. "I will never understand how the Creator chooses those who will be catalysts for change."

Dair chuckled. "He seems to have a thing for small, remote places."

The angel grunted, understanding that Dair was referring to the town of Yellville and the orphaned girl who had mesmerized him. "See you soon," Raphael told him and then shot into the air, his huge wings carrying him faster than the human eye could track.

Dair thought of the village where his next human was located and then transported himself. He swallowed down the ache that was growing in his chest the farther he got from Serenity and told himself that he would do his job, give her the time she requested, and then he would proceed to do anything he needed to in order to win her heart. He did not want to spend the rest of eternity with the ache of her absence in his mind, spirit, and body. Time would not ease it, not for his kind. Once the love of an immortal was given, there was no taking it back. She would hold his adoration, love, and esteem for the rest of time.

Serenity didn't sleep that night. She was in shock. He was real. That's the only thought that kept running through her head before finally moving on to the other implications of such a discovery. He was real. After Dair left, she wrote down their conversation and then she simply lay in bed staring up at the ceiling as if the answers to all of her questions would suddenly appear there. Of all the scenarios she had considered when it came to finally meeting the Sandman, if he even existed, she had never conjured up the idea that he would be interested in her in a romantic way. She had not even considered that he was a man who could feel such things for someone. To her he was a myth who had become a reality—one who had influenced her dream because he had been tasked to do so. That was all she had thought she was to him—an assignment and nothing more, and it didn't bother her in the least to fall into that category with him. But now, now she had so much more to think about than just the fact that the Sandman was real. Now she had to consider that not only was he real but he, in his own words, wanted her.

As she stood staring at her reflection in the mirror in her bathroom, she frowned at herself. "How on earth am I supposed to process the fact that an immortal being is infatuated with me?" she asked out loud. "How am I supposed to respond to him when I don't even know him?"

It was Saturday so she didn't have school to distract her from the situation in which she had suddenly found herself, and it wasn't her Saturday to work at the vet clinic. So she was stuck at home with questions, fears, worries, and more questions bombarding her mind. As if she had known that in that moment Serenity needed a distraction, her cell phone rang and Glory's picture showed up on the screen.

"I'm bored," the twenty-something-year-old said, sounding way too much like a petulant teenager instead of the adult she was.

"You don't work today?" Serenity was sure that her best friend heard the desperation in her question.

Glory paused before she spoke again. "Nooo," she drew out the word. "I don't, and by the way, what's wrong with you?"

Nope, she couldn't get anything past Glory. Though in Serenity's defense, it was more because she sucked at being chill when something was going on in her life that she didn't necessarily want to talk about. But she found that this was not one of those things. She wanted to tell Glory about Dair. Serenity felt that her head just might pop off if she didn't get out some of the crap that was floating around inside it.

"I've got some stuff to tell you," she finally said slowly.

"Want me to come there? Mom's having a good day, so Dad's given me the day off."

Considering the subject matter of the conversation, Serenity decided that it would be best to do it in the privacy of her bedroom. "Yeah, come here. Aunt Darla is taking food to some of the elderly people in town, and Uncle Wayne won't be back until this evening."

"That aunt of yours would feed the whole county if she could," Glory only half teased.

"And then demand that nobody help her with the cleanup. I swear the woman doesn't have a selfish bone in her body. I love her for it, but I also find myself feeling like an egocentric jerk face when I get irritated with other people."

"We can't all be Darlas, Sen. Some of us have to be the mouthy ones, and some of us have to be the obnoxious ones because if everyone went around helping everyone all of the time nobody would be in need of all the kindness, and it would become null and void. Not to mention if we all tried to feed each other the way Aunt Darla does, we'd be a bunch of lard asses unable to get around to help anyone anyways."

"I'll be sure and pass that on to Darla," Serenity said around the laughter that was escaping between words.

"You do that; she'll just deny that she's anything special and then make me a pie."

"Okay stop, I'm going to pee on myself," she laughed even harder. It was so funny because it was utterly true.

"Fine, I'm on my way, bye." Glory hung up and left Serenity still grabbing her side from the laughter that continued to pour out of her as she pictured her aunt making a pie for Glory, all the while arguing that she was not as nice as we always told her she was. The only reason, Serenity imagined that her aunt could in any way not be as good as she was, was if she had a hidden lair of voodoo dolls where she terrorized anyone who didn't like her food. That only made her laugh harder as she headed back to her room to get dressed.

Half an hour later she heard the front door open, because honestly who needs to lock their door when you lived thirty minutes from civilization. Anyone stupid enough to come out that far to break into their house would probably be eaten by a bob cat or a pack of coyotes.

"Please tell me that Aunt Darla made lunch for us because I didn't stop to get us anything and I'm hungry enough to consider cannibalism."

"Couldn't you just start with the cat?" Serenity asked as she walked into the living room with Mr. Whitherby trailing after her.

Glory pinched her lips together and looked from Serenity to the cat and then shook her head. "Nope, you definitely look more filling, not to mention all that fur."

"Okay, enough with the eating of the things that should not be eaten. I'm sure Darla fixed us something." She motioned for Glory to follow her into the kitchen.

"So what's this thing you need to talk to me about?" Glory asked as she leaned on the bar, watching her sort through the containers in the refrigerator.

"Let's get lunch down us first, and then I'll pour out my soul to you."

"I always did love a good soul-pouring. Now, hand over that green stuff I see at the back of the fridge."

Green stuff was a big commodity in their house, especially when Glory and Uncle Wayne were both present. Green stuff was only green gelatin, crushed pineapples, pecans, and whip cream, but it tasted amazing. For some reason when Darla put that combination of things together, she came up with what we all called green stuff, and really it should be called, *so good it makes you willing to steal from your Uncle*, stuff.

"You're braver than I am if you are prepared to face Uncle Wayne when he discovers his green stuff is gone."

Glory held out her hand making a 'give me' motion with it. "Not brave, just smart. I don't plan to be here when he discovers it." She tapped her nose and winked at her.

Serenity just shook her head and pulled out more containers full of the food Aunt Darla made. "I think there's enough for both of us," she said as she motioned to the two counters full of containers.

Glory nodded. "Man, I love that woman."

Forty-five minutes and three full plates too many later, Glory laid on Serenity's bed groaning while Serenity took the floor.

"Why does it have to be so good?" Glory whined.

"Seriously, it's like once you start you can't stop; you just keep shoveling the food in, and all of it looks so good that you can't pick just one or two things, and then, BAM, suddenly you're as full as a tick on a rhinoceros."

"Distract me, Serenity," Glory told her. "Tell me whatever it is you were going to tell me so that I don't think about the fact that I have food clear up to the back of my throat that is threatening to make a reappearance."

"First of all, eww, gross, and second, don't you dare throw up on my bed. You're a grown woman; you're supposed to throw up in the bathroom of some shady club because you're wasted, not at a high school kids house because you couldn't stop eating the food her aunt cooks."

"Now you're just stalling. Spill it, Sarah."

Serenity took a deep breath and then asked, "Remember how we were talking about the Sandman and that whole weird dream I had?"

"The one with the freakishly mature eight-year-old?"

"Yes."

"I remember."

"What if I told you that everything that Emma told me in that dream was true? Would you think I was crazy?" Serenity held her breath as she waited for her friend to answer.

"No," Glory finally answered. "But I would want to know how you know this to be true, without a doubt, based on tangible facts."

She let go of the breath and thanked God for such an amazing friend. "Get comfortable."

"You'll have to settle for mildly miserable until all the food begins to digest. Don't mind the groaning while you explain what the hell you're talking about. Just keep right on going."

"Mr. Sweeney's topic in history yesterday was the folklore of the Sandman."

Glory's head suddenly appeared over the edge of the bed. Her blonde hair fell across her face and she brushed it away impatiently. "Did you know that he was going to be covering that?"

Serenity shook her head. "He said it was a last minute change."

"That's bizarre." She narrowed her eyes, seeming to stare off at nothing before looking back at her. "What did he have to say? Did any of it match what

Emma said?"

Serenity began from the moment when Mr. Sweeny's lecture took a sharp turn into the lore that matched up with what the girl had told her in her dream. Glory, ever the attentive and expressive listener, gasped at all the right places and occasionally added a 'holy hell' when she deemed it necessary. Serenity paused when she finally got to the part where she felt Dair's presence in her room.

"This is the part that worries me. I'm afraid you're going to think I was hallucinating or something just to give substance to everything that I've heard and experienced."

"Well, I always think you are a few heifers shy of having a herd. But seriously, girl, who on earth has their head more tightly screwed onto their shoulders than you? How on earth could I possibly think you were not in your right mind when you have not given any indications of such a thing?" Glory asked.

"Well, you might change your mind when I tell you that Dair was in my room last night and I spoke to him."

Glory's eyes widened. "Did he speak back? Wait, what did he look like? Was he hot? He was hot, wasn't he? I told you he would be hot."

"GLORY!" Serenity grabbed her friend's flailing arm. She tended to get very animated with her hands when she got excited. "Didn't you hear the part where I said a mythical character showed up in my bedroom last night?"

"I heard that, and if you are telling me that you spoke to him, then I believe you."

"Just like that?"

"Serenity, I know you. I know your character, your

heart, and your inability to lie. I mean, let's face it, girl, if ever you wind up playing a poker game that's life and death, we might as well just get your measurements for the coffin."

"I'm not going to be insulted because at the moment I'm just relieved to be able to talk about this."

"Yes, I'm awesome. How could you ever doubt me? Now to the important stuff. Is he hot?"

"Are you really twenty-two? Are you sure they didn't get your birth certificate wrong?"

Glory rolled her eyes. "My best friend is in high school. Can you really have such high expectations for me?"

"Good point," Serenity agreed. "And to answer your question, I have no idea if he's boar butt ugly or hot enough to melt steel. He wouldn't show himself to me."

"So he just talked to you? How did you know he was in your room?"

"I could feel him. It was weird, but I just knew he was there. So I called out to him. But he didn't answer until the third time I said his name. By then, I nearly believed that I was talking to an empty room. But then he spoke." Her face took on a dreamy quality that she didn't recognize as she remembered Dair's smooth, hypnotic voice.

"What's that look for?" Glory asked as she pointed at Serenity's face, nearly poking her in the eye.

"What face?" Serenity attempted to deny what she knew Glory saw.

"Um, the face that says somebody has rocked your world. You have *after an incredible make out* face."

"Okay, what does that even mean, and is it a real thing? And, no, I do not have *after an incredible make out*, face."

Glory clucked her tongue. "You do know where liars go when they die, right?"

She groaned at Glory's go-to saying anytime she refused to admit something to the older girl. "Fine," she gave in, preparing herself for the embarrassment of having to explain that his voice had made her so content that she wanted to be wrapped in his arms and just listen to him for forever. "His voice was. . .well. . .it was like. . . it made me want to. . . I don't know how to explain it," she huffed after her pitiful attempt at an explanation.

"Are you trying to say that his voice was sexy enough to cause an eargasm?"

"Seriously?" Serenity blushed and slapped her hand over her face. After a moment spent gathering herself, she continued. "It *was* sexy," Serenity agreed. "But it was more than that; it was like soothing and hypnotic and shiver-inducing all at once."

"Damn," Glory said as she looked at her with wide, envious eyes.

"What?"

"You're describing the after effects. The burning need now sated, and everything feels super sensitive, but in a good way. You're still floating from the power of it, but now you can focus on the sensations because you aren't distracted by the desire."

She stared at her best friend with wide eyes. "You got all that from me saying his voice was soothing, hypnotic, and shiver-inducing?"

Glory nodded.

"I would like to confirm that your rather descriptive explanation was true, but my V card is still firmly tucked away in my wallet so I can't say that the feelings I felt are in any way the same as those you are describing."

"Okay, how about his voice made you feel as though you had just taken a couple sips of the most perfectly aged wine giving you that warm feeling that runs throughout your entire body."

Serenity looked at her blankly.

"Still no?" Glory asked.

"Not a drinker," she said pointing to herself.

"Well, slap a duck, honey. You're on your own in describing his apparently amazing voice; my repertoire is tapped."

She snorted at her friend who had flopped back down on the bed dramatically. "I appreciate your willingness to share your expertise with me."

Glory gave her a thumbs up. "I knew there was a reason I let you hang out with me. Now," she motioned with her hands to continue. "Tell me more about this Dair with the incredible voice. What did he say to you?"

And so the story continued as Serenity told all, right down to Dair's final whispered words, goodbye. She felt bereft after having relived it through her telling. Now that she was over the initial shock of Dair's blunt truths, she wanted to know more about him.

"Let me just get some clarification here, sweets," Glory said as she turned over on her side and propped herself up on her elbow. "This Dair, immortal legend guy, with the sexy, body-throbbing-inducing voice, told you that he wanted you and you told him to go away?"

"When you put it like that you make me sound lame," she retorted. "I was trying to be responsible. I don't know anything about him."

"Is this where I point out that you spent a week researching him, sat in a class where your teacher lectured about him, and had a dream where a creepy little girl spilled all the beans about him?" Glory looked at her pointedly.

She threw her hands up in the air. "Again with the making me feel lame, Glory."

Her best friend simply shrugged as she looked at her nails. "Babe, I'm just stating the facts. What they reveal is not up to me."

"So, you think I should have just said, *oh you want me, great. Let's just jump into this intense relationship even though you sort of freak me out with the whole myth and immortal background?*

"Or," Glory held up a finger. "You could have simply gone with something like, *I hear what you are saying and while I'm not sure how I will feel a month from now, I would like to get to know you better.* And then you would have gotten a look at the package that holds the voice."

"I can see how your response would have been reasonable, but I was still a little stuck on the whole, *he's the Sandman and he basically has just told me he wants me to be his woman, body and soul.*"

"Well, how do you feel now that you've had a few hours to think about it?" Glory asked.

Serenity tilted her head back on the floor and closed her eyes. "If you are asking me to be honest, then I'm feeling like I'm terrified he won't come back and that I messed up something that could have been amazing."

"You don't need to worry about that." She reached over the edge of the bed and patted her arm. "When a man opens himself up that much, he has no intention of walking away without a fight."

"So what do I do until he comes back?" Serenity asked.

"You live. Because no matter how much your heart wants to make this mysterious guy the center of your universe, your mind knows that allowing your emotions to control you will only drag you down. You can hope, by all means hope, that he returns because you obviously want to spend more time with him, but don't you dare just curl up in a corner allowing your fear and doubts to eat away at you. And when he does come back, because he will, he will find the confident, beautiful woman that he fell head over heels for instead of a whimpering girl pining after a man who has yet to earn her love."

"And there is the twenty-two-year-old my best friend claims to be," she chuckled. But her face sobered quickly as she looked up at Glory. "Thank you for believing me, and hearing me, and for not letting me be a whimpering girl."

Serenity smiled as her friend waved her off as if it were nothing. "Don't go getting all sentimental on me, Sen. It was more for my benefit than yours. You can't honestly expect me to be seen with some sniveling weakling, can you?"

She shook her head. "Of course not, whatever was I thinking," she said with mock shame.

"You weren't. That's what I'm here for. Tell me again about his voice and the things he said to you so I can imagine him saying them to me. You know I have to live vicariously through you for my thrills."

"Glory, that's just all kinds of wrong," she laughed at the unconcerned look on her best friend's face.

"Unless the next words out of your mouth are verbatim repeats from the lovely Dair, please refrain from sharing."

"What if?"

"Nope."

"But," Serenity started again.

"Huh-uh." She was shut down again.

With a resigned sigh Serenity gave in. "His first word rumbled through the darkness. *Yes*, was all he said and yet I felt as if he had just sung me a lullaby."

"Oh that's good. Write that down. But don't stop talking while you're writing. And hurry up. I need to be out of here before Uncle Wayne gets home and tries to hog tie me for eating his green stuff."

"Glory, I love you," she told her.

She raised an eyebrow at her. "Why are you telling me that now?"

"Because what I really want to say would probably keep you from giving me free breakfasts for a month at the fire pit."

"As long as you have more Dair information to share, you're pretty safe from my wrath."

"Then I'll be sure to keep him around for——like—— ever."

"Good call, dream girl, now get back to the story."

Despite all their teasing and ribbing on each other, Serenity really was glad to have a friend like Glory, regardless if she happened to be pushy, bossy, and much too honest. She needed her friend so that she didn't have to traverse the new world that was emerging before her by herself. When Dair came back, she wouldn't have to face all the questions that returned with him on her own. Glory would be there to talk her off the ledge and for that she could put up with any and all of her eccentricities.

Two hundred miles away from the town of Yellville, Arkansas, Emma Whitmore sat staring down at the suitcase in her lap. Her life had been forever changed just five days prior when her parents were shot and killed during a robbery at a gas station. For five days, her life had been total chaos as the state searched for any family that could take her in. Finally, they had found her mother's sister—a sister that Emma knew nothing about. As far as Emma knew, her mother had been an only child. But Emma was quickly learning that adults did not always tell the truth, no matter how much they loved you.

"It's time to get on the bus," the lady from the Department of Human Services said, reaching out a hand for Emma to take.

Emma stared at the offered hand and then stood on her own. She wasn't a baby; she didn't need anyone to hold her hand just to get on a stupid bus. She took her seat by the window, not looking at the lady as she sat down next to her. Emma was sure that the woman had told her her name, but she couldn't remember it. She didn't even remember the aunt's name that she was told she was going to live with.

"Now, Emma, I need you to listen to me very carefully, alright?"

She turned her head to look at the woman.

"I'm going to give you my number, and if for any reason you don't feel safe at your aunt's house, you call me immediately, okay?"

Emma was eight-years-old, but she was not ignorant of the world. Her parents had always been very candid about the things that happened to people in their neighborhood. Her mama had said more than once that the world was the devil's playground, and we were the toys he desperately wanted to possess. She knew that there were bad people in the world, people that let the devil play with them, but she had never faced one in her life. If this aunt was going to be the first play thing of the devil's that she would meet, then she would do it with her head held high and her shoulders pulled back. She nodded at the lady who had been waiting for a response.

"My mama told me that one of the best ways to defeat evil was to face it head on with confident that the battle was already won. She said, 'if you didn't give it a weakness to feed on, then it could not possess you.' I'm not weak, ma'am."

The sadness Emma saw in the woman's eyes told her that she didn't think Emma was strong enough to face what was coming. *Then I'll just have to prove her wrong, right Mama?* She thought to herself as she turned back to look out the window. She watched as the trees and ground rushed past them, taking her closer to a future filled with uncertainty and without her parents in it. Now, more than ever, she would have to lean on all the things her mother had taught her. If she was going to survive and come out on the other side still able to find her destiny, then she was going to have to fight for it. A memory came back to her then from one day during a history lesson. She'd been learning about the different wars in which the United States had been involved. Emma had asked why the U.S. seemed to always have to help other countries with disputes that didn't seem to concern them.

"*Because it was the right thing to do. When the strong stand by and watch those weaker than them being destroyed and do nothing, that is when you will know that our country has become a Godless one. We are strong and have been blessed abundantly; therefore, we will fight when no one else can, and sometimes a clean fight isn't enough to keep us safe or ensure the safety of others we are responsible for. Sometimes, Emma, we have to fight dirty.*"

Emma wasn't sure what her mama had meant by fighting dirty, but deep in her gut she had a feeling she was going to learn very soon what it was and whether or not she had it in her to do it.

Chapter 4

"To see a cup or chalice in your dreams means that a great challenge will soon come your way. The choices you make during the trial will either destroy you or make you stronger."

It had been three days since Dair had seen Serenity. Though he hadn't seen her, he had not left her completely unsupervised. Raphael had been kind enough to keep watch over her, but not without dishing out several jibes about Dair being 'whipped' and having a few too many laughs at Dair's expense. In the meantime, Dair had taken care of two rather easy assignments. Both humans had accepted the direction the dreams Dair weaved for them and had made plans to move forward in the direction he had encouraged. He wished they were all that easy.

"You are getting that mopey look again," Raphael's voice broke the silence that had become the norm for them.

Dair shot him a glare. "I don't have a mopey look."

Raphael laughed. "Dearest brother, I hate to tell you this, but ever since Serenity has come along and tied you up in knots, you have been exhibiting a plethora of new looks that I've never seen on you before. And mopey is most definitely one of them."

He didn't respond. Perhaps, because he knew his friend was right, but he wasn't about to give him the satisfaction of agreeing. It was bad enough that the angel kept reminding him that he was going to have to face the consequences from the Creator at some point. It was a constant dull ache in the back of his mind, one that he kept ignoring.

"You only have two days left, Brudair. Surely the Sandman, lover of the night, powerful immortal, can handle two more days away from his love?"

"When did you get so talkative? The Raphael I remember was one of few words."

His friend shot him a wicked smile, one that should not be on the face of an angel. "Talking has never been this fun before."

"Let's just move on to our next human."

Raphael held his hands up in surrender. "Lead on fearless rebel."

"I liked you better when you didn't talk," Dair grumbled and then closed his eyes, concentrating on the power flowing inside of him like an electrical current. In order to find out who his next assignment was, he simply had to tap into the heavenly realm with his mind. The name was whispered into his mind and just like that he knew where he was supposed to go.

Emma Whitmore, the name filled his mind and he felt a tightening in his gut. After the dream he had weaved for Serenity involving little Emma, he had known that they were tied together in some way. He just hadn't known the reason would be making an appearance so soon. He had seen Emma before, but not as an assignment. It was because she had seen him. She was one of those children so in touch with the world around her that she had absolutely no problem believing in something that most would or could not. He had been on an assignment in her town, weaving for one member of her church. She had seen him while visiting that person in their home. He remembered how she had motioned him to follow her outside and then turned and looked at him with her hands on her hips. She was so small, yet so very brave.

"Who are you and why are you in Mr. Shaw's house?"

"Aren't you scared of me?" he asked her. "Don't you wonder why the adults didn't see me come in?"

She shook her head. "Grown folks miss a lot of things. They only see what's right in front of them and only if it makes sense."

"You're perceptive for one so young."

She shrugged. "I'm a genius; my mama said so."

Dair had decided to tell her about himself, though he didn't fully understand why. Call it loneliness or perhaps simply the need for someone other than the angels and the Creator to know him, but he felt compelled to do so. She had listened attentively and asked a few questions. But mostly she just accepted it.

"I can't say that I would want your job. But then again, even though nobody knows it, you help change the world. That's a pretty big deal."

When he had left her that night, it was with a little less weight on his shoulders as she had allowed him to see himself through the eyes of a child's innocence. She had given him a gift and she didn't even know it.

"Who is our next human?" Raphael interrupted his thoughts.

"Her name is Emma. She is in Yellville, though that is not where she was the first time I met her."

"You have been to see her before?"

Dair shook his head. "Not as an assignment." He quickly filled Raphael in on how he had met Emma and then rubbed his face in a very human gesture. "I knew she would be on my list eventually, I just didn't know it would be this soon, or that she would wind up in Yellville."

"Do you think it might have anything to do with your Serenity?"

"I'm sure she does, but in what way, that I don't know. I'm not often privy to the *whats* and *whys* of the future of humans only that they are very important people."

"Back to Yellville it is," Raphael said as he shot into the air leaving Dair to follow.

Emma's aunt had been an hour late in picking her up from the bus station. When she did finally arrive, Emma had known immediately who she was. She was the spitting image of her mother, only it looked as though life had taken her through the wash and then beat her with a stick one too many times. She looked much, much older than her mother and much less happy. This was a woman who had not had much good in her life. Emma didn't know whether it was by her own doing or because it was simply her lot in life.. She did know that the life she had known in Memphis was just a memory. Once the DHS lady had spoken to her aunt, whose name she remembered was Mildred, she had been very reluctant to let Emma go with her. She kept telling Emma to call her anytime she wanted. Finally, Mildred had taken Emma's hand and drug her to the beat up old station wagon that waited for them in the parking lot.

The wagon had seen much better days. Emma sat in the car trying not to shiver. Either her aunt had some moral objections to using the heater, or the clunker just didn't have one that was operational. Emma would bet on the latter. She clenched her teeth together to keep them from clicking together. Emma tried to distract herself from the cold by staring out of the window and taking in the small town that would now be her home. The sound of the wheels crunching on ice and snow as her aunt navigated the streets reminded her of the few times it had snowed in Memphis. Her mom hated to drive in the snow and would only do it if there was no other option. Emma had ridden with her once and had been blessed with the privilege of hearing her mother's commentary all the way to the grocery store. *Snow seems to bring out the idiot in everyone, Emma,* she told her. *People see white stuff on the ground and suddenly everyone is a stunt driver and their cars are magically indestructible. You'd think they would learn from all the other idiots in the ditches, but nope, they just go right on acting like fools.* Emma smiled on the inside as her mama's words filled her mind. When she let go of the memory and refocused her eyes, she realized they were pulling into the driveway of a house that looked as though it should have been surrounded by a yellow strip bearing the words CONDEMNED written over and over. But because it did not have such a cautionary strip, she deduced that this was her aunt's home and, by default, now hers as well. *Find the good in every situation. Emma Jean, because if you don't you will face a life full of disappointment and sorrow,* more of her mama's wisdom filler her head. She wondered what good her mama would have found in that situation. Knowing her mama she would say something like, *be thankful you have four walls and roof over your head.* Emma would ask, what if it's full of other critters that had taken up residency in it? Where is the good in that? And her mama would answer, *the good is knowing that you would have someone to complain to about the dwelling's management.* No one likes to complain alone. Emma nearly laughed out loud as the car came to a stop. Her mama was wise, but she had a wicked sense of humor too.

Without a word, Mildred slid out and slammed the door shut and Emma reluctantly followed. She ambled after her aunt, dragging her heavy suitcase up the rickety wooden steps and into the house. As she inched slowly into the living room, Emma noticed the faint smell of wet dog. She imagined it was only faint because the overwhelming scent of cigarette smoke saturated everything in the house. Emma's mama had tried to instill in her not to be judgmental, that God loved every person He created, but boy was it hard not to judge her aunt. Just from one glance around her, the first thing she deduced was that Mildred was lazy. Emma had a feeling that wasn't going to bode well for her.

"Now listen up y'hear." The thick country accent came out from the scratchy, dry throat of her aunt. "I ain't got no time to coddle you like no baby. You hungry, you fix your own food. If'in you has to use the bathroom, then go. Don't be wetting the bed neither. I have no idea hows my sister, snob that she was, raised you, but in my house you gonna help. You wash the dishes, pick up the trash, and wipe things down. You ain't living here for free just cause you kin. You gots to earn your way. Now my shows fixing to be on and I don't like to be disturbed so go play outside or to your room. Yours is the first one on the left just down that there hall." Her aunt pointed in a vague direction as her eyes were already glued to the small television directly in front of an old recliner that creaked loudly as she sat down in it. It wasn't from her weight, because Mildred was little more than skin and bones. Her tall form looked near skeletal. Heavy lidded, bloodshot eyes stared out at the television from deep sunken sockets.

Obviously dismissed, Emma grabbed her bag and headed to the indicated hallway in search of her new room—her new life. She took the first door on the left and walked into what could only be described as utter chaos. There were newspapers stacked along the wall nearly halfway to the ceiling. There were trash bags overflowing with clothes and old shoes stacked in one corner, and because the room was so small, about three feet from the door was the bed. It was piled with all sorts of broken and discarded knickknacks that Emma's mama would have labeled as pure junk. The room smelled as if something had died in it about six months ago, but only after it had rolled around on the inside of another dead animal. She tried not to gag as she walked in and was reluctant to set her bag down for fear of irreversibly staining it. She heard a scurrying to her right and turned just in time to see a tiny mouse squeezed through the stacks of newspaper. Immediately following it, an orange cat lunged, swiping a second too late. The cat growled at its escaped meal and twitched its tail back and forth angrily.

"Well, at least I'm not the only one that has to live in this junkyard," she mumbled. She stood there a minute longer before she remembered another thing her mama had told her; *Emma, if you want something in life, you have to go after it. Nobody is going to hand it to you, and if they seem like they're trying to, then there is something in it for them. You can dream all day long about having a hot meal, but if you don't do the work to earn the money to buy the food and then don't get off your rear end and actually cook it, you will end up going hungry, and you will have no one but yourself to blame.*

No one was going to clean this disgusting bed for her. Either she would do it, or she'd sleep standing up. *I'm not a victim*, she told herself. Then she set her suitcase down and pushed the sleeves of her plaid shirt up. It was time to get to work. She sure as heck was not sleeping standing up tonight. With one eye open maybe, but not standing up.

"Just a heads up." She looked back at the cat who was still twitching angrily. "I completely accept work done by animals, so if you or your tiny dinner there wants to help clean up what is obviously your home, then please don't *not* help on my account." Did she really expect the cat and mouse to turn into some Disney characters and begin whistling as they worked? No. But it was nice to have someone to talk to. She had a feeling she was going to get mighty lonely, very fast.

Night had begun to fall when Emma realized that it was getting a little difficult to see in the room. She went to flip on the light but nothing happened. She stood there in the darkening room trying to decide if she should ask Mildred for a light bulb or just go seek one out herself. Her desire to avoid any conflict with the obviously disturbed woman won out and she set off. Rather than searching the kitchen or utility room, she went into the bathroom, hoping that there would be more than one light in it that she could pilfer without anyone being the wiser. She found it, two doors down from her room, and when she flipped on the light, she found what she was looking for. Above the mirror three bright bulbs were sticking out of the sockets. Emma flipped the light back off and waited for her eyes to adjust to the darkness before attempting to climb up on the sink to retrieve one of the bulbs.

Once back in her room a new dilemma occurred. How on earth was she going to get the bulb into the socket when it was way up on the ceiling and she was way down on the ground?

"It appears that you have a bit of a dilemma." Her head whipped around and she saw him—the Sandman whom she had met a couple of years ago. She knew him instantly. He wasn't a figure one was likely to forget. But he wasn't alone; he had, what appeared to Emma, an angel standing with him. She was pretty sure that her estimation of the stranger was correct, as he had huge white feathery wings poking out of the back of his leather jacket and a glow seemed to emanate from him.

"Are you here to see my aunt?" Her voice rose in confusion. She just couldn't imagine her aunt being someone that would change the course of history.

Dair shook his head. "No, little genius, I'm here for you." He reached out and took the bulb from her hand, removed the old one, tossed it into the now overflowing wastebasket, and screwed in the new one. Because of his height, he could have easily touched the ceiling if he'd have wanted to. Emma was frozen in place as she tried to make sense of what he had just told her. She couldn't imagine anything was special enough about her that could influence anything or anyone, let alone the entire course of history.

"I'm only eight-years-old," she pointed out.

"Just because I'm here now doesn't mean that your destiny will be fulfilled immediately. I am simply to put you on the right path through suggestions in your dreams. Age has nothing to do with it," Dair told her.

"Can't you just tell me what to do since I can see you?"

He shook his head. "It doesn't work like that. I don't know what your destiny is. I only know enough to point you in the direction you should go, and I can only relay that information through dreams."

"Hmm, bummer." Emma looked at the angel again and then frowned. "Why's he here? Is my destiny to die?"

The angel smiled at her and it was radiant. "I am merely keeping Brudair company; he is having a bit of a rough week."

Emma thought about this and then smiled with a mischievous gleam in her eyes. "Is it because of the girl from my dream? Serenity, I think is what she told me her name was. She looked like she was going to be, what my mama called, a tough cookie to crack."

The angel burst into a belly laugh while Dair frowned at both of them.

"She is proving to be one of my more difficult assignments," he agreed.

There was a moment of awkward silence and then Dair spoke again. "Why are you here, Emma?"

She tried not to flinch at the thought of her parents, but the pain was still so very raw. DHS had suggested that she talk with a counselor, and she had tried but she didn't know what to say. She was sad but she didn't think it had really set in that they were gone.

"My parents were killed. They were shot at a gas station," she told him as she climbed up on the bed. Emma still wasn't ready to talk about it, not even with an angel and the Sandman. "I guess I should go to sleep so you can do your job."

"I am sorry for your loss, little one," the angel said

as he reached out a hand and placed it on her forehead. Emma felt power rush into her and then peace—like she had not known since before her parents' death—flowed through her.

"Thank you," she told him, unable to think of anything else that would be adequate for the gift he'd just given her. For the moment the pain was at bay and she might actually get some sleep. Emma was asleep as soon as her head hit the dusty pillow.

Dair stared down at the sleeping child and was surprised at how very young she looked. When she was awake her mature vocabulary and confidence made her seem like a much older child, but in sleep all that was stripped away, and she looked like the innocent eight-year-old that she was.

"She has been through much," Raphael said quietly.

"I'm afraid that she will go through worse before her life gets any better." Dair's jaw clenched as he looked around the room for the first time and saw the living conditions that she would be forced to endure. "This woman is not fit to raise a child."

Raphael laid his hand on Dair's shoulder. "We cannot interfere, you know that. The consequences for that is banishment."

"I know. But that doesn't mean it makes it easy to watch." Dair stepped forward and closed his eyes. He gathered his power and allowed Emma's dream to take form and then he gently entered her mind. The dream didn't seem very significant to him. It showed Emma going to the library, and he recognized it as the Marion County Library, where Serenity's aunt worked. That was all and as his part in the dream was concluded, he pulled out of her mind.

"I've made sure she will sleep peacefully," Raphael told him.

"What happened to not interfering?"

"Granting a little child a small measure of peace will not change the course of history or interfere with her free will."

"I know Serenity's and Emma's fates are tied together somehow," Dair spoke up the thoughts that had been in his mind since he realized Emma was his assignment. "And for some reason it doesn't feel like that's a good thing."

"You must let their destiny unfold, regardless of whether or not you agree or like the way it feels." Raphael's words were not meant to be unkind; he was simply reminding Dair that he had no place in the human realm, not really. He was simply a messenger.

"What if I can't?" Dair asked.

"Then you must leave, for good."

Serenity looked into her bathroom mirror after having washed her face. The air hitting her wet skin was cool and she shivered. She looked tired. The dark circles under her eyes did nothing for her already pale skin, and she was pretty sure she might have lost a few pounds, but she didn't typically pay attention to the scales.

"Longest...week...ever," she told her reflection.

She was frustrated with herself even though she had done what Glory had told her. She'd gone on living. She hadn't sulked in her bedroom or curled up in a ball and rocked back and forth as though she'd lost touch with reality. She had gone to school, talked to friends, gone to work, helped at the library, and had dinner with her Aunt Darla and Uncle Wayne who was home for the week. She'd lived, *darn it*. But the one thing she hadn't done much of was sleep. She kept thinking that he would come when she slept, or maybe she'd just been hoping. Serenity hadn't felt depressed as she lay in her bed at night with sleep refusing to take her under. Rather, she just couldn't stop her mind from racing with thoughts about the mysterious Dair. As much as she tried, she just couldn't push him out of her mind. She wondered what he looked like, what he did during the day when he wasn't weaving dreams for people, and where he lived, or *if* he lived anywhere. Did he eat or sleep or have any of the normal human body needs and functions? She hadn't dwelt on that too long because, well, she didn't exactly know him well enough to be concerned with those things. So sleep had eluded her while her mind created hazy images of a mystery guy with an alluring voice.

Serenity brushed her teeth and then headed to the living room to tell her aunt and uncle goodnight.

"I'm going to turn in; I'm so tired," she told them.

"You look a little rough around the edges," Uncle Wayne told her, never one to mince words.

"Thank you for that, oh fish whisperer," she said dryly.

"Do you work at the vet tomorrow?" Darla asked.

Serenity nodded. "Yep, I've got to be there by 7:00 a.m. to let the dogs outside." She looked over at Wayne.

"Any more hunting expeditions planned?"

"Hope not, we found the den of the mountain lion and waited until she came back from hunting. It was freezing but we got her. Hopefully, the Thompson's won't lose any more goats." Serenity nodded and then turned back to go to her room. In her mind she counted, *three, two, one.*

"I got a new one for you," her Uncle Wayne hollered just before she reached her door. She smiled to herself, knowing what was coming.

"Okay," she said as she walked back into the living room. "Let's hear it." Aunt Darla was already shaking her head.

"Relax, Darla, it's not that bad," Wayne told his wife.

"I've heard that before," she retorted.

"Why do squirrels swim on their backs?" He paused for effect and then chuckled as he answered. "To keep their nuts dry."

Serenity couldn't help but crack a smile, though Darla told her laughing at his jokes only encouraged him. Serenity disagreed. She always responded, *I think if we didn't laugh at them then he would just tell more because he would be determined to get a laugh out of us.*

"You're right, Uncle Wayne, compared to your other material that wasn't too bad." Serenity waved goodnight and headed for her room.

She set her alarm on her phone, just in case she actually got some sleep. Being late to work was not something she made a habit of, especially when she knew those poor dogs were waiting to go outside to do their business. Serenity flipped off her light and then pulled back the covers of her bed and climbed in. But just like the other nights, tired as she was, she couldn't sleep. She stared up at the ceiling counting the fan rotations. Nearly a half hour later the blades on the fan began to grow darker. She thought perhaps her eyelids were finally getting heavy, but she quickly realized that she still wasn't the least bit sleepy. He was back.

Serenity shot up and she realized how comical she must have looked but she pushed away her embarrassment. She had more important things to worry about besides being self-conscious.

"Dair?" she nearly whispered into the now completely pitch black room.

"Yes." His voice was every bit as potent as it had been the first time he'd spoken to her. Serenity shook off the effects. *Focus Sarah,* she told herself.

"I wasn't sure if you'd come back," she admitted.

"I told you I would."

She couldn't tell anything by his tone of voice. It wasn't betraying any emotion and it frustrated her. Was he irritated with her for doubting him? Had he been thinking about her all week and worrying about what she was going to say to him?

"How was your week?" he asked.

"Long," she blurted out before she had time to censor herself. He chuckled and, by all that was delicious in this world, that chuckle should be outlawed. Any woman who heard that would want to crawl up in his lap and purr.

"As was mine."

"Really?" Serenity thought she detected a little sadness in his voice.

"It was not my choice to be separated from you, Serenity. Why are you surprised that I would dislike being away?" He wasn't being mean, just stating the facts.

"I guess I'm a little leery. You claim to have intense emotions for me, but you don't even know me."

Again with the chuckle.

"Could you please not do that?" she asked almost breathlessly.

"Do what?" His voice rumbled.

He knew exactly what she was talking about but she answered him anyways. "That little laugh. Could you refrain from it please?"

"I will do my best if you tell me why you don't want me to laugh."

Seriously! she mentally huffed. "It's disarming."

"Hmm, good to know," he muttered and it seemed it was more to himself than an answer for her. "In response to your concerns," he continued in a less flirty tone, which Serenity's dignity appreciated. "We have established that I am not human."

"Definitely established," she agreed.

"And because I'm not human I don't think and feel as a human does. My emotions are much, much more intense. They are not fleeting nor are they given freely to just anyone. My life is much too long to squander such precious things like love, trust, respect, and adoration. I am not meant to have a mate. Perhaps, that also is why my feelings are so strong, because being drawn to you cannot be either of our fates. It cannot be because the Creator never intended the Sandman to have a companion. My existence was to solely be about my task. And I had accepted that. But then you were my next assignment and I was intrigued by the selflessness in you. So I watched you, I listened, and I do apologize if that sounds a little like I was stalking you."

Serenity laughed because he was right, it was pretty

freaking creepy. But she could hear in his voice that he wasn't watching her in a creepy way. He was curious. He wanted to understand her.

"And so because of the things you observed about me, you began to care for me?" she asked.

"I was attracted to you the minute I saw you. But it grew into something more when I got to see beyond your beautiful face."

If he was trying to get brownie points he was doing a good job. Serenity felt her face heat up at the compliment. She'd never been good at taking compliments.

"Your skin is lovely when you blush."

His words took her by surprised and she sucked in a sharp breath. "You can see me?" She was looking around as if that was going to somehow help her see him. *Stop being a moron, Sarah, you can't even see your hand in front of your face.* Serenity chastised herself and then sat still.

"I am the Sandman, the Dream Weaver, the Enticer of Slumber. The night is mine. The darkness is my cloak and obeys my commands. If I do not want to be seen, I can prevent it."

"The girl in my dream, Emma, has seen you," she pointed out.

"Yes." There was a smile in his voice, and Serenity wished so much that she could see that smile. "Children are very perceptive, much more so than adults. Emma saw me when I was on another assignment and she interrogated me. She is quite impressive for an eight-year-old."

"I thought the same thing."

They were both silent for a few minutes. Serenity wasn't sure what to say next. Should she just jump in

with, *hey please stay and hang out so we can see where this goes?*
Could he stay, even if he wanted to? There were just so
many questions, so many *what ifs*. She didn't know
where to start so instead she stayed silent.

"Have you decided whether you want me to leave
or not?" he asked, proving that he was indeed braver
than she.

"I talked about it with my best friend." She waited
to see if he would freak out over the fact that she'd told
someone about him.

"She believed you?" He sounded completely
skeptical. Silly immortal.

"Not all adults are closed minded. Glory knows I
wouldn't lie. So yes, she believed me."

"What did she say?"

Serenity thought back to the many times her best
friend had asked if Dair was hot and then about her
description of what his voice induced. She decided he
didn't really need to know much of what Glory said.
"She thought I should give you a chance."

His silence indicated to her that he was surprised
by her best friend's reaction.

"And what are your thoughts?"

"I," she took a deep breath and let it out before
she finished, "agree."

Suddenly the darkness began to grow lighter until
she could see though her light was still off. She blinked
and let her eyes adjust before looking up. When she
finally did, she found herself having to tilt her head up
and up and up until she finally saw the face of the very
tall, inhumanly handsome immortal before her.

Her throat suddenly felt as if she'd been drinking
sand all day and the hinges in her jaw seemed to be
broken because her mouth would not close. No matter

how much she screamed in her mind for her brain to close her gaping jaws, it just wouldn't happen. As Serenity stared up into eyes so black and clear that she could nearly see her reflection, a brief thought flew through her mind; *I could stare into those eyes for eternity.*

When he cleared his throat it seemed to make something inside her click and her synapses started firing again. She was able to look away from the mesmerizing eyes to the rest of his face. He was beautiful—masculine, no doubt, but beautiful as well. He had black hair, shiny and long on top, sweeping to the side. His skin appeared as smooth as marble and his jaw was strong and defined. His nose was straight and perfectly proportioned for his face and his lips. *My, my.* Serenity purred to herself. His lips, plump without being feminine, curved up in that moment to one side in a little smirk. Her eyes snapped back up to his and the gleam in them said he completely understood that she was basically just checking him out, like looking over a piece of fruit in a grocery store. And much to her chagrin, her next thought was whether or not he'd taste as sweet as the fruit looked. It was one of those moments when she really wanted to smack herself.

"I had the same reaction the first time I saw you," Dair said wrapping her in the warmth of his deep voice again.

It took some work but Serenity finally managed to swallow down the sand. "I, uh, I don't know what you mean." Playing dumb was a good way to go, right? She couldn't very well fess up to mentally drooling over him.

"So you don't find me attractive?" His brow pinched together giving him a boyish cuteness.

"I didn't say that."

"But you didn't say you did either."

"Do you start all your conversations with how attractive you find the other person?"

There was that laugh again. The heat rushed up her neck until Serenity was sure she must be as red as Santa's butt.

"Alright, you win," he conceded. "I will refrain from making any more assumptions because I don't believe I could keep up with your witty banter." He held out his hand then and leaned forward just a bit. "I'm Brudair, and it's an honor to meet you."

Coming from any other man on planet earth that would have been the cheesiest thing she'd ever seen. But from Dair, it was so natural and sincere that instead of laughing she wanted to sigh. Was she pathetic? Definitely. Did she care at that moment? Not even a tiny bit. Serenity reached out her hand and placed it in his larger one. The contact with his cool skin made her want to sigh. "I'm Serenity, but you already know that. It's nice to meet you as well." She expected him to release her hand but instead he simply held it firmly in his own. He straightened and took another step towards her. She felt so small sitting on the bed while Dair stood looming over her. "Would you like to sit?" She nodded to the end of her bed. He nodded in return and stepped to the side, and, in moves that seemed too graceful for such a large person, he sat, barely jarring her at all. He had yet to let go of her hand, not that she minded.

"So what now?" Serenity asked him trying very hard not to squirm under his intense gaze.

"I'm not sure. I've never been in this situation before. What have you done in past relationships?"

Serenity didn't miss the tightening of his lips as he

asked her about other boyfriends. He needn't have worried. Looking away from him, suddenly feeling inadequate she answered, "I've never been in this situation either. I've never dated anyone."

"Then once again you are not like the other humans. I will not deny that I am happy to hear that there have been none before me. I would hate to have to compete with memories."

She looked back at him, thankful that he didn't think her strange for being eighteen and a virgin in more ways than just the biblical sense. She'd never held a guy's hand, not romantically. She'd never kissed anyone or been held in strong arms by a guy who cared for her. "Maybe we could start by getting to know each other a little better. Where did you come from? Where do you live? How long will you be here? Just for a start." She smiled sheepishly as his eyes widened at her sudden rapid fire questions.

"I was hoping I could win you over by my charm, charisma, and good looks before I had to tell you things that might scare you off." Despite the light sound in his voice, in his eyes Serenity could see real worry.

"If you are worried that I will be shocked by what you are going to tell me, then you're right, I might be. But I'm not a coward. I don't run from something just because it's different from me."

"Fair enough. I will hold you to your word," he said as he finally let go of her hand.

She fought the urge to snatch it back. Because ya know, that wouldn't be weird at all. Serenity rolled her eyes at herself.

"I was made by the Creator," he began. "I do not have a home. I have no need of sleep or food, and I can find shelter in the homes of my assignments if I need to get out of the weather." His eyes seemed to grow troubled and she was captivated by the swirling darkness she saw in them. As if black smoke was a part of his iris, it danced in the orbs. "And as for how long I will be here," his stormy eyes met hers as he finished, "I do not know the answer to that."

"But you will have to leave, eventually?" Serenity wanted clarification. She did not want to get so attached to Dair that when he left he took more of her with him than was left behind to cope. A thought occurred to her then. Was he the reason she wound up staying in Yellville in her dream? She wouldn't deny that he would be a major point in favor of staying.

"I wish I could tell you no." Dair looked down at his hands which were clasped in his lap. His large shoulders slumped forward. "I should have already left. My assignment was done the night that you finished the dream. I don't know how long I have before I am sent for."

"Will you be punished?" She didn't like the idea of him being hurt because of her.

His lips twitched in amusement. "Not in the way you're thinking. I won't be flogged or anything. Do you have any other questions?"

Serenity knew he was changing the topic on purpose and she would let him, for now. "Is it hard to adjust as the times change? I mean, how do you keep up with all of it?

"I am merely an observer in this realm, so I get to watch everything, and I pick up on things like the changing lingo and clothing. I've become quite adept at it over the years. I'm usually ahead of the times actually. Knowing what is normal for each of my assigned humans is a necessity for the dream I make for them.

Each dream must be at least somewhat familiar to them."

"What's your favorite decade?" Serenity leaned forward so that her elbows were resting on her legs and her face propped in her hands.

"Until now I'd never had a favorite. I wasn't a part of the human world, just an interloper. It's hard to enjoy something that you never partake in."

She realized then from that statement just how lonely Dair's life must be. To have to watch others have relationships whether with parents, siblings, or significant others but to never get to experience them would be a very lonely existence.

"So, I'm assuming that you don't have any parents?"

He shook his head. "Only the Creator. I have existed for a very long time but I was never a child. I was created just as I look now and I've always been this way." His eyes met hers and she saw the swirling storm in them again.

"Why do your eyes do that?" She pointed as if he didn't know where his own eyes were.

Dair closed them for a few seconds and when he opened them back they were clear and black again. "My emotions tend to cause it. Strong emotions."

She wasn't sure if she was ready to hear what those strong emotions were so she didn't ask. When in doubt, avoidance seemed like the best course of action. The slight smile on his lips told her he knew exactly what she was thinking.

"It's late," Dair said as he reached up and brushed aside a lock of her hair. "I should let you get some sleep. Do you work tomorrow?"

She nodded, unable to speak as his fingers trailed

down her neck. When he pulled his hand away the loss of the cool contact reminded her that she wanted to ask him about that.

"Why is your skin so cool?"

"Last question for the night, Princess."

She frowned at the nickname. Serenity wasn't sure if she liked it or not. But coming from Dair and his sultry voice, she just might let him call her anything.

"When you think of daylight, of daytime, do you associate it with warmth or coolness?"

She considered the question. "Warmth, of course," Serenity answered.

Dair nodded. "And when you think of the dark, of nighttime you probably think of it being cool. I am like the night—cool, a lack of warmth because there is no sun during the night— which is my time."

"There is warmth in you, even if it isn't in your skin," she told him impulsively because she knew it was true.

"Thank you," he said quietly but the gratitude she saw in his eyes said more than his words ever could. "Now I will let you get some sleep."

He stood and Serenity found herself scrambling to her feet. She didn't want him to go, but she knew that he was right. She had to be up early and would be exhausted if she didn't get some sleep.

"So," she said as she looked down at the suddenly very interesting floor. "Will I see you tomorrow?"

Dair took a step towards her and then lifted her chin with a gentle finger. His large hand moved to cup her cheek as her wide eyes looked into his swirling ones. "I couldn't stay away even if you wanted me to. This past week was nearly unbearable for me. I'd not like to repeat it anytime soon."

Heat swept up her body as she felt the blush on her skin.

"So yes, you will see me tomorrow," he continued when she didn't say anything. "What time to you get off work?"

"Noon," she told him and wanted to give herself a round of applause that she actually spoke and didn't just stand there drooling over him.

"Can I meet you there?"

She nodded. Okay, so forget the round of applause; now she couldn't even utter one word. Dair took another step closer to her and then began to lean down towards her. Was he going to kiss her? Would she let him? Glory would probably kill her once she got a look at Dair and then found out that Serenity hadn't let him kiss her. She heard him take a deep breath and could have sworn he groaned, but it was so soft she couldn't be sure. Her eyes fluttered closed as his face came closer. Okay, so maybe she would let him kiss her. Instead of his full lips on hers, she felt them on her forehead. She started to be disappointed but then she felt his strong arm encircle her waist and pull her to him. His body was hard against her softer one, and Serenity couldn't help but notice how sheltered she felt enveloped in his large frame, as if nothing in the world could hurt her as long as his arms were around her protecting her.

"Sleep, good Princess of Peace," he whispered as he stepped away from their embrace. When she opened her eyes her room was empty.

Serenity shivered. "You're not going to stay invisible in my room are you?" she asked the empty room. After several minutes with no response, she took that to mean that Dair was really gone. She climbed back into bed and let out a soft sigh as Mr. Whitherby hopped up next to her. "Well, what'd you think about him Mr. W?"

Her cat let out a low rumble.

Serenity chuckled. "Yeah, he gets my motor running too. But paws off, I don't care which way you swing, that immortal is spoken for."

Chapter 5

"To dream of a snail signifies a long and arduous journey is ahead of you. Beware of starting too quickly. Patience and preparation will be rewarded. However, it could also mean that you have recently stepped in something slimy."

Dair wrapped the shadows of the night around him as he stepped back into the trees that surrounded the house where Serenity was now sleeping. He had left her room abruptly because, had he not, he might have stayed all night just to listen to her voice. He knew that she needed rest. Serenity had a life, regardless of whether or not he wanted to monopolize her nights, and he needed to be sensitive to that. He'd nearly gone back to her several times in the two hours that it took her to finally fall asleep. He could have simply put her to sleep himself, but of course, such actions were outside of his purpose, and he was already crossing the line with the Creator. She tossed and turned and talked to her cat until finally her breathing grew slow and steady. It was then that he finally allowed himself to think about the fact that he had spoken to her, and she had seen him and had not asked him to leave. Sarah Serenity Tillman wanted to know him.

His lips spread into a wide smile and his head fell back as his eyes closed. The crisp winter air flowed over him and rustled his hair. He didn't even shiver in the cold mountain air. All his thoughts were on the brunette who had stolen his heart.

"She wants you to stay?" Raphael's voice intruded on his moment but still the smile didn't falter.

He turned to look at the angel. "She does."

"How long?"

Dair shrugged. "Until she wants me to leave."

"And when she begins to age and you stay the same?"

"I'll love her still."

"But how will she feel about looking like your mother instead of your mate?"

Dair knew that Raphael wasn't trying to be cruel. But that didn't stop the frustration that gripped him. Being reminded that he could not truly have a life with Serenity, not a human one, was painful.

"I don't know what then," he finally admitted.

"Perhaps, it is something you need to bring to her attention," Raphael recommended.

Dair knew his old friend was right, and he would talk to her about it, but it might be later rather than sooner.

Emma tried to be as quiet as she could. She opened the door to her room and looked down the hall to the bathroom and then back in the direction of the living room where she could hear the yelling. If she didn't have to pee so badly, she wouldn't even consider leaving the safety of her hovel. But she knew if she didn't make a run for it very soon, things were going to get messy. She bit her bottom lip as she fidgeted from foot to foot, building her courage internally.

All she had to do was push open the door a little further, hope it didn't creak, hurry soundlessly to the bathroom, shut the door, hope it didn't creak, pee, wash her hands, and then return just as quietly. She could do that right? She jumped when she heard a loud crash against the wall. *Maybe I can hold it until whoever that is leaves*, she thought as she began to close the door.

"You can go; I'll keep you safe."

Emma turned at the sound of Dair's voice. He was in his usual black: black pants, black long sleeve shirt, and black jacket and boots. She had told him that his clothes were a tad over the top, considering his job. He didn't seem to care.

"It sounds bad out there," she said and pointed out the door just as another loud crash erupted followed by some cursing.

"Nothing is going to happen to you," Dair told her as he walked over and pulled the door quietly open. "Go do what you need to and I'll be here keeping watch."

Emma didn't know if Dair could really do anything to protect her or not. He was, after all, just the Sandman, not a guardian angel. But something in his dark eyes told her to trust him. And she had to pee so badly by that point that there really was no other option. She darted out the door and made it to the bathroom and closed the door as quietly as she could behind her.

Business done and hands washed, she peeked out the bathroom door to find Dair standing in the hall with his huge frame nearly taking up the entire space. His arms were folded against his chest as he stared in the direction of the noise. He made a motion for her to come on with his hand, but his eyes never left the front of the hall. She dashed back and leapt onto the bed turning in the same motion so that she landed facing Dair who was closing the door behind them.

"How long has that been going on?" he asked her gently as he knelt down on the floor across the room from her.

"Since early this morning," Emma told him.

"Has anyone come in here?"

She shook her head. "My aunt stuck her head in just after the banging on the door started. She said, *don't you leave this room for nothing; if you do I'll take a switch to your backside.* But that was at least a couple of hours ago. Since then there's been nothing but screaming, cursing, and things hitting the wall. I would have obeyed had I not had to go to the bathroom, but I haven't had an accident since I was knee high to a grasshopper, that's what my mama always said, and I wasn't about to have one just to keep from getting a switch to my butt."

"Knee high to a grasshopper, huh?" He smiled at her.

"I know, I'm not much taller now, but believe me, I used to be shorter." Another crash had them both looking at the door.

"Emma you need to get out of the house for a little while," Dair told her as he stood. "Raphael," he called out as he looked up at the ceiling.

Her eyes widened as the angel appeared out of nowhere standing next to Dair.

"You shouted?" The angel's brow rose when he too heard the screaming. He looked back at her and his lips tightened.

"Can you take Emma to the library?" Dair asked

him. "I have a feeling Darla would love her." He didn't mention that meeting Darla had been a part of the dream he'd given Emma.

"Yes," was all Raphael said.

Emma stood on her bed and put her hands on her hips. "Wait just a second; I don't need a babysitter." She pointed at Dair. "My mama raised me to take care of myself."

Raphael held up his hand when Dair started to respond. "Ms. Emma, you are mistaken. Dair is not sending me with you as your babysitter. He is sending me as your guide. You have only been in town for a day so he assumed you did not know where the library was located. Furthermore, you will not know who Darla is and I can be of assistance there as well."

Emma studied the angel briefly and though she knew he was just humoring her, he was most definitely a babysitter, she appreciated it none the less. "Alright then, you can walk me to the library. How am I going to let my aunt know?"

"I'll take care of it," Dair said quickly. "You two just go." He handed her the coat lying on the end of the bed. Emma had already gotten dressed and put on her shoes. She'd done that when the pounding on the front door had started.

Raphael took her hand and smiled warmly. "Close your eyes." She did as she was told. "Okay, you can open them."

Emma's blinked several times as the sunlight made her eyes water. The cold morning air swirled around her, and she pulled her coat closer against her. She and Raphael were standing on the sidewalk in front of the small house her aunt called home. It wasn't an ugly house, just an unloved one. The paint was peeling off of the trim and several of the windows had foil over them from the inside. It looked like a sad clown, complete with a faded red door as the nose. A fine layer of snow blanketed the ground and sprinkled the trees, and it was the only thing that could be called beautiful in regards to the house.

"Are you ready?" Raphael asked her.

Emma looked away from the house to the angel. He looked like a regular person in jeans and a sweater and coat. His wings were gone as was the glory that seemed to encircle him. She nodded at him and fell into step beside him. But then she stopped as her head tilted and she looked up at him.

"Won't people find it a little strange that we just suddenly appeared on the side walk out of thin air?"

Raphael gave her a sly smile. "Being an angelic being does give one a few powers you know?"

Emma looked up at him waiting for him to elaborate.

"Why don't we begin walking so you do not freeze and I will explain it?"

"While you're at it, you can tell me what people, in a town where everyone seems to know everyone, will think about some huge, strange man walking with a little orphan girl down the street."

"I, like Dair, am only seen when I want to be seen. And even then I can control how much people perceive. For example, right now as we walk down the street when people look at us they see what they would expect to see. Maybe a big brother walking with his younger sister, or a mother with her daughter. Complete with the same skin tones and attributes. However, once we are out of sight they simply forget that they ever saw us."

Emma thought about this for a moment, her eyes roaming over the people getting in and out of their cars in the parking lots. A few glanced their way, but for the most part they were engrossed in their own comings and goings. "That's a handy trick." She paused and puckered her lips, still considering the myriad of dilemmas that could result from being accompanied by a huge celestial being.

"So when we get in this library, if someone asks me who you are, what am I supposed to tell them?" she asked.

"Just tell them I'm your guardian angel." Raphael smiled.

"Really?"

He nodded. "I'll take care of the rest."

Emma wanted to ask more questions but held her tongue as they continued down the street. If Raphael said he could handle it then she would trust him. It wasn't like she had a whole lot of people to rely on since her parents had died, she couldn't really afford to go turning away the ones she did have. She remembered one day she and her mama had been at the park and Emma had been asking question after question to her mother, and after answering them each, finally her mama had smiled and said, *child, sometimes the question is formed in our mind not so we can ask someone else the answer but so that we can find the answer our self.* Of course, Emma had pointed out that by asking she was indeed trying to find the answer. But now that she was older, because eight is indeed much older and wiser than six, she understood that her mama was just looking for some peace and quiet.

They crossed a somewhat busy street and made a left onto another road. The snow crunched nosily under their feet and Emma found herself fascinated with the different designs the tires made in the snow. Had Raphael not grabbed her jacket a couple of times and directed her in the right route, she just might have walked off into the street to follow the patterns and swirls.

"We are here." His deep voice pulled her eyes up from the pavement. There was a red brick building with a sign that said Marion County Library. What the sign actually read to Emma was *Safe Haven*. She'd never needed a safe haven before; her home had always been safe before. But she'd never appreciated a public library so much as she did that moment.

She followed Raphael to the door and walked inside when he held it open for her. The warmth swathed her immediately. She smiled as she walked further into the building. The smell of books rushed into her nose and right behind that the smell of cookies followed.

"You just missed story time, but you made it in time for treats." A cheerful voice called out from around the corner of one of the many bookshelves. Raphael pushed her gently in the direction of the voice, and as they rounded the rows of books, Emma found a group of children sitting on a large carpeted area. Each hovered over a small white paper plate containing a cookie and some grapes next to a juice box.

"Hi." That same cheerful voice grabbed Emma's attention from the room full of children. "I'm Darla."

The woman held out her hand to her. Emma took it and returned the warm smile given to her by the woman named Darla. "I'm Emma and this is my guardian angel." She motioned to the huge form next to her. Raphael bowed his head slightly to Darla who didn't even flinch at the words, guardian angel.

"It's very nice to meet you and we are honored to have a guardian angel in our library," Darla said to Raphael, not missing a beat, with the same warm smile. "Please come in and have some snacks with us." She motioned for them to follow her. As they walked up to the carpeted area, all of the children stopped what they were doing and looked up at Raphael with wide, curious eyes. He gave them a nod and a smile and that was all it took for them to accept him.

"Kids, this is Emma. This is her first time here at story time so please give her a warm welcome," Darla announced to the group.

Emma took a seat on the carpet with the other kids while Raphael sat in the offered chair. Immediately Emma was bombarded by questions from the others and in no time she was swapping stories with the group. They wanted to know everything about her, but Emma wasn't ready to share her pain with others yet so she gave them a watered down version of how she ended up in Yellville. After their snacks, Darla and another librarian set up tables for them with craft supplies. Darla explained that they would be making Christmas ornaments for their trees using duct tape and proceeded to show them how it was done.

An hour and a half, ten rolls of duct tape, and many torn strips stuck to the table later, they finally finished their craft. As the kids began to leave with their parents, Emma found herself extremely hesitant to go. She wasn't ready to leave the safety of the library and return to the sad clown house that seemed weighed down with the hard life her aunt had lived. As she stared at the ornament she'd made, Emma's heart broke a little more because it was Christmas. There should be a tree to hang the ornament on, but for her there wasn't. It should be a time of joy and happiness and yet, instead, only grief filled her.

"If you're constantly waiting around for your circumstances to change so you can be happy, then you will lead a miserable life, Emma Whitmore," her mother's voice echoed in her mind. Emma's mom was big on finding joy in every circumstance. She didn't like complainers because she believed that each person was master of their own destiny. You were either happy or not happy because you chose it.

"You're thinking awfully hard," Darla's voice interrupted her thoughts.

She looked up at the librarian and nodded. "Yes ma'am. It seems lately I have a lot of hard thinking to do."

"Well, you're welcome to come here and do that thinking anytime you want."

"Thank you," Emma smiled. "I suppose I better be getting home."

"And where is home, exactly?" Darla asked.

"I live with my aunt Mildred just a few blocks over," Emma told her.

"Mildred Jones?"

"Yes ma'am." The alarm on Darla's face did not go unnoticed by the eight-year-old. Emma realized that in a town this small there weren't many secrets. Darla seemed to be thinking something over as she looked at Emma, and finally—seeming to come to a decision—she nodded.

"My niece, Serenity, does mentoring for the elementary schools. I don't think she has a student right now. Would you be interested in that? Basically she can pick you up, bring you here, and help you with your homework; also she'll do crafts with you and sort of be like a big sister."

Emma knew what she was doing. Darla was worried about her and trying to find a way to help without being too obvious about it. She appreciated it, though she hated feeling helpless. "That would be nice." Darla beamed, obviously pleased and relieved. "Great! I'll let her know and she can pick you up from school on Monday. If your aunt has a problem with it, I'll be happy to talk with her." Darla's voice had taken on a stern tone, and Emma realized that this sweet woman was no pushover despite her easy going disposition. She had mama bear written all over her face.

"I doubt she will care, if she even notices," Emma admitted. She stood to go and Raphael was immediately by her side. Just as she reached the door she turned and looked back at Darla. "What's your niece's name again?"

"Serenity. Serenity Tillman," Darla answered.

Emma felt her stomach drop as the name registered with her brain. Serenity Tillman was the girl from her dream. She also had realized that the library she was standing had been the one from her dream the night Dair had come to see her. Looked like she was right on track to fulfill her destiny. Now if she could just not be too human and screw it up.

Serenity would like to say that she didn't look at the clock every five minutes as she went about her mundane tasks at the clinic. She would like to say that her foot didn't tap impatiently and that she didn't keep looking out the window wondering if Dair would show up early, or how he would show up even. *Would he just pop up or would he use the door like a normal customer? Or would he just wait for her in the parking lot?* (She really hoped he would just wait outside).

"You seem anxious today," Jackson said as he finished drying a golden retriever he'd just bathed. "Everything okay?"

How to answer that? Did she simply say, yes, everything is fine? Or did she go for honesty and bust out with, nope, not okay because I met an immortal legend last night who admitted to being 'in like' with me and wants to pursue a relationship, and I said yes and now I can't wait to see him again? That probably wouldn't go over too well. "I'm fine, just a little distracted with some stuff." Okay, so that wasn't lying, it was just veering from the real issue. Veering was okay, right? At first she didn't think Jackson was going to leave it alone but finally he just shrugged.

To her relief, the end of her shift came without any tall dark strangers popping out of thin air into the middle of the veterinary clinic waiting room. Serenity wrote down her hours on her time card as she clocked out, her hands practically shaking. Part of her wanted to run to the parking lot, but the other part, the one with some dignity left, wouldn't let her feet go faster than a normal walk.

When she reached the front door, Serenity took a deep breath and let it out slow before pushing it open.

Jackson had said he would lock up so she didn't have to do anything other than walk out to her car. True to his word, Dair was waiting for her. His huge frame was leaning against her car with his arms crossed over his chest. The black clothing and dark hair and eyes made him look dangerous. His legs were crossed at the ankles and he looked for all the world that he had nothing better to be doing than standing there waiting on her.

Serenity's steps nearly faltered as her eyes met his. The smoldering look he had zeroed in on her had her heart speeding up and her palms growing clammy. She attempted to rub them inconspicuously on her jeans, but the crooked smile he shot her told her that the move did not go unnoticed.

"Hey," she said once she was standing a few feet from him. His masculine scent blew in her direction as the winter wind kicked up, and she wanted to get closer, but again her dignity kept her in place.

"Hello, Serenity." Dair's smooth voice reminded her of those Dove chocolate commercials where they showed the melted chocolate being stirred making her want to dip her whole hand in and not just a finger. It was dark and rich and quite possibly made him as lickable as a spoon covered in the stuff. *Don't think about any licking of any kind Sarah,* she chastised herself.

"How was your morning?" he asked her.

"Long," Serenity answered honestly, which seemed to be a recurring theme when it came to his absence. This brought a chuckle from him which had her blushing.

"As was mine," he admitted completely unashamed.

Needing to look away from his intense stare, Serenity glanced down at the frozen ground. The snow that had fallen the previous night was quickly being turned to brown slush as people and cars continually mucked it up. After a few minutes of awkward silence, she decided she was being ridiculous. So what if she embarrassed herself, she wasn't going to change who she was to impress Dair, sexy immortal or not.

"So what do you want to do today?" she asked him as she once again met his dark eyes. He had pushed off of the car and was now standing at his full height, causing her to have to tilt her head up to look at him.

He shrugged his muscular shoulders. "I'll go with whatever you want to do."

"Well, I hate to break it to you, but there isn't a whole lot of exciting things to do in the quaint little town of Yellville. So our options are limited. We could grab a pizza and head back to my aunt and uncle's house."

"Pizza sounds good. Will your aunt and uncle be home?"

Serenity shook her head. "Darla is taking some soup to a friend that just had surgery, and Wayne is helping a neighbor brand some cattle."

"I can see where you get your helpful nature."

She shrugged as she motioned for him to get in the car. "If not me, than who? I don't think we should wait on someone else to help if we are able."

Dair walked around to the passenger side and somehow folded his large body into the front seat. "That's not the behavior I'm used to seeing in humans," he admitted.

"That's sad," she said as she started the car and made her way towards the Mama's pizza, Yellville's lone pizza joint.

"I've been thinking of things I wanted to ask you,"

Dair said as he tapped out a rhythm with his hand on his thigh in a strangely human fashion.

"Oh?"

"Nothing too personal," he said quickly.

She smiled. "Okay, shoot."

"Favorite color?"

Serenity glanced over at him noticing once again the deep black onyx eyes and for an instant she wanted to say black, which would have been truthful. But she decided that that might come off a little too cheesy. So she answered with her next favorite color. "Teal." The slight upturn of his lips told her that he knew she wasn't being completely honest.

"Favorite kind of music?"

"Singer/songwriter type stuff like Brandie Carlisle or The Civil Wars."

"Favorite food?"

"Well, I'm from the South so pretty much any good, home cooked meal."

She pulled into the parking lot of the pizza place and held up her finger. "Hold the rest of those. I'll be right back." Serenity shouldn't have bothered saying anything because Dair was already getting out of the car.

"You don't really believe I would let you pay for our meal do you?" He shook his head. "I might not have ever dated, but even I know that the male should be providing the food for his female."

Serenity's head tilted to the side as her brow furrowed. "That's a very archaic way of putting it." She followed him inside and decided not to protest when he went to the counter and paid for the pizza. She also decided to ignore the way the cashier was unable to tear her eyes off of him as she rang him up. Once back in the car her mind was still mulling over what Dair had said.

"What are you thinking so hard about?" he asked her after several minutes of silence.

"The whole *the male should be providing the food for his female*. It sounds so caveman like. We live in a different time now. It isn't necessary for men to hunt for their food and the women to wait for them to bring home something for them to cook."

Dair nodded. "I understand that, but the changing times haven't changed how humans were fundamentally designed."

"And how is that?"

His eyes narrowed as he looked at her. "Why do I think I might be walking into a trap?"

Serenity laughed. "I promise not to jump to any conclusions. I'll let you make your point."

He continued to stare at her. Finally, he decided she was being truthful. "Males and females were created with specific roles in mind. That's not to say that they can't adapt to other roles, but from the beginning of their creation, man was created to provide, protect, and shelter his female. Woman was created with the drive to nurture, support, and love. She is his helpmate and her role is just as vital as his. When the whole women's rights movement came about, it was hard for most of us immortals to watch. The roles became so distorted and the need to prove equality became more important than fulfilling the Creator's plan for man and woman. I am not saying that a woman is in any way weaker than a man. In some ways she is much stronger. All I'm saying is their roles are different, and when they are living out those roles, they have much more contentment than when they are fighting against the design originally intended for them. So even though men no longer go out and hunt, or battle enemies, there is still a very strong drive in them to provide for and protect their families. I think that many men would never confess to that because of how society has emasculated them. Television shows make the men in families out to be a joke instead of being the leader of the family. They portray wives as being manipulative and unwilling to allow their male to take responsibility for his family. Not very many males will stand up to this because they would be crucified as a sexist pig. Those who think that the feminist movement hasn't affected this world in both positive *and* negative ways are blind."

Serenity was speechless. Not because she didn't agree with him, but because Dair seemed so passionate about the topic. She had to admit there was something very, very attractive about a man who was willing to take control, to lead, and to protect. "You feel very strongly about this," she observed out loud.

"I've watched the world for centuries and in so many ways humanity shoots itself in the foot because they rebel against their very design. It's frustrating not to be able to do anything, to just be a spectator."

Serenity turned into her aunt and uncle's driveway, parked the car, and climbed out with Dair following. "I can understand that. So, forgive me if this seems insensitive, but you're not human."

Dair smiled. "Correct."

"But yet you still have the same drive as human males? Everything you've described, you feel that?"

"It seems so," he admitted as they entered the house and headed for the kitchen. Dair set the pizza on the dining room table and waited for Serenity to hand him a plate.

After his speech, she wasn't surprised when he put a slice of pizza on the plate he was holding and then held it out to her. She laughed. "Is this you hunting for me?"

Then his entirely too sexy lips split into a smile that had her heart speeding up. "It is a small thing, I know. But to provide a meal for you brings me satisfaction. I'm as surprised as you are."

She took a seat and Dair took the one next to her. Their knees were so close they nearly touched and, silly as it was, Serenity desperately wanted them to. Once again Dair seemed to know what she was thinking because he shifted his leg until it was resting against hers. When she looked up at him, her eyes a little wider than usual, he winked at her. Her face immediately flushed and she looked down at her half eaten pizza. The immortal should be banned from smiling or winking. It was just too sexy.

"Do you have any questions for me?" he asked just before taking a large bite of his own slice.

"Let's go with the same ones you asked me."

He swallowed before responding. *Even his swallowing is sexy,* she thought to herself and then mentally kicked herself for thinking such a thing.

"My favorite color is red, my favorite music is classical, and my favorite food is pizza," he said and grinned as he held up his nearly eaten slice.

Serenity laughed; she couldn't help it; the darn guy was entirely too cute, among other things, for his own good. After lunch Serenity washed their plates while Dair watched her. She didn't want to admit it, but his attention was slightly flattering.

"So do you need to eat?" She asked attempting to distract herself from his scrutiny.

Dair shook his head. "I do not need sustenance to live. But, I can eat and do enjoy doing so on occasion."

There was another pause and he simply continued to watch her.

"You aren't going to offer to help?" she asked as she glanced at him over her shoulder.

A wicked grin spread across his face and his dark eyes seemed to smolder. "I know that it would be the gentlemanly thing to do, but if I come over there to help you, I lose the incredible view that I have from my current vantage point."

Serenity was so shocked by his blunt comment that she dropped the dish she had been drying. Dair moved so fast that she hardly saw him. He caught the plate before it could hit the floor. Breathless from more than just his speed, all she could do was stare at him.

"Did I scare you?"

For a moment Serenity couldn't find her voice. She cleared her throat before finally answering. "Which time? With the comment or the action?"

"Both," he answered as he took a step towards her and another until he was standing less than a few inches from her.

"I wouldn't say scared so much as shocked."

His eyes roamed over her face and it nearly felt like a caress. When she licked her lips nervously, she saw and heard his sharp intake of breath and nearly smiled. She was glad at least that she wasn't the only one affected. He felt the chemistry between them. That put her at least a little at ease. She felt more on equal ground.

"I'm comfortable around you. I find it hard not to say what I'm thinking. Though I will confess that I have managed to keep most of my desires to myself."

"Most of them?" she asked hesitantly.

"Most," he agreed as he reached out and gripped her waist with one of his large hands. He pulled her closer.

Serenity had to tilt her head farther back to look up at him. It might have been better if she hadn't. His heated gaze left nothing to wonder about. He desired her and he was fighting that desire with everything he had.

"It is so new to me," he whispered.

"What is?" she asked just as softly, not wanting to break the moment.

"This need. I'm like a man who has been denied anything to drink for decades, and you are the first glimpse of something, the only thing, that will quench me. I've never felt something so consuming. Does that make sense?"

Serenity nodded. "I'm beginning to understand that feeling myself."

"You desire me?" His voice held awe and yet a hint of disbelief.

"Have you looked at yourself in a mirror? Only a blind person wouldn't desire you and that was only if you didn't speak. As soon as you opened your mouth, they'd want you too." She wasn't embarrassed by her openness, not when Dair was looking at her with such yearning. "So what do we do now?"

His lips twitched. "Do you really want *my* suggestion?"

Serenity chuckled as she looked away, needing a moment to collect herself. "I suppose your suggestion would include some sort of physical touch."

She felt his finger touch her chin and slowly he lifted her face to look at him. "Does my touch bother you? Please be honest with me. Because if it does then I will stop. I won't like it," he admitted, "but I will always respect your wishes."

"I think I like it a little too much," Serenity told him.

"So you don't want me to stop?"

She slowly shook her head.

"Good." His voice was nearly a growl. "Because it would be very, very hard for me to be near you and not be able to touch you."

"Is this moving too fast?" she asked suddenly. "I mean, we've only just met. The physical attraction is off the freaking charts; I'm not questioning that. I think we have chemistry and that can't be helped but what about the emotions?"

"How do you feel about me?" Dair's hand tightened on her waist.

"I don't know. I like you. You're different from the guys in my high school. You're more confident, commanding, and interesting."

"That comes with age. They are young and unsure of themselves. But then some males come by being dominant naturally. I didn't realize until my feelings for you started just how dominant I am."

"I guess I'm in like with you," she said with a small smile.

Dair thought about this and finally gave a single nod. "It's a start. One day you will be hopelessly in love with me."

Serenity didn't tell him that was exactly what she was afraid of. Falling for an immortal who didn't belong with humans wasn't the smartest thing a girl could do. She decided that it was time to change the subject. "I have a secret obsession," she said as she stepped back from him. His hand dropped from her and she instantly wanted it back.

"Oh?" Dair's eyes sparkled with mischief. "What might that be, Princess?"

"Video games," she answered with a wry smile and then turned and headed out of the kitchen. She didn't look back to see if Dair followed. She knew he did because she could feel his black onyx eyes on her. Serenity pushed the door to her room open and grabbed her TV remote off of the desk. She sat on the end of her bed and patted the space beside her as she looked up at him.

"I believe you will have a slightly unfair advantage in this competition," Dair told her as he sat down next to her and took the controller she held out to him.

"Naw, you're a dude. According to Glory, video games are like standing up to pee for a guy; it just comes naturally." The look on Dair's face at her words was all it took to remove any embarrassment she might have felt over the comment.

"Then I should hope that my video game skills are adequate or you will be worried about me using your aunt's bathroom."

Dair's comment caught her off guard and Serenity let out an un-lady like snort. She shook her head at the obviously pleased with himself immortal and pulled up the game menu. Expertly clicking through several different screens until finally reaching the one she wanted, Serenity pointed to the right side of the TV. "Okay, you are on the right, and I'm on the left. It's a split screen but we are racing each other. Controls are pretty simple. The thumb joystick is what moves you forward and backward and turns you. The arrows move you side to side. You ready?" She looked at him with a raised brow.

"Is this where you humans would say something like get prepared to eat my dust?"

Serenity laughed. "Yah, maybe twenty years ago. How about we just see if you can keep your car on the racetrack and then you can talk smack."

Little did either of them know that it would be the beginning of many days spent getting to know one another while battling it out through video games—be they war, racing, or adventure.

"So when will I get to meet your aunt and uncle?" Dair asked as Serenity walked him to the front door, which Dair insisted on using despite his ability to appear and disappear from anywhere.

"Um," she brilliantly replied, caught off guard by his question.

"Isn't that what the guy in a relationship does? He meets the guardian of the female they are, for lack of a better term, courting, correct?"

She shot him a smirk. "Is that what we're doing? Courting?"

"In a manner," he said as he took her hand and lifted it to his lips. Dair pressed a gentle kiss to it, and Serenity felt the tingles clear up her arm and down into the pit of her stomach.

"Well, I'll ask Darla about doing dinner."

"Great," he smiled at her. "May I come to you tonight to tuck you in?" His eyes held the roguish gleam she was becoming accustomed to when he was teasing her.

Serenity's mind danced with all the possibilities of being tucked in by Dair. She blinked several times feeling her face flush. "That would be nice," she finally said after clearing her throat.

"Then I shall you see you tonight, my princess of peace." He leaned forward and pressed a kiss to her forehead. Serenity had to clench her fists together to keep from grabbing onto him and holding him to her. Suddenly he was gone and the room felt darker without him. She thought this was interesting, considering he had told her that the darkness was his element. Shouldn't the darkness have fled with him, rather than growing stronger in his absence?

Flopping down onto the couch with a loud sigh, Serenity shook her head. "Oh, brother. Girl, you have got it bad."

She didn't want to admit it but really there was no point in denying it. Denying truth never made it any less true; it just made it harder to accept it once there was no longer a way to avoid it.

Chapter 6

"To dream of birds can mean a variety of things. Eagles represent a strong desire to travel and to conquer new horizons. Hawks represent a desire to hunt, fight, or protect one's territory. Robins represent a desire to nest and raise a family. Mockingbirds suggest that you are the type of person who runs his mouth a little too much but says very little."

Darla moved efficiently around the cozy kitchen as she finished up the meal she was preparing for dinner. Serenity could tell she was excited, which made her happy but also irritated her just a bit.

"I don't see what the big deal is," she said for the fifteenth time.

Darla stopped in mid-stride and turned to face her. "The bid deal is that it's a boy."

Serenity's lips tightened as she attempted not to smile. She wanted to laugh at the expression she was sure would be on Dair's face at being called a boy. Serenity knew that Dair was anything but a boy.

"And?"

"Well, you've never had a boy over before."

She knew what Darla wanted to say was, FINALLY, you do something normal. But what she didn't know was that Dair wasn't normal. In fact, nothing about the situation was normal. But as she thought about the Sandman who was slowly stealing her heart, she realized she didn't want normal. Normal, she decided, was highly overrated.

"Up until now, no boys have interested me," she admitted honestly.

Darla nodded. "Well, it's not like you've had a massive selection to choose from."

Serenity laughed. "No, I suppose not."

"I've told Wayne to be on his best behavior." Her aunt winked.

"You know that Wayne only cause him to want to do the exact opposite, right? In fact I bet right now he is out there in the living room going through his wide array of joke books trying to find one that is sure to cause Dair the most embarrassment possible." Serenity could tell Darla wasn't worried in the least.

"The boy needs to prove he can handle a little bit of your uncle."

Serenity groaned. "That's asking a bit much at the first meeting, don't you think?"

Darla continued what she had been doing as she shook her head. "If he's as awesome as that smile on your face claims he is, then Dair will be just fine."

Dair took a deep breath as he stood on the porch of Serenity's aunt and uncle's home. He couldn't believe how nervous he was over meeting a couple of mortals, admittedly these weren't just any ordinary humans. They were the guardians of the woman he was falling for. It was important to him that they like him because he knew it would be important to Serenity as well. He held two roses in his hands, one white and one red. Letting out one final breath he lifted his hand and knocked on the door.

The door opened and Serenity stood looking at him with a shy smile spread across her beautiful face.

"Happy to see me?" he teased.

"Perhaps." She grinned wider and then motioned for him to enter.

Dair held out the red rose to her. "For you."

"Thank you."

"You must be Dair!"

He looked up to see Darla come bustling out of the kitchen with a wide, friendly smile beaming on her face. It was one of those smiles that was so genuine the receiver couldn't help but smile back.

"And you must be Aunt Darla," Dair said as Darla wrapped her arms around him in a tight hug.

"It's so nice to meet you. You know it's not every day that Serenity invites a young man home."

Dair stepped back from the hug and glanced over at a now blushing Serenity. He gave her a quick wink before looking back at her aunt. "I'm glad to hear that."

"I hope you're hungry," Darla said as she motioned for him to follow her, "because I've cooked up a feast just for you."

Serenity laughed. "She's so kindly going to let the rest of us partake of the feast she made especially for you."

Dair reached for her hand and pulled her with him as he followed after Darla. "Well, even the plebeians have to eat." As they entered the kitchen Dair saw that Wayne was already seated at the table. He stood and reached out a large hand to him. Dair met the man's eyes and saw mischief dancing behind them as he shook Wayne's hand.

"Dair, I suppose?" Wayne asked.

"Yes sir," Dair answered. "It's nice to meet you Uncle Wayne. Serenity has told me a lot about both of you and thinks very highly of you."

"Well, come on in and have a seat," Wayne told him and motioned for Dair to take a chair at the table.

Once they were seated Darla started bringing over plates for each of them filled with delicious smelling food. There was roast, potatoes, carrots, corn, peas, rolls, and macaroni and cheese. Dair didn't have to eat, but he enjoyed it when he did. He waited until everyone was seated and for Darla to begin eating before he picked up his own fork and began. Serenity sat at his right and kept shooting him sly glances, each of which he returned with a wink that drew a lovely flush to her skin.

"So Dair, how old are you?" Wayne asked.

Dair swallowed the bite he had just taken before answering. He had thought about the questions he might be asked and came up with some answers that he hoped wouldn't raise suspicion. "I'm twenty."

Wayne nodded. "Are you in school or do you work?"

"I plan to go to school, but right now I'm just traveling a bit. I guess you could say that I have inherited good fortune and have the means to do so."

"How did you end up in Yellville?" Darla asked.

Dair had expected this question but had struggled to come up with an adequate answer. He knew he needed to have something better than just 'passerby.' As much as he hated to flat out lie to Darla and Wayne, he didn't really have a choice. "I recently purchased some land in the mountains. I've been looking for a place to build a cabin, and Arkansas is one of the most beautiful places I've ever been that still has any wild land left to speak of." He knew that he couldn't get away with saying he had family there because Darla probably knew just about everyone in the town.

"We have lots of people who buy mountain homes for retirement or just use as summer homes. Although you are much younger than the people we usually get. But then I guess if I had the money to do what I wanted with and didn't have to work, I probably would as well." Wayne nodded.

"I want to work. I don't want you to think that I'm in anyway lazy," Dair explained. "I'm just trying to find a place to get settled before deciding on what to do next." He glanced over at Serenity hoping that maybe he could gauge how he was doing by her expression. She smiled and nodded at him approvingly.

"Okay," Wayne said suddenly. "Time to get down to the important stuff."

Dair set his fork down and wiped his mouth with his napkin. "Okay." He waited, expecting Wayne to ask him what his intentions were towards Serenity. This was something he had considered as well. He didn't want to scare them by saying that he wanted Serenity for his own for all time, though that was true enough, but he wanted them to understand that he wasn't just playing the field, as he'd heard human males call meaningless dating. Serenity was important to him and Dair wanted to make sure that Darla and Wayne understood that.

Wayne cleared his throat before he started. "An old widow bought an antique from a shop. . ."

Serenity let out a loud groan but Wayne just ignored her and kept right on going.

"And brought it home. As she was polishing it up a genie burst from it and said, 'You have awakened me from my slumber! I shall now grant you three wishes!' The widow asked for a cottage in the country. The genie nodded his head, and suddenly she found herself holding the deed to a little place outside of town. The widow then asked for enough money to be wealthy for the rest of her days. The genie nodded and suddenly they were surrounded by piles of money. 'You have one more wish,' the genie said. The widow pointed to her pet cat and said, 'Ever since my dear husband died this cat has been my faithful companion. Please, turn him into a handsome young man who will make love to me just as my husband did.' The genie nodded and disappeared. Suddenly there was an extremely handsome young man standing where her cat used to be. The woman gasped with joy, but the man just glared at her. After a few moments, he finally said, 'Well, I bet now you are sorry you got me neutered!'"

Dair laughed, not only because of the joke but because he had seriously thought Wayne was about to grill him, not tell him a dirty joke. Once they'd all collected themselves, Dair shot Serenity a shy look before turning back to Wayne. "Okay, I've got one for you then. I don't think the ladies will find it too offensive," he said, shooting Darla a quick wink. "Why doesn't a chicken wear pants?"

Dair waited with eyebrows raised, giving them time to think it over and answer. After a few seconds, he answered his own question.

"Because his pecker is on his head."

Wayne was laughing so hard the table was shaking. Dair glanced over at Serenity whose mouth had dropped open. He reached across and gently pushed her chin up and winked.

"I think he's a keeper, Serenity," Wayne said as he took a deep breath, composing himself after the boisterous laugh. "Any man that can tell a joke like that and keep a straight face. . . yep, he's a keeper."

"Glad to know that's your standard, Uncle Wayne," Serenity said dryly.

"Who's ready for dessert?" Darla spoke up before Wayne could retaliate.

An hour later, they were still gathered around the dining room table, only playing cards—rather than delicious food—were spread out before them. In all the millennia that he'd been alive, Dair had never played cards before; he'd never had any reason to. But he was a fast learner and picking up the game they called crazy eights with no problems. Wayne kept trying to distract Dair with dirty jokes. What Wayne didn't realize was, though the dirty jokes weren't distracting to him, the blush that continued to get redder on Serenity's lovely skin definitely was a distraction. So in a roundabout way, Uncle Wayne was being successful.

"Did you let them win?" Serenity asked him later that evening as they stood on the porch. The cold night air was crisp and refreshing and was helping Dair clear his head of any ungentlemanly thoughts.

"No, why do you ask?"

"I just figured an immortal who is as old as you are would be, I don't know, better at stuff."

"Better at stuff?" he asked with a small crooked smile.

Serenity shoved his shoulder. "You know what I mean."

"I'm afraid, my lady, that I do not know what you mean. What *stuff* are you implying I should be better at because of my immortally old status?" Dair's eyes twinkled with mischief as he spoke in a style that was definitely not from her time period.

"Oh forget it, you punk," she laughed.

"For your information, they won because I was

distracted by a certain lovely woman who kept shooting her uncle dirty looks.

She slapped a hand over her eyes. "UGH! Those jokes. . .they were terrible. I mean, each one just kept getting worse and worse."

Dair grabbed her wrist and pulled it away from her face. "They were quite vivid; that's for sure."

"You aren't helping."

He shrugged. "I didn't mind, especially since your face kept getting flushed." Dair pulled her towards him, so close that their bodies touched, and she had to tilt her head back to look up at him. "I had a very nice time tonight, Serenity," he told her as he met her gaze. "You have a wonderful family."

"I'm glad you came," she said and then licked her lips.

Dair bit back a groan as he watched her tongue slide across the plump flesh. *Eyes up, Dair*, he told himself and forced them up to her own eyes. He realized that it wasn't any better. Serenity was looking at him with a hunger that nearly matched his own. He leaned down and kissed her forehead, lingering only for a second to breathe in her sweet scent, and then he stepped back putting much needed distance between them.

"I'd better go."

She nodded but then frowned. "Is that your truck?" She pointed to the beat up Chevy parked in the driveway.

He smiled at her. "You didn't think I could drive, did you?"

"Not exactly," she admitted. "I just figured that since you didn't need to drive then maybe you had never learned to."

"I have to do something in my spare time," he told her with a smile.

"Where'd you get the truck?"

Dair could tell she was wondering if he had stolen the vehicle. He hadn't, not exactly. "I borrowed it from an acquaintance. I figured that it was the mode of transportation that your aunt and uncle would expect."

"Borrowed?"

"I might have used a little persuasion to get a gentleman to allow me to commandeer it. But, I'm returning it in actually better condition than when I took it. The transmission was about to go out in it, and I had Raphael use a little divine intervention to keep it running longer."

"Well, I suppose that isn't technically stealing." Serenity grinned. "And you did help the guy out even if he will never know it."

They were quiet for a few minutes simply looking out into the clear winter night. The bright stars lit up the sky giving them a stunning view of the rolling land around them. Finally Dair broke the comfortable silence.

"Thank you again," he said as he stepped down off the porch and towards the truck. He turned and continued to walk backwards. "Perhaps, I could see you tomorrow?"

Serenity shrugged with a small smile. "Perhaps."

Serenity felt as if she were floating as she walked to her bedroom. She called a hasty goodnight to Darla and Wayne and then headed to her room to get ready for bed. It was a little earlier than her normal bedtime, but she was eager to drift off. There was no use in denying it; she missed Dair already and she hoped the Sandman would show up in her dreams tonight. After washing her face and brushing her teeth, she changed clothes and quickly climbed into bed. But like a kid on Christmas Eve, Serenity lay in her bed, staring up at the ceiling, too excited to close her eyes. As it grew later and her eyes finally grew heavy, Serenity faded off to sleep, and her last thought was of a certain immortal who had captivated her in just a matter of days.

He didn't come, Serenity thought as she sat at the kitchen table eating breakfast the next morning. She had been sure that Dair would show up to tell her goodnight, but he hadn't, and she was more upset about it than she cared to admit.

"Why the long face?" Darla asked as she washed the morning dishes.

Serenity shrugged. She couldn't very well tell her aunt that she was disappointed that a guy she was crushing on hadn't shown up in her bedroom that night. No, she imagined that wouldn't go over too well. "Just feeling blah."

Darla nodded. "I've had those days. This cold weather probably isn't helping."

Serenity knew that the weather had nothing to do with her poor mood. She didn't want to be depressed over a boy, immortal or otherwise, and yet no amount of telling herself to snap out of it was doing any good. She took her plate to the sink and handed it off to her aunt who refused to let her help. She had finally given up trying. "I think I'm going to go into town; maybe a little holiday shopping will cheer me up."

Serenity flipped on the radio in her car and turned it to one of the stations that was playing holiday music all day long. She tried to think about the gifts she needed to get, but her mind kept drifting back to onyx black eyes and lips too full for their own good. Unable to focus, she decided that instead of shopping, she'd go pay Glory a visit. If anyone could cheer her up, it would be her best friend.

"I had a feeling I would be seeing you on this cold Sunday," Glory said as she opened her front door and motioned for Serenity to enter. "So who kicked your puppy?"

Serenity huffed out a less than enthusiastic laugh. "I look that downtrodden?"

Glory rolled her eyes. "Who the hell says things like that? Downtrodden? What are you seventy-five?"

"Dair came over for dinner last night," she told her as she plopped down unceremoniously on the well-loved couch.

"Well, did he kick one of your puppies or something? I would have thought hanging out with him would have put an extra pep in your step, not reduced you to a sulking three-year-old."

"No, he was great, but I guess I just thought he would come by to say goodnight. But," she looked away from the scrutiny of Glory's gaze.

"Ahh, so you've got it bad. Is that what you're telling me?"

Serenity closed her eyes and leaned her head back on the couch. "How did this happen? I was all prepared to be aloof and mysterious and not let him get to me, and now I'm waiting up for him at night hoping he will throw me a bone."

Glory snorted. "That's pretty funny considering you work in a vet clinic."

"Ha, ha," she responded dryly.

"So, I'm guessing you came over here for old Glory to cheer you up?"

Serenity nodded. "Are you free today or are you helping with your mom?"

"Dad's taken her to the beauty shop to get her *do* done. So, I'm free for a little while."

"How's she doing?" Serenity knew that Glory didn't really like to talk about her mom, but she wanted her best friend to know that she cared.

"Good days and bad days. Today's a good day. Can't be too thankful for those."

"And here I am complaining about a boy."

Glory waved her off. "I live vicariously through you, my little bird. So, by all means, complain away and while you're at it, please be sure to give me any juicy details that you feel should be omitted."

"Exactly, why would I give you details that I feel should be omitted?"

"Because those are always the best ones."

Serenity laughed and knew she had done the right thing by coming to Glory. She wasn't sure how her friend stayed so positive, but it always seemed to rub off on those around her, and for that she was grateful.

That night would be the second night that Dair would be unable to see Serenity. He had planned on going and seeing her at some point during the day but plans had changed. He and Raphael had gone to check on Emma and, after finding her hiding in the closet of her room, decided that they couldn't leave her alone, not with Mildred high as a kite and entertaining every sort of miscreant known to man.

"Where on earth does she find these men?" Dair asked Raphael as they sat in the dark room while Emma slept. They had taken up sentry at her door planning to take out any person who headed in her direction. More than likely, none of these individuals would be too sorely missed. The day had seemed to drag as they listened to fights and other sounds that no child should ever have to hear. Raphael had attempted to distract the young girl with magic which wasn't really magic at all, but simply his divine powers. She had been fascinated at first but slowly she lost interest and began to withdraw within herself.

"They're drifters mostly. Apparently, Mildred has herself a reputation for entertaining," Raphael explained, the disgust in his tone evident. "I'll never understand people like her who waste the life the Creator has given them. Don't they realize they only get one? Haven't they any desire to do good? Don't they want to leave the world having enhanced the life of just one other person?"

"You know as well as I do that many only seek selfish gain and temporary pleasure."

"It is such a waste." Raphael walked over to the window and opened the dilapidated blinds. "You have no idea what little Emma's destiny is?"

Dair wished that he did, but this was one of the times that the Creator wasn't giving anything away. All he knew was that she and Serenity were tied together. "No, sometimes I get little flashes when I prepare their dreams but with Emma I get nothing."

"She's tied to Serenity."

Dair nodded confirming what they'd already talk about before.

"I have a feeling that whatever it is they will do, it is very, very important."

Dair agreed because otherwise he would not be involved, though he hadn't voiced it out loud. Truth be told he not only did he know their fates were entwined but that it wasn't going to necessarily be a happy outcome. He looked over at the sleeping child when she started to stir. Dair walked over to her and placed his hand on her forehead. "Sleep, little Emma. Have good dreams and worry not for you have your own two guardians watching over you."

Two days passed before Dair was able to see Serenity again. He and Raphael had made sure that Emma made it to school safely, and then Dair was called away on a follow-up to another assignment. By the time Tuesday night rolled around, he was aching to see her.

He appeared in her room wrapping the shadows around himself as he watched her sleep. Just as she always did, she took his breath away.

"I didn't think you were coming back." Her voice broke the silence and stirred something deep inside of him. He hadn't realized she was awake.

"How did you know I was here?"

"I can feel you."

Her declaration had him reeling. She could feel

him? How was that even possible?

"I don't understand it either," she admitted. "But I just know when you are near. It's like an electrical buzz in my veins and it hums throughout my body."

Dair walked over to her bed and sat down on the edge of it close to her. She turned so that she was lying on her side looking up at him. Her hair was wild around her, making her look like an alluring siren.

"I wanted to see you; I just had things I had to take care of."

"Another assignment?"

"One of the things was an assignment; the other was just someone in need of help." Serenity must have picked up on the sorrow in his voice because she reached out and placed her hand on his.

"Are you alright?" she asked.

Was he? He didn't even know. There was just something about the entire situation with Emma and Serenity that had him feeling uneasy. "Honestly, I'm not sure."

"Who is this person that needs help? Is there something I can do?"

Despite his dismal mood, Dair found a smile pulling at his lips. This female who continually thought of others was once again willing to help, even a perfect stranger. "I actually think you will be meeting her regardless of what I want. Her name is Emma." Dair waited for the recognition to dawn on her face.

"Wait, Emma? As in *the Emma*? The Emma that was in my dream?" She sat up and pulled the covers close as a shiver ran through her. Dair wanted to wrap her in his arms but he was still a little unsure of whether or not she would welcome his touch.

"Yes. But her name is actually Emma Whitmore."

He waited for her reaction before continuing. When she just continued to look up at him with worried eyes, he decided to tell her the rest. "Emma has moved to Yellville. Her parents were killed in a shooting and her aunt now has custody of her."

"Oh wow, her aunt lives in Yellville? Who is her aunt?"

"Mildred Jones." Dair immediately saw the recognition of the name in Serenity's eyes.

"She's living with *that* woman?" Her eyes widened and her lips drew into a tight line.

He nodded. "Raphael, one of the angels and my closest friend and I have been looking out for her."

Serenity let out a long breath. Too concerned about the child she ignored the whole angel part. "That is not a safe place for her, Dair. Everyone knows Mildred and knows her reputation. How could anyone give her a child?"

"I won't let anything happen to her," he promised and meant it with every fiber of his being.

"Neither will I," she gritted out.

Dair reached up and ran a finger across her flushed cheek. "So fierce, my princess of peace," he told her and saw her eyes soften as she looked at him. "You have no idea just how amazing you are."

"I'm nothing special, Dair," she said and tried to look away, but Dair held her chin to keep her head from turning.

He leaned down until his lips were inches from hers. "Never say such a thing again. Even if the Creator hadn't singled you out for whatever destiny it is He has for you, you are still special. You give of yourself even when others don't appreciate you. That sort of selflessness is not common." His eyes held her for a few minutes more and then he finally gave into the burning desire. He needed to taste her, yearned to know her lips in an intimate way, and couldn't hold himself back any longer. He moved slowly to give her time to tell him no, but he could see the surrender in her eyes and the need as she leaned towards him. Dair felt her warm breath on his face and her respirations increased. He wondered if her heart was pounding out a rhythm as hard as his was. He released her chin and slid his hand down and around to the back of her neck. Serenity's eyes grew heavy with yearning and slowly closed as Dair finally pressed his lips to hers.

In that moment he was sure there must be a halleluiah chorus being sung somewhere because something so good could not possibly go uncelebrated. He felt her move, climbing up so that her body was pressed to his. Dair used his other arm to wrap it around her waist and pulled her on to his lap never breaking the kiss. Serenity sucked in a deep breath at the bold move and he took advantage of the open access she gave him by slipping his tongue into the warmth of her mouth. Dair had never kissed anyone before, but he was sure that it wouldn't feel like that with anyone else. He was also sure that he would want to do it more often than not. His grip tightened on her neck as he deepened the kiss, needing to be closer to her, to somehow crawl inside of her and be a part of her. Was this what it meant to be one with your mate? As his hand slid up her back, pulling her tighter against him, his mind drifted to more intimate thoughts, and he realized that if kissing Serenity was this intense, he didn't know how he could survive being more intimate with her, if that day were to ever come. He pulled away from her lips but not because he was in any way done with her. His lips traveled across her jaw and down her neck. Serenity's head fell back, giving him access to her smooth skin, and he took full advantage of it. He knew it was getting time to stop, but as his lips and tongue tasted her flesh, Dair found that he couldn't pull away. And when Serenity reached up and began running her fingers through his hair, he knew he was quickly reaching the point of no return.

When his hand slipped from her back and up to her collar, pushing it down further so he could trail kisses across the exposed flesh, he let out a low growl. "Princess, tell me to stop." To his surprised, and if he was honest, delight, Serenity didn't tell him to stop but instead pulled his head closer and lower. Her chest rose and fell causing the swell of her breast to rise up and greet him with entirely too much eagerness. Dair ripped his mouth away from her and turned his head. His own breathing was unsteady, and his hand shook as he moved her collar back in place, covering the delicious skin that he so badly wanted to explore.

They were both quiet as they attempted to gather themselves. Dair hoped that Serenity wasn't feeling rejected, because that was the furthest thing from his intentions. He simply was trying to protect her virtue. No man who would take something so precious before he made a woman his in the eyes of the Creator deserved such a gift. No matter how badly Dair wanted to claim Serenity in every way possible, he would not disrespect her in such a way.

"That was...unexpected."

He finally turned to meet her gaze. His brow drew together as his head tilted and he studied her. "Really? Because I was pretty confident that the passion between us would be explosive and I do believe I was right." He loved the blush that covered her skin and loved the way the warmth of it felt against the hand that was still holding the back of her neck.

"I didn't mean that; I just meant I didn't realize what a floozy I was." She laughed a little. Dair could tell she was truly embarrassed.

"Hey, look at me," he told her when she glanced away. Her eyes found his and he hoped she would see the sincerity in them when he spoke. "You have nothing to be embarrassed about. I was very close to begging you to let me relieve you of these frustrating clothes so that I could make you mine in every way. If anyone should be embarrassed or ashamed, it's me. Given just a few moments longer, Princess, and my hands were going to begin wandering to places that should only be touched by your husband." She was speechless. Her mouth dropped open slightly and then closed only to repeat the action several more times. Dair chuckled and pressed a soft kiss to her lips. "Surely, you aren't surprised to find out that you are so desirable."

"Well honestly, I've never cared whether a guy desired me."

"Is it cruel of me to be happy that you've never felt that way about another male?"

Serenity laughed. "Only if it's cruel of me to be glad that considering your age, you've never been with other girls."

Dair wrapped both arms around her waist and pulled her closer to him, his larger form allowing him to lay his cheek against her hair. The floral scent of her shampoo was nice, but it was the scent beneath that, her scent, that had his mouth watering. Dair had never dealt with the feelings of desire and had to admit that he wasn't exactly sure how to handle them. They were much more intense than he had ever imagined, and he truly wondered how mere mortals kept their control. His body nearly shook with need for her. Serenity pulled back to look up at him, a frown marring her beautiful face.

"Are you okay?" she asked.

"Aside from the fact that your body feels incredibly good against mine, your scent is making my mouth water like a man whose thirst hasn't been quenched in a century, and everything inside of me is screaming for me to take you and to claim you like some primal beast—yes, I'm okay." Her eyes widened at his declaration and he could tell she was struggling with how to respond.

"Perhaps, I should get off your lap," she suggested and started to move.

Dair tightened his grip on her and slowly shook his head. "I'm not ready to let you go." Those words meant so much more than just letting her climb back into bed and out of the shelter of his hold. He truly knew that he would never be ready to let her go. Dair realized then just how badly he wanted to be human, to have a human life span so that he could share it the Serenity. He wanted to marry her, love her, have babies with her, and grow old with her. There was a time when he wondered how humans could get into relationships knowing that their days together were numbered. They would not have an eternity together, and yet now he realized that it only made their love and commitment all the more precious. Two imperfect souls come together—becoming one and sharing joy, hurt, sorrow, love, and so much more—all the while never knowing if they will even have one more day together. They weren't promised a tomorrow. Their days were appointed by the Creator, and though their lives on earth were not even close to the splendor that their home with their Creator would be, it was still priceless in its own right. The relationship between male and female, mate and mate, husband and wife was a precious gift. It was a covenant between the man and woman and their Creator. It was to be protected at all costs and to be nourished beyond all other relationships—save the one they had with their Creator. And Dair wanted that with a desperation that scared him. He didn't just want it with any female. He wanted it with Serenity, his princess, his love.

Serenity laid her head against Dair's chest allowing the rhythm of his heart beat to soothe her. She felt raw and exposed after having experienced something so intense with Dair. Deep in her bones she could feel that what they had, what was building between them, was not an everyday sort of crush. It was deep, ardent, and all encompassing. As Dair's lips had demanded her response, to which she more than happily answered, Serenity was sure she had felt their souls connect. Was it realistic? She didn't know. Did it make any sense? Absolutely not. But there it was in all its unbelievable glory, a connection she had never felt with anyone—and knew she might never feel with another—had bridged itself between them. He had claimed he wasn't ready to let her go, and she was far from ready for him to release her. She wanted to be sheltered in his arms forever and shielded from the dark things in the world. Dair made her feel safe for the first time since her parents' deaths. He made her feel treasured and adored. She didn't know how she was going to handle it when he left, because she knew he would eventually have to leave. There was no two ways about it. Dair was immortal with a task appointed to him by the Creator and she was human. She just didn't see a way that they could be together.

Serenity felt his hand slide down her hair to her back repeatedly petting her, comforting her as if he understood her pain. And maybe he could feel it the way she had felt his soul. Her arms slipped around his waist and his back muscle's flexed against her hands. He was so strong, so solid, and she imagined if things were different he would be a man who stuck. He would be a man who would take a wife and never let her go. He would stick it out through every obstacle, every joy, and every pain, and he wouldn't want them to just be surviving, he would want them to flourish. Dair would want there to be passion and desire, want, and love. Yes, he would be a man who stuck, and yet she couldn't have him.

"You have school tomorrow," he whispered into the dark room. "I need to let you get some rest."

"Will you stay?" The words were out before she could bite them back.

Dair stood up holding her in his arms as if she weighed no more than a child and laid her in her bed. He pulled the covers up to her chin and then walked around to the other side of the bed. To her surprise and delight, he laid down next to her, on top of the covers, and wrapped a strong arm around her midsection pulling her close to him.

"Dream of me, Princess," Dair whispered into her ear.

"Then weave me a dream, Sandman," she said softly, "and then we can dream together."

As her eyes grew heavy, she heard Dair's voice telling her to sleep and to open her mind to him and to let him in. That was no hardship she thought as sleep finally claimed her.

Chapter 7

"To see a squirrel in your dreams means that you will soon make one or more new friends. While you should take advantage of the opportunity, be wary of being too trusting too soon. Take care not to reveal the location of your stash of nuts."

Emma's first day of school in Yellville wasn't nearly as scary as she had first thought it would be. Of course it could be because of the huge angel, though invisible to everyone else, had stayed with her throughout the day making sure everything went smoothly. Emma had told him several times that she didn't need a babysitter. Raphael's response had been that maybe he would learn something too, since he had never gone to elementary school. She couldn't imagine what an angel, who had been around since the dawn of time, could learn in the second grade, but then again she and her parents use to watch the show *Are You Smarter than a Fifth Grader* and her parents got questions wrong all the time. So maybe the angel could learn something. She had to be careful not to talk to him though because it would look like she was talking to herself. It was bad enough that most people already knew that she was living in a shack with her drunk aunt; she didn't want them thinking she was crazy as well. Emma could see the look in the teacher's eyes, a look her mama would have said was pity, and it made her grit her teeth. She didn't want anyone's pity. Emma just wanted to be treated like a normal girl.

By lunch time she had met two girls who had the potential to be friends. Penny Jane and Charlotte had both seemed to take Emma under their wings.

"Do you have any brother or sisters?" Penny Jane asked as she pulled her sandwich and chips from her Hello Kitty lunch box. Emma couldn't help but look enviously at the sandwich, after having been unable to identify the slop on her tray that the school was trying to pass off as food. Realizing they were still waiting for an answer, Emma forced her eyes away from Penny Jane's lunch.

"Nope, I'm an only child."

"That must be awesome," Charlotte said with awe in her voice. "I have six brothers and sisters. Six! And I'm number four so I never get anything new. All my clothes were worn by the older girls, all my toys were played with first by them, and even my hair brush used to be my older sister's. It must be nice not to have to get used stuff."

Listening to Charlotte go on and on about her grievances, that was one of her vocabulary words her mom had constantly taught her, she couldn't help but once again hear her mother's voice. *You remember to be thankful for whatever your circumstances, Emma Jean, because no matter how much you think you want something different, different doesn't always equate to better.* Her mother had been right. How many times had Emma wanted to move away from Memphis, away from the big city to a country house where she could have horses and rabbits? And here she was in a small, country town, and things were definitely not better.

Lunch continued with a constant flow of conversation from Charlotte and Penny Jane. She'd never seen two girls talk so fast. And half the time they finished each other's sentences so the flow was never broken; they just kept right on going. Emma glanced at Raphael from the corner of her eye and nearly laughed when she saw him watching the two girls with wide eyes. It was obvious he hadn't spent much time around eight-year-old girls. Poor guy didn't know what he had signed on for.

By the end of the day, Emma was ready to get away from the stares from the teachers and the whispers and pointing from her immature classmates. Emma's mama had always told her that being so smart was a blessing and a curse. It was a blessing because school was easy for her, almost too easy, but it was a curse because it made her an outsider. She often found it hard to be around kids her own age because they just seemed so clueless to her. Emma tried not to be judgmental, especially since it wasn't their faults that their IQ levels probably didn't come anywhere close to her own. They were simply products of their genetics, as was she. As she and Raphael exited the building, Emma took a deep breath letting the cold air fill her lungs. It was refreshing after being cooped up in the school all day.

"I don't really want to go back to Mildred's yet," she told Raphael as they started walking. Based on a few glances from other kids she knew that Raphael had made himself visible. She didn't give envious glances to those getting into cars where there was heat, walking was her only mode of transportation unless she wanted to take the bus, which she didn't. Walking was good for her she told herself anytime she wanted to whine about it. *Be thankful you can walk, Emma Jean.* That's what her mama would say. Man, she missed her mama. It was as if a hole had been ripped in her heart where her mother used to be, and now her heart didn't beat right anymore. The rhythm was off, like someone clapping to music but their hands met two beats too late. And Emma didn't know if it would ever be right again.

"How about we go back to the library and see that nice librarian?" Raphael suggested.

Emma thought that sounded like a much better idea than going back to the house where her aunt lived. She couldn't call it home. She had no home, not anymore.

"So, did you learn anything?" Emma finally asked Raphael as they crunched through the snow. Emma loved the sound of snow beneath her shoes. The crunching sound was somehow gratifying because when you walked in snow you could see your progress. If she looked back behind her, Emma would see her footprints in the compressed snow and be able to see how far she'd gone. Sometimes, when there was no snow, when the sidewalks were dry, walking felt unproductive, as if she were standing in one place—going nowhere—simply just moving her legs. Yes, she liked the snow beneath her shoes; she liked that, until new snow fell or others walked over her steps, physical proof would show that she had indeed gone somewhere. And for some reason it was important to her that she not remain stagnant, another vocabulary word from her mama. Her attention was drawn away from the crunching when Raphael began to answer.

"At first no, but then we went to lunch. There I learned that some eight-year-old girls have no need of air when they are talking."

Emma burst in to a fit of giggles that had her holding her side as Raphael paused with her on the sidewalk. The look of exasperation on his face only had her laughing more. When she finally gained some control of herself a single brow on Raphael's face rose. "Are you quite done?"

"I'm about as done as a frozen Christmas turkey," Emma grinned.

"What exactly does that mean?"

"It means that I've not yet begun to laugh at your horrid expression over energizer bunny eight year olds."

"You don't seem eight," Raphael pointed out.

Emma shrugged. "On paper, I'm more like twenty—according to my test scores anyways." Emma continued to chuckle under her breath as they started off again. When they finally reached the library, she was pretty sure her toes were so frozen they just might break in half. She and Raphael stomped the snow from their shoes before entering the library. The warm air rushed over her as she walked into the foyer with Raphael on her heels. Emma was immediately greeted with a smile from Darla that was just as warm as the air filling the room.

"I was hoping you'd come back," Darla grinned as she rounded the counter with arms already open. Emma had figured out that Darla was a hugger. As the kind woman knelt down and wrapped her arms around her, Emma bit her lip to hold in the emotions that continually seemed to threaten her control. She used to get hugs every day. She used to come home to a smile and the chatter of her mama asking her all about the school day. But those days were just memories.

Darla pulled back and held Emma's shoulders and studied her face. Emma met her eyes, having been taught to look at people when they were talking. "I don't suppose you'd be willing to help me take care of a little problem would you, Emma?"

Emma considered that whatever problem Darla had, it was nothing compared to her aunt's issues. "Sure, I can help."

"Yeah!" Darla exclaimed in a way that only she would be able to pull off as genuine. "I seemed to have baked too many cookies, and I would hate for them to go to waste."

Emma smiled up at the librarian. "Well, you're in luck, Mrs. Darla, eating cookies just happens to be one of my best problem solving skills."

"None of that *Mrs.* stuff, it's just Darla," she said with a wink and motioned for them to follow her.

An hour, and ten chocolate chip cookies too many, later, Emma sat helping Darla scan returned books back into the library reference system and place them on the recirculation cart which, Darla said, they would then use to return the books to their rightful place on the shelves. Emma was just happy to be doing something productive instead of hiding in the closet or talking to a mouse and a cat. She had decided the other night, when the mouse that shared her bedroom wall had stopped and stared at her as she spoke, that she definitely needed to get out more. Christmas music played from an old radio on the counter and she and Darla sang along. It was strangely comforting. Emma was pretty sure that if she didn't have the library to come to everyday, her life would be miserable. It was bordering on that already, but that was only when she was at her aunt's house.

Emma and Darla both looked up when the door to the library opened and in walked a girl Emma immediately recognized from her dream. It was Serenity in the flesh. She smiled a knowing smile at her and

Emma knew that Serenity recognized her as well.

"I see my aunt has put you to work," Serenity said as she walked over to the counter.

Darla clucked her tongue at her niece. "You know better than that. Emma here wouldn't take no for an answer. I had some crafts she could do, but she insisted on helping."

"Ahh, so you've met your match?" Serenity asked her.

Darla looked over at Emma and winked before looking back at Serenity. "How was your day?"

Serenity shrugged. "It was a day. I can't wait for Christmas break. I need a breather from school."

"Well, it's only one week away. I think you can make it until then," Darla told her.

"So, Emma," Serenity said and looked at her. "Darla mentioned that you might be interested in the mentoring program that the elementary school does with the high school students. I don't have a student right now. How would you feel about me being your mentor?"

Emma didn't point out that if it was academics Serenity would be mentoring her in, she would be wasting her time. More than likely, Emma's knowledge far surpassed Serenity's. But she did want a friend; that was something everyone needed regardless of their IQ. "That would be good," she answered.

"Great!" Serenity said and Emma could see her aunt's influence in her. "Let's get started then. You can come with me to the vet clinic and help me take care of the animals."

Emma perked up at this idea. "What kind of animals?"

"Mostly dogs and cats, but we occasionally get a

reptile of some sort or goats, horses, and cows."

"Horses?" Emma smiled.

Serenity laughed. "So we have an equine lover?"

Emma nodded. "I've always wanted a horse. I've read a lot about them. They are said to be great animals for people with handicaps and mental illness. They're intuitive and can pick up on the emotions of their caretaker."

"I've heard that too," Darla said nodding. "Well, you go on with Serenity and when you two are done, come back to the house for dinner. Don't you worry about your aunt, Emma; I'll let her know where you will be."

Emma didn't want sweet Darla to have to talk to her aunt, but neither did she want to talk to Mildred herself.

"Better not to argue with her." Serenity held out her hand for the young girl to take. "She'll just do what she wants whether you want her to or not."

"All right," Emma finally said, standing and slipping on her coat. She took Serenity's hand and allowed her to lead her towards the door. She looked back at Darla just as they began to step out into the cold air. "Don't go in, Darla," she said attempting to keep the worry from her voice, "to my aunt's house I mean. Don't go inside, okay?"

"You don't worry about me, honey; I've dealt with the likes of Mildred Jones before. You just go on and have fun with Serenity, and I'll see you girls tonight."

Raphael suddenly appeared next to her. She hadn't noticed that he'd disappeared, but she quickly realized that she was the only one who could see him. "Do not worry about Darla. I will make sure she is safe. Dair will be with you and Serenity," Raphael told her.

Emma nodded her head slightly and then turned to follow Serenity to her car.

Serenity waited for Emma to get her seat buckled before backing out of the parking spot. She was glad that Emma had been willing to go with her, considering they had met in a dream. Serenity was worried she might have been too freaked out. When her aunt Darla had mentioned Emma to her and asked if she would mentor her, even though she knew Serenity had stopped mentoring, she didn't mention that she already knew her. She did however agree to mentor her without hesitation. She knew from her talks with Dair that Emma was going to be someone important in her life and probably the lives of many others.

"I don't want to assume, so I'm going to ask," Serenity began. "Do you remember me from the dream Dair weaved for us?"

Emma nodded. "Yep, but I already knew you were here. Dair told me."

"Yea, he told me about you too. I'm so sorry for your loss, Emma. I want you to know that you are welcome in Darla's and Wayne's home anytime." Serenity hoped that Emma could hear in her voice that it was only concern and not pity that she felt for her.

"Thank you," Emma told her and that was all she said about it. "So about this vet. . .is that where you work?"

Serenity nodded. "It's my part time job. I really like working with animals. They're great listeners and aside from the occasional trouble maker, they don't complain or gripe at us."

"They're also very loyal," Emma pointed out. "I've never had a pet, but I read a lot about dogs. It was always interesting to me how they train dogs to rescue people, find drugs, and comfort those who are sick. Animals are truly amazing creatures."

Serenity was a little taken aback by the young girl's knowledge. It wasn't every day that she came across an eight-year-old that liked to read about horses and dogs. The eight-year-olds she had been around were more concerned with sparkly things and American Girl dolls.

As they pulled into the parking lot, Serenity's lips spread into a ridiculous smile at the sight before her.

"You've got it bad girl," Emma said from beside her.

Serenity's head snapped sideways to look at her. "That obvious?"

"Wipe the drool off before you get out," Emma said as she grinned and opened her door.

Dair stood leaning against the building, relaxed as if it wasn't twenty-eight degrees outside. Serenity climbed out of the car and followed Emma to where Dair stood.

"Raphael told me you would be here," Emma told him.

Serenity looked at Dair and then down at the girl. "Raphael, as in the angel right?"

Emma nodded and said with a shrug. "He's sort of my guardian angel."

Serenity looked back at Dair and smiled her thanks because she knew it was his doing that Emma had someone looking after her when others could not.

"How are my two favorite ladies?" Dair asked as he pulled the door open for them to step in out of the freezing wind.

"Excellent," Serenity said and had to fight not to throw herself in his arms.

Emma shook her head and Serenity heard her mumble. "Girl needs a bib."

Dair laughed as he looked down at her. "Emma, I take it you are here to help Serenity clean kennels and exercise dogs?"

Emma nodded. "Cleaning dog poop beats sitting in my room talking to a mouse and a cat any day."

Serenity's heart hurt at the words but she wasn't going to let Emma see it. When her parents had died, the one thing she hated most was the pity in people's eyes. She wouldn't do that to Emma.

"Let's get to work. The sooner we start the sooner we can be finished," Serenity said as she waved them to follow her to the back. She was glad that Jackson had the day off; she didn't want to see how he and Dair would interact.

"She seems to be having fun," Dair's breath whispered against her skin as he spoke from behind her. Serenity was bathing one of her regulars, a small and perpetually happy little pug named Pugsly. Sometimes it amazed her at how unoriginal owners could be when naming their pets. She felt Dair's arms snake around her waist, his large hands resting on her stomach. Serenity wanted to lean back against his firm chest. She wanted to sink into his embrace and see where it led, but Pugsly, wet and shivering, was looking up at her with pleading eyes. She smiled down at the dog and finished washing him. Dair stayed behind her simply holding her. When she finished rinsing the pug, Dair released her so she could lift Pugsly and set him on the table. She began to dry him off as Dair stepped around the table and watched her.

"You have a habit of staring," Serenity pointed out to him.

He didn't look the least bit bothered by her statement. He folded his large arms across his broad chest and leaned his shoulder against the wall. "I like to have something to think about when I'm away from you."

Okay, what was a girl supposed to say to that? Serenity bit her bottom lip as she peeked up at him while she continued to dry the little pug. Dair's smoldering eyes met hers and she quickly glanced back down. He was so intense, so overwhelming at times, that she found it hard to breathe. Serenity cleared her throat before she spoke. "Could you go check on Emma for me?" she asked. Cowards way out? Yep, but she needed to collect herself and she couldn't do that with his roaming eyes.

She didn't hear him move. Suddenly his lips were pressed against her ear. No other part of his body touched hers, and yet his warm breath heating her skin was igniting passion as if he were plastered against her. "Are you running from me, Princess?" His voice was deep and velvety smooth, coaxing her to respond to him.

"No," her voice squeaked and she had to clear her throat before she continued, "not running, just need to breathe."

"You can't breathe with me?" She was surprised to hear hurt in his voice. Serenity was glad that Pugsly was one of her better behaved dogs because he just sat on the table patiently waiting while Dair grabbed her hips and turned her to face him. His eyes were doing that smoky, swirly thing. She had touched a nerve.

"I . . . it's just," Serenity stumbled to explain but nothing would come out. Dair's intense stare had her speechless. He stepped closer and when she attempted to look away, he grabbed her chin gently, but firmly, and forced her to look up at him.

"For the first time in my long existence, I finally feel like I *can* breathe, because of you. Am I smothering you? Is that what you mean?"

Serenity could see that Dair was truly worried about what she had said, and yet she hadn't mean it in the way he was thinking. She needed to explain but she wasn't always good with words, especially when she was emotional, and Dair stirred deep, powerful emotions in her. But she didn't want him thinking that he was doing anything wrong, so for him, she would try.

"You aren't smothering me, Dair," she finally spoke. His body didn't relax and his eyes were still swirling. "What I meant was that your presence is so intense sometimes, that it's all consuming. I feel as if the air is being sucked from the room, and the only thing that is going to fix it is either you leaving or me giving in and…," she paused, unsure if she should finish.

"Giving in and what, Princess?" His narrowed eyes dared her to be honest with him.

"Giving in and going to you. Giving in to the need I feel to be in your arms. Giving in to the need to taste you, to have you fill me with your breath as you kiss me. When you kiss me it's like there's no me and you; there's only us, as though we are—"

"One," he interrupted.

She nodded, her eyes wide as she realized he felt it to.

"Why don't you give in?" he asked and she saw his shoulders relax just a little.

Serenity knew she needed to talk with him about her fears, but she wasn't ready for that heavy conversation. It had only been a couple of weeks and things were already very intense. "I'm not ready to answer that question." She waited for his reaction because she imagined it might hurt his feelings that she didn't want to share her emotions with him. But he surprised her.

"When you are ready, I will listen." He stepped back but his eyes didn't leave hers. "Just don't wait too long to come to me. I can't help fix the issue if you don't tell me what it is."

Serenity watched him head out of the tub room in search of Emma. Her heart was pounding in her chest as she leaned back against the table to keep from collapsing to the floor. He was going to be the death of her, or at least of her heart. How would she ever recover once he left? How was she supposed to tell him that the reason she didn't give in was because she was scared about how she felt about him? If Serenity let herself, she would fall in love with Brudair. He would own a piece of her heart, her soul, and when he left, he would leave a gaping hole. She should probably ask him to leave now before that could happen, but it was like her body rebelled against the idea. Her lips would not form the words and her lungs would not give her the breath to speak. She wanted whatever time she could have with him. At least then she would have memories.

Serenity heard a whine coming from behind her and turned to look at the little pug. She laughed at the forlorn look on the, *it's so ugly it's cute*, face. "I'm pitiful, aren't I, Pugsly?" His head cocked to the side as though listening to her. "Do you think I should let him go?" His head tilted the other way. "And now I'm asking advice from a dog," she said as she picked him up and headed for his kennel.

Dair stood just outside the tub room door. The air shimmered around him as he shifted so that mortals could no longer see him. He should be ashamed for standing there listening to Serenity, but it was killing him not to know what she didn't want to talk about. *Should I let him go*, she had asked the little dog. What did she mean by that? Did she think she was somehow forcing him to stay? Did she not realize that he was fighting to find a way to be with her?

"Why are you standing out here when Serenity is in there?" Emma's voice had him tensing. He had forgotten that she could see him when others could not, unless he specifically prevented her.

"She said she needed to breathe," Dair said honestly.

Emma looked up at him and nodded as though she understood. That had him curious. "What?" he asked.

She shrugged. "Nothing, it's just that you can be a little heavy."

"Heavy? What does that mean?"

"It's obvious that you love her, and when you're with her it's like whatever power it is that you have is constantly reaching for her."

Dair's brow rose as he stared down at the little girl. She was way too insightful for her age. He had to admit that when he was around Serenity, he had a hard time controlling the power he wielded. It was as though the shadows that he carried with him wanted to wrap around her and cover her to keep her safe. He imagined it must be because of his own need to protect her and his power acted accordingly.

Dair watched as Emma continued to wipe down empty cages, and he couldn't help but wonder what it was this remarkable child would do to change the course of history. He imagined that whatever it was, it would be significant.

"Are you going to be coming to dinner?" Serenity asked him as they walked to her car. They had finished up all of Serenity's tasks rather quickly once Dair had stopped staring at her and helped instead. After cleaning out litter boxes for the better part of an hour, he realized that he much preferred watching his beautiful princess work—rather than scooping himself.

"I will be by later tonight. Please give my apologies to your aunt that I can't make it. I have some business to take care of." Dair hated leaving her, but he had to continue to do his job. If he did not, he would be forced to move on sooner rather than later.

"Okay, I'll let her know," Serenity said as she opened her car door and started to sit down. Dair wrapped an arm around her waist and pulled her against him before she could make it.

"I don't like to leave you," he told her. "And I like it less when I don't get a proper goodbye."

Her eyes snapped up to his. "What is it you want, Sandman?" she asked and he was glad to see that his confident princess was back.

"A token, to remember you while I'm away." She laughed at his chivalrous tone. He wanted to groan at the sound. That laugh did strange things to him.

She seemed to think about his request and then a wicked gleam filled her eyes. She stood up on her tiptoes and wrapped her arms around his neck, pulling him down towards her in a tight hug. To anyone else, even Emma sitting in the car, it would simply look like a sweet embrace between a boyfriend and girlfriend. But Dair knew differently. And if he hadn't buried his face in her hair, anyone watching would have known as well. Instead of simply hugging him, Serenity had pressed her face against his neck. He had felt her warm breath before he felt her mouth close down on the tendon there. His arms tightened around her which seemed to do something to Serenity because the suction of her mouth suddenly became even more intense. Dair wasn't entirely sure what she was doing, but he hoped she never stopped. Just as that thought filled his mind, cool air was hitting his neck as Serenity pulled away. He had to grit his teeth not to ask her to continue. Dair closed his eyes, attempting to regain some shred of composure, and when he opened them he was looking down in the smug sea green eyes of Serenity.

"What was that?" he nearly growled.

She grinned. "It's called a couple different things. Some call it a hicky and some call it a love bite. But you can call it my token. Perhaps, now you will have no trouble remembering me."

"I definitely won't have trouble remembering, but tell me, my lady, how on earth am I supposed to leave you now?"

Serenity's eyes widened as though she was suddenly just realizing the effect her stunt had had on him. "You liked it?"

"You couldn't tell by the death grip I had on you?" Dair's hands had moved to her hips and he held her in place, unsure if he was attempting to steady himself or her. He was so new to not only the emotions he felt for Serenity but also the physical sensations that she evoked in him. It was more powerful than he could have ever imagined it would be.

She smiled up at him, obviously pleased with herself. "I'll have to remember that."

She started to step back from him but he found it impossible to let her go. Serenity placed her hands over his and gently pried them loose. Her large eyes looked up at him and were filled with concern. "Are you alright?"

Taking a deep breath he stepped back to clear his head of her smell so that he could think. "Just a little unsure of how to handle emotions I've never felt before." He motioned for her to get in her car. "You have to be freezing. I'll see you tonight. Be safe."

"You too," she told him as she shut the door.

Dair watched her back out of the parking spot and pull out into the street. The tightening in his chest grew worse as she drove away. He knew he was going to have to go to the Creator soon. Dair had no idea what he would say or what he would do if the Creator said no. But his feelings for Serenity were growing stronger every day and the thought of leaving her was one that he couldn't stand.

He closed his eyes and focused on his next assignment, allowing the information to flow into his mind and pull him where he needed to go. When Dair opened his eyes he was standing in the room of rundown home that reeked of stale cigarette smoke and sour clothes. The room itself was neat and tidy. The small bed in the corner was made with a blanket that looked too thin to add any real protection from the cold. There was a desk on the opposite wall that looked as though the addition of one more item would cause the entire mess to go crashing to the ground. Stacks of books covered the top, but on closer inspection Dair saw that the books were arranged in alphabetical order by author. They were all books on science and health: cell development, DNA studies, stem cell research.

Whoever this person was, they were very interested in the human body. Dair took up his post next to the one window in the room and prepared to wait for the arrival of the room's occupant. Dair had reached his destination earlier than necessary, but he knew the sooner he finished with the assignment, the sooner he would be able to return to Serenity. He groaned and rubbed his face as he realized how pathetic he had become. The constant ache inside of him to be near her was something he didn't understand. Was it normal or something different because of who and what he was? Dair wasn't sure and added it to the list of things he would need to ask the Creator. Dair was pretty sure the Almighty was the only one who would be able to answer him.

Two hours later, long after the sun had set and the stars lit the winter sky, Dair's charge arrived home. He was a young man who looked to be between nineteen and twenty years of age. He was tall, thin, and very studious looking with round glasses. He had a sharp beak like nose and a narrow mouth. It was a kind face, though unassuming and certainly not handsome. He was plain, just someone a person would pass on the street and never notice as nothing remarkable stood out about the young man.

When the young man finally decided to go to sleep, Dair felt the dream begin to weave in his mind, and he quickly saw that though the man did not appear remarkable, his actions one day would make him stand out far above the rest.

Dair began the dream by showing the man a vision of his college graduation. Then he was opening an acceptance letter to medical school. Dair felt the man's emotions over the idea, and he used his power to magnify those emotions, hoping to influence him to no longer wonder if that path was an option, but rather to pursue it in earnest. This man needed to graduate from medical school; he needed to become one of the leading researchers in cell mutation and development. He needed to do these things because he and the team he would one day lead would find the cure for many terminal illnesses. He would then go on to take his research to third world countries, using his own money to help fund relief and aide to children. Dair saw the man's purpose, his contribution to history in its entirety, and he had to wonder why the Creator was allowing it. He continued to weave the dream, allowing small glimpses of his future and of the possibilities open to him if he followed his desires. He needed to pursue his passions, instead of buying into the lies that were telling him he would never amount to anything because no one in his family ever had.

When Dair pulled out of the human's mind, he stood for a few moments staring down in awe at the man the Creator had purposed for such a great task. He was not a rich person. He didn't come from a family with a history of Ivy League school enrollment. He wasn't the son of a famous person or political figure. He was a nobody in a poor part of a city, born into circumstances that should make him a statistic. As it always did, it amazed Dair who the Creator used for such seemingly impossible tasks: the unassuming, the underdogs, the ones society deemed unworthy. Yet their Creator made them worthy.

"Be strong, Wilson Turner," Dair whispered, having taken the man's name from his mind. "Do not let others dictate what your purpose will be. For your journey will be a difficult one, a selfless one, but one that only you can travel. Be strong."

Dair left the future scientist to his dream, hoping that Turner would indeed follow the path he was destined for. There was no guarantee that the young man would follow the suggestions Dair had planted in his mind, but perhaps, it would make him think harder before deciding he couldn't succeed.

Dair thought of Serenity and quickly found himself standing outside of her bedroom window. The light was still on and he could see her shadow moving around through the thin curtains. He was eager to see her, and hold her, and he gave no second thought to using his power to appear in her room. His eyes opened just as he felt the heat of the house and every part of him, except his betraying eyes, froze. *Turn around,* he yelled at himself and yet his body refused to move. It was as if the connection between his mind and his limbs had been completely cut off. When his eyes finally met Serenity's, Dair was surprised to see that she was calm, not freaking out like he clearly was.

"Perhaps, you might want to knock before you just appear?" she asked with a small quirk of her lips.

Dair nodded. He wanted to say something, anything, but it was useless. So instead he stood there looking like an idiot, a perverted idiot at that.

"Could you turn around for a sec?" He could tell she was trying really hard not to laugh, and that was the only reason he was finally able to move. Dair nodded and then willed his body to turn away from a very beautiful, but very dressed only in a towel, Serenity.

Chapter 8

"If you dream you are standing naked in the park, it probably means that you need to spend some time in nature away from the modern inconveniences of the world."

Serenity bit her lip as she quickly slipped into her sleep clothes. She was trying very hard not to laugh at Dair, but it was difficult. He was usually so calm and collected. To see him at a complete loss, with shock and awe on his face, was something she really wished she could have gotten a picture of. She knew she should probably be embarrassed at having him see her only in a towel, but she figured it covered more than a bathing suit did, so really she had nothing to be embarrassed about. If she was honest with herself, she was actually flattered at the response on Dair's face and in his eyes. There was no mistaking the desire that flared in their black depths as he drank her in. A girl could get used to being looked at like that.

"Okay, I'm decent," she finally told him. She watched as he turned around slowly as if he expected her to suddenly yell, *just kidding now I'm naked as the day I was born*! When he was finally facing her again, the look in his eyes had her breath freezing in her lungs.

"I am so sorry for just barging in like that, Serenity," Dair said in a low, velvety smooth voice. Serenity wasn't sure if he was trying to ensnare her with his voice or not, but it was working.

"Uh, Dair, you're going to have to turn that stuff off."

His head tilted to the side and his brow furrowed. "What stuff?"

"The sexy as sin voice and the come hither bedroom eyes," she said and motioned with her hand, waving towards his face as if that explained it all. "That mess has got to go." Her words had the opposite effect. The room seemed to suddenly darken, like the lights had been dimmed somehow and the temperature dropped just enough to cause chill bumps to raise all over her skin. Serenity knew from the many times Uncle Wayne had told her about dealing with predators that she wasn't supposed to run. But with the way Dair was looking at her in that moment, everything inside of her was screaming run. The scary part was that she didn't know if it was telling her to run *to* him or *away* from him. *Way to go hormones, you're totally making this easy on me…not,* she told herself.

"We are in your bedroom," Dair told her unnecessarily as he took a measured step towards her.

"Your powers of observation are astounding; now could you please bring the hotness down a notch?"

"You said I have bedroom eyes, and I feel I should point out that it's appropriate since we are indeed in your bedroom." He sounded so logical, as if she should have come to the same conclusion as well.

Serenity looked around for something to get his attention—something to snap him out of *Don Juan* mode and back into the *maybe it's not a good idea to use my powers on my girlfriend* mode. She saw a glass of water on her night stand, and just as he was taking another step towards her, Serenity snatched it up and flung the water right in Dair's face. Serenity stood staring at a now dripping wet—which only made him hotter, dammit—Dair. Her mouth hung open like a landing pad for any flying insects that might happen by, and her hand was frozen in midair with the empty glass still tilted towards the immortal. Had she really just flung water in his face? She watched as he reached up with his hand and wiped his eyes, nose, and mouth dry. Yes, yes she had.

"Are you back?" Serenity asked hesitantly.

Dair continued to attempt to dry his face with the sleeve of his jacket as he answered. "It seems that I lack some control in my desire for you. I'm guessing that the water was the only thing you could think of?"

She felt her face flush. "Yah, about that. See you were stalking me in a *totally I'm going to devour you* way, and I honestly didn't know that I would stop you. So I had to do something before you were able to touch me. I thought about using the lamp, but I like that lamp sooo," she said as she drug out the last word.

"I apologize if I scared you."

Serenity could see that he was truly worried that she was scared of him, but what he wasn't understanding was that she was not afraid of what he would do to her. She was afraid of what she would let him do to her. "I'm not scared of you, Dair. I just think that our attraction for each other is intense, and perhaps distance is a good thing at the moment."

"You're a virgin?"

Serenity's eyes widened. *Okay, that was not what she was expecting.* "Yes, I'm most definitely a virgin. That isn't something that I'm willing to just give to anyone."

"It's for someone you love?" he asked.

"Yes, but not just love. It's for the one person that I will commit myself to for life."

"Your mate?" He paused and then corrected himself. "Your husband?"

She nodded.

"That is another thing that is different about you," he responded.

"Well, to be honest, until now, it hasn't exactly been a hardship. But, with you, it's. . . I." She let out a deep breath. "Well, let's just say I understand why people don't wait. I'm not saying I agree or that I will change my plan, but I totally get it."

They sat staring at one another for several minutes. It wasn't an uncomfortable silence but Serenity didn't enjoy the distance between them. Finally she let out a resigned sigh and scooted across the bed until their knees where touching. "Would you consider me needy if I said I want you to hold me?"

Dair grinned at her and the effect on his handsome face took her breath away. "I always want to hold you. Do you consider me needy because of that?"

She shook her head. Serenity wasn't surprised when he scooped her up as though she weighed nothing and sat her on his lap. His strong arms encircled her waist, pulling her tightly against his chest. Despite how it sounded, a little cheesy she admitted, it felt right to be in his arms. It felt as though it was where she belonged—where she would always belong. Serenity felt his breath on her neck as he buried his face in her hair. He took several deep breaths before whispering, "You smell amazing."

She didn't know what to say to that so she just snuggled in deeper against him.

"How did things go with Emma tonight?" Dair asked, his voice muffled because he had yet to raise his face from her neck.

"Well, Darla was in heaven having someone to dote over. And I think Emma had a good time. It was really hard to take her back home."

"Did you take her by yourself?"

Serenity could tell by the sharp tone that he did not approve of that idea. "No, we all took her back. Darla was trying to convince Emma to let her ask if she could stay the night at our house, but Emma was insistent that she not rock the boat. She was worried about how Mildred might behave I think. I honestly didn't think Aunt Darla was going to let her out of the car. She kept telling her things like make sure you put something in front of your door while you're sleeping and keep shoes on while you sleep in case you need to escape quickly. Emma had to remind her that she had a guardian angel, which seemed to appease Darla a little considering she doesn't doubt for a minute that Raphael truly is an angel. I asked her about it and she said 'there's purity in him that isn't in others', so I'm just going with it."

"I wish there was something more I could do to help her," Dair told her. The sorrow in his voice broke her heart. And she understood how he felt because she wanted nothing more than to snatch Emma from her aunt and never let her return to the wretched woman. Serenity had found herself wondering how Mildred had ended up such a wretch while her sister had obviously fared much better. What choices had she made that had veered her so far in the opposite direction of her sister? Part of her felt sorry for the woman, but then the other part of her knew that life was full of choices, and it wasn't always just the cards a person was dealt that determined their lot in life. Rather, it was what they did with the hand that mattered. There had to have been a point when Mildred Jones had the opportunity to choose something better for herself. For whatever reason, she let that opportunity pass her by.

"What are you thinking about?" Dair asked. She felt his hand begin to stroke her arm and she shivered under his gentle touch.

"Choices," she answered softly.

"What about them?"

"Just how they never truly only affect the person making them. Our choices always affect those around us, those close to us, even if the effect is not immediately apparent; eventually the choices have consequences."

"So do you ever think you should make a choice based solely on what you need or want? Or do you think you should always consider those who might be affected by that choice?" Dair had pulled back now and she could feel his eyes on her face.

"That's the million dollar question, isn't it?" Serenity turned to look up at him. "Is there a time when I should only think about myself? It sounds so bad when it's put like that."

"I think that as long as your choice isn't going to harm someone, or put them in danger, then sometimes it has to be totally up to you regardless of the effect on someone else's life. That's not to say there aren't times when you do need to consider others, but seasons of life change, circumstances change, and there are times when you have to take care of yourself without worrying about everyone around you."

Serenity wanted to agree with Dair, but in the back of her mind, something nagged at her. She still wondered about whether she should leave her aunt and uncle after she graduated. Was it okay to think of herself at that point? Would it be heartless of her to leave them here after everything they'd done for her?

"I should let you sleep," Dair told her as he

reached up and brushed her hair from her face. His fingertips grazed her skin and Serenity found herself leaning into his touch. He chuckled at her response to him and that did nothing to cool her desire for him.

Climbing off of his lap took effort because she truly would rather sleep in his arms than in her bed alone. But she understood that it probably wasn't totally appropriate for her to be sleeping with a guy in her room, even if they were just sleeping. Okay, so it *was* totally inappropriate, and her aunt Darla might faint if she saw it, but that didn't make her want it any less. "Damn hormones," she growled under her breath.

"They complicate things, don't they?" Dair smiled down at her having heard her grumbling.

She felt the heat on her neck as it rose up her face clear to her hairline. As she laid back and look up at the boy, well really man, who held her heart, she decided that it was a whole lot more than hormones that complicated things between them.

"Sweet dreams, Princess," Dair whispered as he leaned down and pressed his lips to hers. It wasn't nearly long enough, but then she figured she could never get enough of his kisses. He could kiss her a million times a day, and still she would crave more.

"See you tomorrow?"

He ran a finger down her cheek and nodded. "Definitely."

"Dair," she said quickly before he could do his disappearing thing.

"Yes, beautiful?" Her heart fluttered at the endearment. "What we talked about earlier, the whole mate or husband thing." She paused, unsure of how to ask her question without being too embarrassed. "Have you ever thought about. . . I mean, would you consider.

. . I was just." Thank goodness he saved her.

"Have I thought about marrying you?" He knelt down beside her bed so that his face was level with hers. His deep black eyes bore into hers as he leaned closer. "The answer is yes. I will not deny that I have dreamed about the idea of making you mine in every way possible. To have you vow before the Creator and man that you are mine, and to give you the same vow, is my heart's desire. To share in the intimacy of physical love—to be the man gifted with your body, your heart, your soul—would be nothing short of a miracle."

Serenity couldn't breathe. She hadn't expected that answer. And as his words penetrated her mind and heart, she hoped that he did not ask her the same question because she feared she would yell out, *Yes! Please take me now!* Now, wouldn't that be a tad embarrassing? He must have seen that very answer in her eyes because he shot her one of his sexy smirks and, with one last quick kiss, he was gone. She reached up and turned her lamp off, allowing the darkness to engulf her room. As her head hit the pillow, Dair's words continued to wreak havoc on her mind, and images of a wedding, a wedding night, and a lifetime with him consumed her thoughts.

"You just had to go and end with *the man gifted with your body,* didn't you, Sandman?" she grumbled into the empty room as she attempted to get comfortable. With thoughts of Dair and the possibilities of what it would be like to be his in every way dancing through her head, getting comfortable was a losing battle. She felt something then, the cool air that alerted her to his presence, but when she looked around her room he was nowhere to be seen.

"If you're there, it's your fault I can't sleep; do

something about it." She pulled the covers up tight to her chin as she curled into a ball on her side, and as she felt the familiar effects of his power, she smiled to herself and thought, *make it a good one, Sandman, make it a good one.*

Dair stood at the foot of Serenity's bed watching her sleep. A subtle smile was on her lips as she slipped into the dream he had made for her. He had a feeling he would get an ear full tomorrow, but to see her blush would be well worth it. He hated to leave her, but he knew that if he stayed any longer, especially knowing what her mind was getting to experience in its sleeping state, he would crawl into her bed to hold her. He was also pretty sure there would be kissing after he woke her up. Nope, he definitely couldn't stay. With one last look at his love, he closed his eyes and traveled to Emma's house.

"I was wondering if you would show tonight," Raphael said as he stepped around the dark corner of the rundown home.

"Has everything been quiet?"

Raphael shrugged. "For the most part. A man came by earlier, but Mildred had what he wanted, so there was no fighting. They did, however, get high together and Mildred kept calling for Emma to come make them something to eat. I wouldn't let Emma leave her room, and finally I went out to Mildred and her guest and subtly suggested that he leave and she go to sleep."

"By subtle you mean?" Dair's eyes narrowed.

"I might have used a little influence on them, though I did not make myself known," Raphael said with a sniff.

Dair chuckled. "You're crossing over to the dark side."

"No, I was protecting a child. I didn't harm either human in any way, though the thought did cross my mind." The angel glanced up at the night sky and then back at Dair. "How is your female?"

Dair could tell he wanted to ask more. "She is well." He waited, knowing that Raphael wouldn't be able to keep quiet.

"What are you going to do?"

"I'm going to the Creator."

Raphael's eyes widened. "When?"

"Soon."

"What are you going to ask?"

"Honestly, I have no idea. But I don't want to keep a secret, especially when He already knows."

"What if He tells you that she isn't for you?"

Dair felt as though a fist had wrapped around his heart and began to squeeze. He didn't want to even consider that the Creator would tell him to let Serenity go. "I don't know what. I feel as though I belong to her. I've been walking this earth since the beginning of time; always something was missing, until her. How does a being live without air to breathe? She's my air, Raphael."

"Then I hope for your sake, brother, you get to keep her."

Emma couldn't believe how quickly the days flew by. But it was the nights that seemed to drag. She had woken up that morning and pulled out the small calendar her mama had given her and to her surprise saw that it was Christmas Eve. How had she not realized it was so soon? School had been out for a week, and she had spent every moment she could at the library or with Serenity. With all of the present wrapping Darla had her doing at the library, she would have thought that she'd have realized Christmas was literally right on top of her.

She climbed out of bed, already dressed with even her shoes on. It was a Darla request and so she honored it. Emma pulled her long hair over her shoulder and re-braided it the way her mama had taught her and then headed for her bedroom door. As always, she stopped and listened before she opened it. The house was quiet, which meant Aunt Mildred was still asleep or gone. She hoped it was the latter. When she opened the door and stepped out into the hall, she was greeted with a nod from Raphael who was standing guard, as usual, between her room and the living room. She had to wonder if he got bored standing in the hall all night. She had asked him once if he ever got tired, and he had informed her in his flat, no nonsense way that angels did not require sleep.

Emma made her way to the bathroom to take care of her morning business and then headed back to her room. Raphael followed her in and she saw that Dair had appeared as well.

"Mildred left this morning, but she will be back very soon. We should probably leave before she returns. I saw that she had a list of grocery items in her hand," Raphael told them.

"She was going to the grocery store?" Emma frowned. "That's new." Emma had never actually seen her aunt bring home groceries that she had bought herself. Usually the way her aunt acquired food was as a form of payment for the 'goods' that she sold out of her home. Emma figured accepting groceries for payment was much easier for her aunt than actually having to get out and go do something that might require the slightest bit of energy. "Why are you worried about us being gone before she gets back?" Emma asked the angel. Mildred had never tried to stop her from leaving before.

"She was muttering something about putting you to work to pay for your stay."

Emma could tell that Raphael didn't like having to tell her, but it didn't hurt Emma's feelings. Why should she be hurt over a woman who she didn't really know, nor did she care for? For her, living with her aunt was simply a season of her life that would pass. She wouldn't always be a child and she would not always need the room Mildred begrudgingly provided. One day Emma would be able to care for herself, and then she could put the time she spent with her aunt behind her.

They left the house quickly with both Dair and Raphael keeping a wary eye out for her aunt's beat-up old, what use to be, blue station wagon. They walked more quickly than usual and Emma found herself having to pay close attention to the slippery sidewalk and roads. She found herself wondering what things Darla had planned for the day. Even though she dearly loved her time with Darla, she was hoping Serenity would be by to take her to the vet so she could be around the animals. Regardless of what the day held, she knew that as long as she was away from her aunt, it would be a good one.

As they entered the library, the familiar smell of books hit Emma and she found herself smiling. This place had truly become her home. Darla and the other staff always welcomed her with open arms and they never treated Raphael differently, despite his huge size and somewhat intimidating demeanor.

"I am so glad you are here." Darla's voice carried from the small office that was to the right of the checkout desk. She came rushing out in her usual exuberant manner, smiling as if Emma and the two guardians with her had hung the moon. "Hello Dair, Raphael." She nodded to them and then wrapped Emma in her usual hug.

"Darla," Raphael's voice rumbled.

Dair simply nodded in return.

"How are you doing this fine Christmas Eve morning?" Darla asked her.

"I actually didn't even realize that today was Christmas Eve. It's hard to believe that I've been here for over two weeks already."

"Time does fly when you're having fun," Darla sighed.

"So why are you so glad we're here?" Emma asked.

"Oh, right." Darla clapped her hands together and then rubbed them as if warming them. Darla was about to say something more but was interrupted by screeching tires in the parking lot. They all turned to look out the window and see what the commotion was. Emma's stomach dropped to her toes when she saw her aunt's car parked right outside the front door of the library.

"Emma, go to the back please," Darla said, her voice suddenly taking on a tone that Emma had never heard before.

Emma shook her head. "I'm sorry ma'am, but I can't do that. I can't leave y'all here to face my problem."

The door flew open with a resounding snap as it struck the wall behind it. Mildred Jones stormed in, looking wild-eyed and as crazy as Emma had ever seen her. Emma swore if she had been a dog she would have been foaming at the mouth.

"Mildred, you cannot park your car in front of the door; it's a fire hazard," Darla told her calmly.

Raphael and Dair had stepped closer to Emma forming a protective barrier around her. She knew that they wanted to protect her from her aunt, but there wasn't anything they could do. Mildred was her legal guardian and had never really done her any harm. She didn't see any way for them to help her, at least not right then.

"I ain't staying. I come to pick up my ward. I didn't give her no permission to leave the house, and yet I sees her walking down the street, with two men no less." Her gaze shifted to Emma and her glazed-over eyes narrowed. "How you think it looks, girl, for you to be walking around with men old enough to be your father? I ain't raisin no whore."

Emma was surprised that Mildred remembered seeing them considering Raphael's ability to sway minds, and she wondered if it had anything to do with all the drug use and alcohol. Maybe her mind was just too gone to be able to be influenced like others.

"ENOUGH," Dair's voice rumbled over Mildred's. And pulling Emma from her thoughts about her aunt. "You will not call the child such vulgar names or you will face my wrath.

"And who's you be for me to care? That brat is mine. She livin' in my home, eatin' my food, sleepin' in the bed I be providing, and she's goin to start earning her keep. Now, come on, girl, ya hear? I have people coming for dinner and I won't be letting them go hungry."

Emma stepped forward to follow her aunt but Darla gently took her arm. "You don't need to go with her, Emma. She's been drinking and is probably high as a kite as well."

Emma looked up into the worried eyes of the woman who she'd come to think of as her real aunt and smiled gently. "I'll be okay, Darla. I'm not a victim and I'm tough. If I don't go with her now, I have a feeling it will be worse for me later on." Emma could tell that it took everything in Darla for her to release her and let her walk out of the library. She didn't want to disappoint her, but she knew that her aunt would take her anger out on Emma if she didn't just do what she wanted. Cooking dinner for her aunt and her low life friends wouldn't be that bad as long as Emma could lock herself in her room before they all arrived.

Even though she heard Darla tell Raphael to make sure she made it home in one piece, Emma didn't look back as she climbed into the back seat of her aunt's car. She didn't want to see the worry in their faces. Instead, she leaned her head back and closed her eyes and thought of happier times. Emma drew on her memories of past Christmases with her parents. If her mama and daddy were still alive they would be in the kitchen with the Christmas music turned up loud while they cooked Christmas dinner. Her mama would let her help make the dressing and baste the turkey, and she would even let her eat some of the cookie dough from the sugar cookies they made every year. The whole house would smell of good food and be full of laughter and music. They weren't the perfect family, but her parents worked hard to make the holidays special. He mama always used to tell her, *Emma, memories are important and making good ones can sometimes be the difference between simply surviving through difficult situations or thriving.* As she sat in the back of that car, with stale cigarette smoke swirling around her, Emma realized exactly what her mama had been talking about.

Two hours later, Emma stood in the kitchen in Mildred's house admiring the 'feast' she'd prepared. The preparation had consisted mostly of simply heating things up because her aunt had only bought stuff that needed to be tossed in a pan and warmed or thrown into the microwave. Green beans, mashed potatoes, as well as macaroni and cheese were all microwavable. The turkey she bought was already cooked and simply had to be heated up in the stove. The dressing was Stove Top from a box. None of it was difficult for the girl to manage. She simply followed the directions on the backs of the containers. Her aunt had left her alone for the most part, only coming in a few times to gripe and complain about Emma *thinking she could come and go as she pleased.* Emma simply ignored her and listened to the Christmas music she had playing in her head.

Once the table was set and all the food was laid out, Emma started to slip off to her room. But her aunt grabbed her arm and turned Emma to face her.

"Where do you think yer going?"

"I figured you would want me out of the way so that you and your guests could have a nice time," Emma told her. She fought the urge to pull her arm out of the tight grasp. Her parents had never handled her so roughly. Oh, she had been spanked on occasion but never had her mama smacked her or hit her out of anger.

"I wants you out here where I can be keeping an eye on you. You can serve us and make yourself useful."

Emma didn't like the sound of that. "Are you sure? I'm terribly clumsy at times." She was fibbing but she figured it was allowed if she was attempting to protect herself. Emma had a feeling being around the type of men her aunt entertained would not be in her best interest.

"Well, you better not spill anything on my guests or you'll be punished. Didn't my dear sister teach you bout sparing the rod n spoilin the child?"

Emma nearly snorted out a laugh. The idea of that woman spouting out Bible verses was about as ridiculous as a politician swearing on the Bible that he would be honest and put the people's best interest first. Truly it was laughable. But Emma swallowed it down and simply nodded at her aunt.

One by one, Mildred's friends began to arrive and with each new person the leering looks and snide comments increased. Emma couldn't bring herself to appear meek or afraid. She wouldn't give them the satisfaction of thinking they were getting to her. Instead, she met their gazes head on with a challenging one of her own. Her mama and daddy hadn't raised a coward, and she would not lower herself in front of the likes of those people.

"She's a pretty little thing, Milly," one particularly shifty man said as he licked his fingers after having ripped his piece of turkey apart. Emma stood in the kitchen waiting for her aunt's orders. Every so often her aunt would yell, 'fill that glass, girl' or 'get us more food, you ingrate'. Emma bit her tongue over and over to keep from saying things that would only cause a flare in her aunt's temper. She endured the looks from the men and the snide comments from the women. The final straw was when a man her aunt called Rat reached out and ran a finger down her cheek as she refilled his glass. Nobody would touch Emma without her permission. Her mama had always told her that her body belonged to herself, and no one had the right to touch it in any way.

Emma couldn't stop her hand from flying up and slapping the disgusting appendage away from her face. Her eyes narrowed on the man called Rat, and she gritted her teeth as she spoke. "Didn't your mama teach you any manners? I do not want you to touch me; please don't." Only her mama's insistent reminders to be respectful had Emma saying please, though she knew this man did not deserve her respect.

"She's a feisty one, Mildred," Rat laughed as he continued to watch her. "You should sell her; she'd bring a pretty penny."

"Sell her," Mildred snapped. "She ain't but. . ." She paused and looked over at Emma. "How old are you, girl?"

Emma straightened her shoulders as she stepped back away from the table. "I'm eight years old."

"See, she's only eight. What would I be selling her for?"

Rat's eyes lingered much too long on Emma, causing her stomach to roll. "She's only a few years away from breeding age; until then she could be put to work in a man's house cooking and cleaning."

"Why can't she just be kept in my house to cook and clean? She's my kin," Mildred said as she smacked her food.

"She needs to be trained by a man if she's to be a proper slave."

Emma was pretty sure she was going to vomit all over the floor if she had to listen to any more of Rat's disgusting talk of selling her and making her a slave to a man. Emma wasn't stupid; she knew exactly what kind of slave he was talking about. She would run away before she let that happen. *I'm not a victim*, she told herself. It was her mantra as she continued to listen to the disgusting, vile people who sat around the table eating food in celebration of a holiday that they didn't even understand. When Mildred raised her glass and hollered, 'Merry Christmas and all that crap', Emma wanted to stomp her foot and tell them all how disgraceful their behavior was at such a time. They were supposed to be celebrating the birth of Jesus, and instead they spoke of disgusting acts and illegal things that no eight-year-old should ever have to hear about.

As the night grew later, the group became increasingly sluggish due to the alcohol they consumed and the drugs they were openly doing in front of her. When they were all finally gathered in the living room—lying around like lazy, fat rats—she began to walk slowly backwards toward her room, keeping her eyes on them all the while. As she made her way down the hallway, her eyes roaming the group wearily she wondered where Raphael was. She couldn't see him and so she thought maybe he was standing guard using whatever cloaking power it was that angels had. She didn't wonder about it too long because she was simply too tired to give it any more thought.

As she closed the door behind her, she turned the lock and then pressed her back against it and slowly slid to the floor. She wasn't a victim, but that didn't mean she wasn't scared. Emma knew she would be foolish to not be afraid. The people currently on the other side of her wall were shameless, morally bankrupt degenerates with no conscience; at least that's what her mother would say. They had nothing left to lose and her daddy told her those kind of people were the most dangerous sort. She was only eight years old. She had ten years left until she would be considered an adult. How was she going to survive ten years with a woman who cared nothing for her and would do nothing to protect her from the likes of people like Rat?

Emma didn't realize she had fallen asleep sitting there on the floor until she was startled awake by the sound of the doorknob to her room turning. She reached up to make sure the lock was turned and let out the breath she hadn't even realized she was holding. The knob continued to jiggle and Emma heard a string of curses from a deep yet very slurred voice. She stood up but her stomach seemed to remain on the floor as she backed away slowly from the door toward the window. Her eyes darted to the bed where her coat lay and in the process noted that Raphael still wasn't there. When the jiggling turned into the sound of a shoulder against the door, she knew she needed to get out of there.

Emma grabbed her coat and quickly shoved her arms into the sleeves. As quietly as possible she pushed the window open, though she was sure whoever was on the other side of that door could hear her panicked breathing. Thankfully, Raphael had thought ahead and already greased the old, rusted window so that it wouldn't make any noise should she ever need to use it to make a hasty exit. Emma could feel the cold air on her face as she began to climb through the window. She didn't flinch when she heard the door give way to another hard shove but she tried to move more quickly. She thought she was going to make, but her movement was impeded by the prickly leaves on the bushes planted right in front of her window. Her first leg was touching the ground and she had begun to lift the other when he grabbed her.

"Gotcha," the deep voice growled. She recognized the voice—Rat.

Emma attempted to pull her leg out of his grasp but he was much too strong for her. His other hand took hold of the braid in her hair and yanked her head back. She let out an involuntary cry as a sharp pain radiated through her scalp. He jerked her through the window and back into the dark room. Emma's arms flailed out in front of her, desperate to grab anything that she could use to pull herself away from her attacker. It was useless. Her arms were just too short. When he tossed her onto the bed, she looked around frantically for anything that she could use as a weapon. A hand connected with her face before she could get her arms up to block the blow. She screamed inside her mind for Raphael. He was her guardian, her self-appointed protector, and though she didn't know why he hadn't been there that night, she knew he would come. He had to, because if he didn't, things much worse than being slapped across the face were going to happen.

Raphael took in a sharp breath as the desperation of Emma's cry filled his mind. He knelt, head bowed in reverence, before the Creator which was the only reason he had not been with Emma that night. He had done as Darla asked and made sure the child arrived to her aunt's safely, but then his Maker had called and he had to answer. Raphael had known it would be about Brudair but he had been surprised by the Creator's questions.

"The child is in need," the deep voice said as it radiated into his soul and covered Raphael in peace that only the Creator could give. "You have been guarding her?"

"Yes," he answered honestly.

"Continue to do so. The purpose I have for her is great, and she will bear many burdens before she fulfills it. Go now, keep her safe, but do not interfere with her free will. Understand this Raphael, what happens tonight must happen. She will become the woman I have destined her to be partly because of her experiences."

"As you will it," Raphael responded. He did not stand until he had traveled from the Creator's presence. When he arrived outside of Mildred's home, he immediately felt the darkness and evil that saturated even the air around the shack. Raphael's head snapped around to the window on the side of the house where Emma's room was located and he immediately appeared inside of the room.

"STOP." The power given to him from the Creator had the man, whose hand had been reared back to hit Emma once more, frozen. "Emma come here." She climbed quickly from the bed but before she moved to Raphael's side she pulled her leg back and kicked the man in the shin.

"That's for being such a nasty person," she snapped and then hurried to stand behind Raphael.

Raphael's lips twitched at the young girl's spirit. She was a fighter and based on what the Creator had said about the burdens she would face, she was going to need to be a fighter.

Using his will alone, Raphael turned the unmovable man to face him. The fear in his eyes was unmistakable, as was the utter hatred. This was a man that did not like to be humiliated and would retaliate for such a thing. The man's eyes widened further when Raphael took a step toward him.

"This child is under my protection as ordered by the Creator. To stand against the Creator is to face your own destruction. You will not touch her again. If you attempt to, you will face my wrath. Now, leave." Raphael gave the man a small push with his power, forcing the man toward the door. He could tell that Rat was trying to turn around and face him, but he was powerless to do so under Raphael's command. Once the door was closed, Raphael turned to look down at Emma. Though her face was bruised from a blow that he had not been there to stop, she held her chin up high and her shoulders were pulled back. She was beaten but not defeated.

"I am sorry that I was not here," he told her as he knelt down before her. He attempted to make his tone sound gentler for her sake.

"The point is that you got here in time," she told him. "It could have been much worse than a smack across the face."

"Are you alright?" He was glad to see that she was holding herself together, but it also worried him that she wasn't shaken by the incident. "Would you like to go to Darla's?"

Both of their heads turned toward the living room as they heard a crash followed by an unintelligible shout. She looked back at him and nodded. "I think that's a great idea."

When they instantly appeared in front of Darla and Wayne's front door, Emma frowned at him. "How come we walk everywhere in town if you can just do that?"

"Because it would probably alert the other humans that I am not normal if we suddenly appeared out of nowhere. Although if it only happened once they wouldn't remember but repeatedly and it gets harder to influence them to forget the shock."

"Oh, right, that makes sense."

Raphael knocked on the door, even though the house was dark and it was obvious that everyone inside was asleep. It was late, but he knew that Darla would not care. After several minutes, the locks on the door began to turn. When the door was finally pulled open, it was a drowsy Serenity that stood before them. She took one look at Emma and her eyes narrowed in on the puffy, swollen cheek. "Who did this?" she asked him at the same time motioning for them to enter. Her voice was tight with emotion and Raphael could tell she was attempting to keep her cool for the sake of the child.

"One of Mildred's acquaintances," he told her.

"Where were you?" Serenity snapped. "You said you would protect her. How did this happen?"

Raphael's face didn't change as he answered. "I had been called by the Creator and was in his presence at the time of Emma's attack. As soon as I was aware of the trouble, the Creator sent me to intervene."

"It was one strike too late, don't you think?" Her voice was growing louder with every question. She had a right to be angry; he would not deny her that. But his response would probably only anger her further, so he simply said nothing. The only thing that consoled Raphael's shame at not having been there was that he knew he would be with her from now on with the blessing of the Creator behind him. She would still face adversity, but he would be able to protect her from most of the evil that came her way.

The room was suddenly illuminated in bright light as Darla and Wayne came rushing into the living area, flipping the switch as they did so. Darla's eyes took in the room quickly and then found Emma.

"Did she do this to you?" Darla hurried to her and knelt in front of the child. "Did your aunt hurt you?"

Emma shook her head. "It was a friend of hers they called Rat. I had locked my door but apparently that particular lock had not been tested against nasty, drunk men. I tried to get out the window but he caught me."

Darla wrapped her arms around Emma and pulled her tightly to her chest. The girl suddenly looked like the eight-year-old that she was. She laid her cheek on Darla's shoulder, and when she looked up at Raphael, he saw the sheen of tears in her eyes. He was thankful for those tears because it was not healthy for her to keep those emotions bottled up inside. Tears were healthy; they were like a cleansing waterfall to the soul and, once released, would wash away the pain.

"I don't like to cry," she sniffled as she closed her eyes causing the tears to fall. "It makes me feel like a victim and I am not a victim."

Darla shook her head. "Crying doesn't make you a victim, Emma," she told her as she rubbed her back to sooth her. "You become a victim when you let the trauma overtake your life instead of dealing with it and letting it go."

"Tears are good for you," Raphael said. When she opened her eyes back up, he knelt down. His large frame seemed to make the room shrink. His face was almost level with hers as his eyes met Emma's. "They are a gift from the Creator to his creation. Tears release endorphins in the mind that help soothe and comfort. They cleanse the eyes and relieve stress, thereby lowering blood pressure and taking strain off of the heart. He created you with tears and nothing he created is bad. Those tears you are holding in are necessary, Emma. Let them fall, let them heal, and let them remind you with each one that you are not alone."

Chapter 9

"To dream of Christmas while it is Spring or Summer means that you are subconsciously remembering some long-forgotten pleasant experience of your childhood. To dream of the Grinch means that you are subconsciously burying an unpleasant memory."

Serenity motioned for Raphael to follow her into the kitchen once Darla had gotten Emma tucked away in the spare bedroom for the night. She knew by the worried look on the angel's face that he thought she was about to go off on him again for not being there when Emma needed him. And though she was still angry over it, she knew yelling at Raphael wouldn't change the events of the evening. But she had something more important to talk about.

"Tomorrow morning is Christmas." Serenity rolled her eyes when he stood there and simply blinked at her. "As in there are usually presents under the tree from Santa for little girls and little boys."

"Emma will not have presents at her aunt's house, I'm sure," Raphael said dully.

"Yes, I know. We've gotten her a few things ourselves, but we don't want her to think that Santa has forgotten her, now do we?

"You desire for me to go and get her presents?"

"Ding, ding, ding, give the angel his prize," Serenity said dryly. "Yes, we want you to get her presents." She held out a list and some money to him but he only took the list.

"I do not need your money."

Serenity's brow scrunched up. "Are you sure? You do realize that stuff isn't free. You can't just say, *hey, I'm an angel so give me what I want.*"

This time Raphael rolled his eyes at her. It was such a human gesture that Serenity couldn't help the huff of laughter.

"I have been on this earth much, much longer than you. I learned the concept of commerce and goods without any trouble, believe it or not."

Serenity's eyes widened. "Did you just use sarcasm? Wow, I'm impressed. It was a little stiff, but you're making progress."

"I didn't realize I was trying to make progress."

"Raphael, we all have stuff that we need to make some progress on. Now, as much as I know you like small talk, off with you. You've got shopping to do."

"I do not like small talk," Raphael told her with a slight crease in his forehead.

"And we digress." She blew out breath. "I was being sarcastic, Raph; just go with it."

He simply looked at her for a moment longer before disappearing.

"Where did he disappear to?" Darla asked as she walked into the kitchen looking more worried than Serenity had seen her in a long time.

"Okay first doesn't it freak you out that a man who claims to be an angel just up and disappears from your kitchen? And second I sent him on a mission. He's going to be Santa."

Darla smiled. "That was good thinking. And you need to remember Serenity that some of us experience things in our life time that make us very aware of the unseen world around us. I think the Good Book puts it as entertaining angels unaware. Some of us are simply aware."

Serenity was tired to delve into that rabbit hole with her aunt. She'd just accept it for what it was. Darla wasn't crazy and therefore obviously had simply accepted the supernatural world as being real. Serenity's mind drifted back to Raphael and the gifts and she hoped that something as small as making Emma's Christmas a little brighter would be enough to help heal the ordeal the young girl had been through that night. But she knew she could hope until the world crumbled and that wouldn't change the fact that pieces of Emma's innocence had been taken from her. Because of that she would never be the same.

"You go on to bed, Darla," she told her aunt. "I'll wait up for Raphael and make him help wrap the presents. It's the least he can do."

"Don't be too hard on him, Sarah Serenity. We can't begin to understand what kind of obligations he is under."

Once again the way Darla referred to Raphael with such casualness baffled her. "I forget sometimes that you are way too chill for any normal adult."

"Back in my day it was cool, not chill," Darla smiled at her as she headed towards her room.

"Back in your day you all also thought pants that looked like they had bells at their bottoms were *cool*," she said and drew out the word. "So I don't know if I'd be too proud of what happened back in your day."

Darla simply laughed at her and hollered goodnight leaving Serenity standing in the empty kitchen wishing Dair was with her and Raphael would hurry.

"What a Christmas," she muttered under her

breath.

"What a Christmas indeed," a small voice said from behind her.

Serenity's head whipped around to find Emma standing in the doorway where her aunt had stood only moments ago. "What are you doing up, chickadee?"

Emma shrugged. "Couldn't sleep."

Serenity sighed. "I can understand that. But you do know Santa can't come if you're awake, right?"

Emma's lips quirked up in a small smile as she shook her head at her. "You can't honestly believe someone with my IQ could possibly still believe in Santa Clause, could you?"

"Well, I don't know what your IQ is soooo," Serenity hedged.

"Fair enough," Emma agreed. "I'm two points below Albert Einstein's score."

Serenity propped a hand on her hip and offered Emma a bemused smile. "I don't know Einstein's IQ either."

The eight-year-old copied Serenity's pose and added a head tilt of her own. "What exactly do you know?"

As Serenity stared down at the young girl who had been through so much, her stomach clenched inside of her. What did she know? She knew that if she'd been in Emma's shoes tonight she wouldn't be able to have a light hearted conversation in the kitchen of people she'd only known a couple of weeks. She knew that she would be a mess of blubbering tears and snot and the whole nine yards if some scary, nasty man had attempted to put his hands on her. But she didn't share those things with Emma, not yet. "I know that little girls need to be in bed if they want Santa to come," she finally told her.

Emma's hand dropped from her hip and she let out a resigned sigh. "Fine, I will go to bed, even though I know Santa Clause is not going to be trotting in here on some reindeer, plopping himself down a chimney, and unpacking a pack that seemingly never empties." All of this she said as she began walking backwards toward the hallway.

"Hey, Emma," Serenity called just as the girl began to turn around to walk to Wayne and Darla's spare bedroom. Emma looked back at her with large, trusting eyes. "Even if there's not a Santa, you still are not forgotten."

Emma's eyes lit up with what Serenity could only describe as hope. A smile stretched across the young girl's face as she spoke, "Of course I'm not. God didn't create me just so he could go and forget me."

"No, I suppose he didn't," Serenity whispered as Emma continued down the hall.

The house was quiet after everyone had gone to bed. Serenity was left to her thoughts as she sat in the kitchen at the small dining room table. She had to continually push her mind away from the *what could have beens* and *what might have happened* had Raphael not arrived when he did. She knew that it would do no good to dwell on things that hadn't happened or couldn't be changed. So she thought of Dair instead and wondered how his night was going. He had told her that he might be gone longer than one night because he had several assignments to complete. Serenity had asked him how he knows when he has a new person to see and he had shrugged and said, "I just do." She could tell he had never given it a second thought. Why would he? It was what he had been doing since his creation. Like, breathing was second nature to her; making dreams was the same to Dair. So instead of sitting and dwelling on all that she couldn't fix, she pulled her phone from the pocket of her flannel pajama bottoms and dialed Glory's number. It had been days since she'd gotten to talk to her best friend, and if anyone would know what to say to keep Serenity's mind busy it would be Glory.

"It's late," Glory's voice chirped through the receiver when she finally picked up.

"That's all you have to say to me? For all you know I'm calling with a crisis."

"Are you?"

Serenity bit her lip. "Well, it's a post crisis."

"Post crisis is not a crisis and therefore does not require the same kind of courtesy a crisis would. So again I say, it's late."

"Aren't you even the least bit curious about the post crisis?" Serenity taunted.

There was a pause before Glory let out a long sigh. "Good grief, Sarah Tillman, would you spit it out already. Getting information out of you is like trying to get milk from a slug."

"Um, Glory, milk doesn't come from slugs."

"Exactly, so you should totally feel my pain. Now give me the post crisis details and don't leave anything out."

"You're grouchy."

"It's late."

"You said that."

"And yet you have yet to fill me in on the post crisis. What. The. Hell. Serenity?"

"Okay, okay, geeze, sometimes it's hard to believe you're an actual adult." Serenity hurried on before

Glory could add her two cents. "So Emma showed up on our door tonight…" She told Glory every detail starting from when Darla had told her about Emma's aunt coming up to the library to take Emma home. As she spoke she felt her blood getting hot all over again. By the time she had finished the story, Serenity was ready to take a bat to Mildred's to see if this Rat character was hanging around.

"Is she alright?" Glory's voice was considerably softer than it had been when she'd first answered the phone. "I haven't met this little Emma yet, but from what you've told me she's one smart cookie and tough. How is she handling things?"

"Honestly, I'm a little shocked as to how well she's taking it. I feel like she should be a blubbering mess. I mean she's shed some tears and it's obvious that she isn't unaffected but she's actually holding it together really well."

"She doesn't have a choice," Glory told her. "For Emma there is no plan B. Her parents are gone, this Mildred chick is all she has, and she knows that she has to make the best of what she's got. I imagine little Emma knows that what's done is done, and all she can do is move forward."

"I think it's past time you and Emma met," Serenity pointed out.

"I have to agree, little pet. You have been remiss in your duties as a best friend and have not kept me apprised of all of your comings and goings."

"You do realize that this best friend thing works both ways, right? You haven't been ringing my phone."

Serenity could see the shrug she knew her best friend was no doubt giving her. "True, but I have an excuse. I have a job. All you do is go to school, like that's important or anything."

Serenity laughed. "Yes, you're right my graduating is of no consequence at all. How wrong of me to not make sure you are better informed before I worry about getting to class and getting my work done."

"Now, we are finally making some progress," Glory said in her most haughty voice. "I will come to your home on the morrow to meet the child."

"You're weird."

"You love me," Glory sang.

"Yes, yes I do. It's late; go to bed." Serenity laughed when Glory let out a few of her favorite expletives before finally hanging up. She wasn't surprised that she hadn't said more on what had happened with Emma. She knew that it would be hitting too close to home with Glory. Serenity felt guilty for even telling her something like that over the phone, but then she knew that Glory would want to know before she met Emma face-to-face.

Her phone dinged letting her know that she'd received a text. It was from Glory.

"I'm fine. Quit worrying bout me."

Serenity smiled to herself. Glory knew her too well.

She texted back. "Don't flatter yourself. I'm more worried about me and Emma if you don't get some sleep. You'll be a bear tomorrow."

Glory responded with, "Grrr. Night."

Serenity let out a sigh as she set her phone on the table and stretched her arms out in front of her. She knew that Glory would be fine, but she still hated that memories would no doubt be dredged up because of the topic of their conversation. Glory's life hadn't been an easy one. She had wonderful parents, no doubt, and they loved her. But, unfortunately, parents couldn't pick their family members and family didn't always mean friendly or loving. She didn't want to go down that road tonight so she tucked those memories away for another time. Just as she was about to stand, she felt the temperature in the room drop a couple of degrees.

"Hey."

Serenity's head whipped around at the sound of the deep, silky voice. "What are you doing here?" she whispered through the smile that was threatening to split her face in half. She hadn't realized how badly she had wanted to see him or how much she had needed him.

"What's wrong," Dair asked as his eyes narrowed and he knelt down in front of her.

She shook her head, unable to say anything for fear that she would turn into a blubbering mess and tell him about the events of the night and then beg him to make it better. Instead she just reached for him and, like she knew he would, Dair wrapped her in his strong embrace. His hand stroked down her hair and back and his whispered words soothed her. "I felt you."

His words had her pulling away to look at him. "What do you mean you felt me?"

He started to do the whole shoulder shrug thing but when she frowned at him he stopped. "I could feel you were upset and that you needed me, like a string is attached to my soul connecting to yours and your soul was giving it a tug."

"How come I can't feel you?" she asked, then watched as Dair closed his eyes and his face was completely relaxed. She wondered what he was doing but didn't have to wonder long because then *she* felt him. Cool waves of concern flowed through her and she knew it was Dair's concern for her.

"Why, I mean, how," she stuttered as he opened his eyes to look at her.

"I don't know," he answered, obviously having understood what she was asking. "I don't understand it either. But I'm not complaining."

Serenity smiled. "I'm not either."

"Now, will you tell me what has you so upset?"

Serenity bit the inside of her cheek, giving herself time to think, to figure out how to explain the events of the night without causing Dair to flip his lid. In the end, she decided that there was no way for her to explain little Emma being attacked in such a way that wouldn't have Dair fuming. Better to just rip the Band-Aide off quickly she decided.

"Emma was attacked by one of Mildred's scumbags tonight." The words flew out of her mouth before she had a chance to even consider that maybe she should first tell him that Emma was alright and that she was safe. Dair started to stand and Serenity could feel the air around them growing colder as his temper flared. "Wait, wait, Dair." She stood quickly and grabbed his arm. "Maybe I should have mentioned that she's here and she's safe."

"What happened?" The room seemed to dim as his power began to grow, and she could tell he truly was on the verge of losing control. Serenity had no idea what sort of power Dair wielded, other than being able to create dreams, but she imagined an immortal being was no weakling.

Serenity told him all that Emma had told her, and once she was finished she waited. Dair stood in the middle of the small kitchen. He was still as stone and his inhuman beauty was harsh as the anger and obvious frustration at having not been there washed over him.

"He didn't." He paused but she knew he wasn't going to continue and she didn't blame him. Serenity didn't like to think about what could have happened either.

"No, he didn't touch her, not like that."

Dair let out a slow breath that seemed to help him gain some control. "I'm sorry that I wasn't here to be with you. I know it must have been hard for you to handle."

She knew how he meant it, and Serenity appreciated that he wanted to be there to support her and that he cared enough to want to care for not only her but Emma as well. "We managed. Besides, Emma is one incredible little lady. She's made of stern stuff."

"Where the hell was Raphael?" he growled, his previous anger coming back full force. "I thought he said he would be watching over the child."

"He said he had been summoned by the Creator." Serenity didn't miss the way Dair's shoulders tensed.

"That would have been the only thing that would have kept the angel away. He takes his responsibilities very seriously. I imagine he is not handling this well."

"I reamed him," she admitted. Dair shot her a sideways glance and a small smile appeared on his lips.

"How did he handle that?"

She shrugged. "He took it like a man."

"Speaking of the angel," Dair said as he cocked his head to the side, "where is he?"

It was Serenity's turn to slip on a sly smile. "I sent him on an errand. He's playing Santa tonight."

"Presents for Emma?"

"Yep," she said popping the *p* with her lips. "He's so jolly; I figured he really fit the part."

Dair laughed.

It was only a few minutes later when Raphael appeared in the kitchen with his arms loaded down with bags. Serenity's eyes widened. "You don't mess around do you?"

"I am not sure what you mean by that."

Serenity waved him off. "Never mind. Let's just see what the damage is." They began going through the gifts and she was happily surprised to see that Raphael had done really well. He got Emma some challenging puzzle games, a cute pair of snow boots, a stylish scarf, hat and mitten set, several boxes that appeared to be some sort of girly crafts, and some books. Well, not just some books, he had actually gotten her seven books, and they weren't just your run of the mill books. These were classics like *Beowulf*, *Of Mice and Men*, *1984*, and *The Iliad and the Odyssey*.

"Do you think she will like these books?" Serenity asked as she flipped through a copy of *The Scarlet Letter*.

Raphael's brow scrunched together. "She said that she was extremely intelligent. All of the books in the children's section seemed much too juvenile for her. These books seemed to be more appropriate."

Serenity just shook her head. She went and grabbed the wrapping paper from the hall closet and enlisted Dair and Raphael to help her get the presents wrapped and under the tree. Once the work was done, she thanked Raphael for his help and then turned to Dair. "I'm going to go to bed. If Emma's anything like I was at her age, she'll be up in just a few hours—too excited to sleep."

Dair's eyes twinkled with mischief. "Is that my hint to come and tuck you in?"

Serenity's cheeks flared with heat as she glanced at Raphael from the corner of her eye, but he wasn't paying them a bit of attention. She gave Dair a subtle jerk of her head to follow her.

Dair watched Serenity walk towards her room. His eyes didn't leave her form as he spoke to Raphael. "Thank you for being here for the girls."

There was a long pause before the angel answered. "I am sorry that I was not there to protect her."

"No one expects you to be perfect, old friend," Dair said, his voice low. He didn't wait for Raphael's response. He knew no words would comfort the angel. He would deal with what he considered his failure in his own way.

As he entered Serenity's room, he pushed the door gently closed behind him and smiled when she tensed at the click that filled the silence. He stood there watching her, mesmerized as she brushed her long brown locks. She was beautiful. Her inner beauty only made the outer that much more incredible, and he was left breathless because she had chosen him.

"Are you just going to stand there?" she asked him, though her eyes did not meet his.

"What would you have me do, Princess?"

"Why do you call me that?"

"It's your name. Sarah Serenity literally means princess of peace. It's fitting if you ask me. So again, I ask you. What would you have me do?"

She paused and then finally looked up at him. Her eyes were full of the longing and ache that he felt inside of his own soul—an ache that only she could fill. Dair couldn't remember a time in his very long existence ever feeling a need so strong as he did in that moment. He needed to hold her, to know that she was safe in his arms. Dair took a step towards her; his eyes held hers as he took another and another until he was standing inches from her. Serenity's head tilted back so that she could look up at him. His hand reached up of its own accord, and his fingers brushed her hair from her face and then sank deeper into the thick strands until he was cupping her head.

"What are you doing to me?" he whispered as his eyes roamed over her face. "When I'm away from you all of my thoughts are for you. When I'm with you, regardless of how close I am to you, it is never close enough. What, Sarah Serenity, are you doing to me?"

Her breathing quickened and at some point her own hands had ended up on his chest and were now wrapped around his shirt as though she had to grasp him in order to stay standing. Serenity's eye were glazing over, held captive by him.

"I'm not doing anything," she finally answered and it came out in a breathy voice that had Dair's stomach clenching with desire.

He leaned closer until his mouth hovered just above hers. He could feel her warm breath on his face and smell her sweet scent, and it only incensed his passion for her.

"I'm going to taste you now," Dair whispered against her lips and he could literally feel his mouth begin to water for her. She nodded, unable to say anything and that had his confidence growing. He felt his own breathing increase just before his lips pressed against her. Her warmth flowed over him as she pressed herself closer. The hand that wasn't wrapped in her luscious hair wrapped around her waist and pulled her even tighter against him. When Serenity's lips parted allowing him entrance into the moist depths of her mouth, Dair fought the urge to lay her down on the bed, knowing it would only lead to things for which they weren't yet ready. It was nearly his undoing when she slid her hands up his chest and shoulders until her fingers were running through his hair. Her soft groans and mewling were a red flag that it was time for him to stop.

Dair ripped his lips away from hers, pressing their foreheads together. He couldn't speak, not yet. All he was capable of in that moment was breathing while attempting to stay upright. Serenity's eyes were closed and her chest rose and fell as the breath rushed in and out. Dair could feel her heart pounding against her chest as she pressed closer to him. Dair's eyes followed her tongue as she slowly traced her lips with it.

"Careful, love," he told her in a near moan. "I can only take so much."

To his surprise she chuckled as she opened her eyes and pulled back so she could look up at him. "I assure you that I am not purposefully trying to tempt you."

"Princess, your very existence is enough to tempt me. I'm afraid there is nothing you can do to keep me from desiring you."

Her lips pursed crookedly as she thought about his words. "I bet I could come up with a way to be less appealing. What if I never brushed my hair or bathed? Bet you wouldn't want to get close then."

"Your scent is the most intoxicating thing I've ever smelled. I have a feeling that would only draw me closer."

"I'm not sure whether to be flattered or grossed out."

Dair shrugged. "Just being honest." They stood there staring at one another for several minutes.

Neither of them was ready to let go. Dair didn't think he would ever be ready, not in this lifetime or the next. As he brushed a stray strand of hair from her face he whispered, "I need to let you get some sleep."

She nodded and then rose up on her toes to press a sweet kiss to his lips. She was out of his arms before he could deepen it. Dair watched as she climbed into bed and then he turned off the light for her. "Sweet dreams, Princess," he told her. Serenity smiled at him as she drifted off to sleep. To his surprise, Dair felt a dream being drawn to his consciousness and realized it was for his Serenity. His brow furrowed as he thought about the fact that he hadn't known beforehand that she was on the agenda. Closing his eyes, he reached into her mind and began to build the dream for her. Dair watched as Emma and Serenity hung out at the library together. The dream consisted mostly of Serenity pursuing a relationship with Emma. He wondered why this was the dream he was to give her when Serenity was already on that path.

Dair didn't have time to contemplate it further because as soon as the dream was complete he felt the call of his Creator. His chest tightened as he gave Serenity one last look before traveling from her presence and into the presence of pure light. Dair knelt as he entered the Creator's presence, and the warmth that enveloped him brought him immediate peace. Dair attempted to slow his breathing as he waited—for what, he wasn't sure. It had been centuries since he was last summoned to the Creator, and he was not foolish enough to think that this was some coincidence. It had to be about Serenity.

"Brudair," the deep voice rumbled and Dair's hands clenched into fists as he attempted to remain calm. "It has been long since our last meeting. You have done your work well."

"Thank you," Dair said reverently.

"As of late, you have become enamored with an assignment that you were given. She is special, Sarah Serenity Tillman. She will serve a much bigger purpose than you can imagine."

"I am more than enamored with her."

"You love her," the Creator confirmed. "And yet, love is not an emotion you were created for."

The air rushed from Dair's chest as though he had been punched. It was one thing to know something, but then to be told by the very being who knitted you together was something else entirely.

"Am I not capable of love?" he asked, still not daring to raise his head.

"That is not what I said. I said you were not created for it. You have served me faithfully. The number of lives that you have helped is countless. You have helped shape history for the better and yet you will never truly know the impact you have had simply by making the dreams that inspire and guide."

"I'm honored to serve you. Can't," he said then paused and took several slow breaths, "can't I love her and serve you at the same time?"

"There are times that you are allowed to see the puzzle, not just the particular piece that you are weaving in the moment. Sometimes you get to see exactly what will happen if your assignment follows the path laid out for him. Then there are other times that I deem it better for you not to know. I think it is time you see the greater picture when it comes to Sarah Serenity Tillman and Emma Whitmore."

That was all the warning he got before his mind

was suddenly bombarded with images. Serenity was climbing out of her car in the driveway that he recognized as Mildred's. The woman's house came into view as he watched Serenity walk to the front door. Her face was one of restrained anger. She pounded on the door as she called Mildred's name. But when the door finally swung open, it wasn't Mildred who stood there.

Dair felt all of his muscle's tense as the man who had answered the door leered at his Serenity. He looked as though he hadn't bathed in weeks—his hair was greasy, his teeth yellow, and not all of them there. But it was his eyes that Dair would never forget. They didn't have the glassy look of a drug addict. This man's eyes were dark, soulless, and filled with complete evil. The longer he stared at Serenity the more wild the gaze became. It was obvious he was excited about the unexpected intrusion. Dair could practically see the man salivating, and it just confirmed even more that there was no conscience left in the human standing before Serenity.

"I'm here for Emma," Serenity told him sternly.

The man laughed. "Well, she can't come out to play, but you. . ." His eyes followed down her body and back up again. "You can certainly come *in* and play."

Dair knew that Serenity was protective of those she loved. He knew that she was strong and fearless when she needed to be, but he was still shocked when she shoved the man back and stormed into the house calling Emma's name.

He wanted to go to her, needed to protect her, and yet he couldn't move. Instead he could only watch in his mind's eye as the woman he loved argued with Mildred, who had emerged from the hallway. Both of their arms were flailing wildly as they yelled at one another. Emma then appeared from the hallway as well, and the fear on her face could not be hidden. That seemed to set something off inside of Serenity. But before she could move towards the girl, Rat suddenly had a gun pointed at her.

Dair choked on the air that wouldn't go into his lungs. He couldn't breathe as everything seemed to suddenly move in slow motion. He could tell that Serenity knew the man intended to pull the trigger. Resolve settled in her eyes settled on Emma. Her mouth was moving but Dair couldn't hear anything above the roar of his blood pulsing through his body. When Emma was finally by her side she started to push Emma behind her. The whole time Serenity was whispering to Emma, the man with the gun was steadily talking, describing in disgusting detail how he planned to use Serenity. He planned to kill Emma and then Serenity would be his. Serenity's head snapped up at that comment and she shoved Emma behind her just as she had said she would. She lunged towards the man to keep his attention on her and off of Emma. And so when the gun went off, little Emma was safely out the front door.

Dair watched helplessly as Serenity fell to the floor. The shot was pointblank in the chest. Blood seeped out around her body and though he could hear Mildred yelling, and the man yelling back, he couldn't take his eyes off of Serenity's still form. Suddenly the scene changed and he was no longer in that death-filled house. His breathing was still ragged as he tried to gain control of himself after seeing his worst nightmare come true right before his eyes. Finally, he looked around and saw that he was in a huge room filled with thousands of people all staring up at a stage that was decorated in red, white, and blue. On the center of the stage was a podium and standing at the podium was a pretty black woman dressed in a red suit. She stood tall and confident as she stared out at the cheering crowd. After a few moments, she raised her arms and the room fell into expectant silence.

"First, I must give glory to God because, you see, if not for Him, I would not be standing here today. Long ago, when I was a small girl, He delivered me from the hands of some evil people and gave me angels, in many forms, to protect me. One of those angels was a young teenage girl name Sarah Serenity Tillman. When I was eight years old, she saved my life by standing between me and a man with a gun. She died that day." The woman paused. The woman, Dair now realized, was a grown version of Emma Whitmore. She seemed to be collecting herself. Once she was sure the tears would remain at bay, she continued. "She died that day so that I might live. So the only reason I stand here on this historic day as the first female President of this great country is because God deemed it so. And because Serenity saw my life as something worth saving. There is no greater sacrifice than to give up one's life for another. Think of the world we would live in if we all lived in such a way. Think of all the good that would be done if we valued others, as Sarah Tillman valued me, above ourselves. I stand here today honored that you, the people of this nation, have deemed me worthy to be in a position of leadership. I vow to you that I will strive to put your worth above my own. My life for yours. My sacrifice is to protect all of you. When I think about what it means to be the Commander and Chief, my mind is drawn back to a scripture that I think every great leader should read. It comes from the book of

John, chapter 19 starting in verse 10. It is Pilate, a governor in Rome at that time, speaking to Jesus after the religious leaders of that day had turned him over to the government to be executed. Pilate says to Jesus, 'Don't you realize I have power either to free you or to crucify you?'" Emma paused as she looked up over the crowd. Dair could see the emotions welling up in her eyes—could almost feel her conviction himself. Emma took a breath and then continued, but this time she didn't look down at her notes; her eyes were for the people. "Jesus's response is a reminder to me of my place in this world. He says, 'You would have no power over me if it were not given to you from above.' " Another purposeful pause. "I too would not be in this position if God had not allowed it to happen. I have no power, not without His say so. And so I will forever be humbled and daily remind myself that I am held to a higher standard. I will stand before my Creator one day and answer for my actions as your president and how I long to hear the words, 'Well done, my good and faithful servant.' " Finally she ended her speech with, "My life for yours; my sacrifice is to protect, serve, and value every person of this great nation above myself."

The room faded and Dair found himself once again kneeling before the Creator. He couldn't move. He felt as if everything inside of him had died the moment he saw Serenity still on the floor of that disgusting house. Though he knew it had not yet come to pass, he felt as if it had really happened. Probably because he knew that it would. Serenity would die to save Emma's life so that she could fulfill the Creator's plan for her to become the first female president. And he knew that there was a bigger reason behind her being president of such a great nation than just that she was female. She would do great things for the Creator and for her country. No doubt she would change lives for the better. But why Serenity? That was the question now repeating itself in his mind, in his soul. Why Serenity?

"Is there no other way?" Dair finally spoke. He was almost afraid of the answer and yet he had to ask. He had to know if there was anything he could do to change the outcome of Serenity's future. Did she have to be the one to die?

"Emma Whitmore is destined to change the course of history for the greatest country on the planet. She must become the leader she is needed to be. If Emma does not become president, then her nation will continue down the path of destruction until they have immersed themselves in their own immorality to the point that they no longer recognize right from wrong. They will be desensitized beyond any other nation at any point in history. Tolerance will be preached as a way to ignore and accept depraved acts. Entitlement will become the peoples' cry to every want and desire, regardless of the harmfulness of their desires. They will serve themselves and I will remove my hand from them. I have sheltered, blessed, and watched them flourish at times. I have also wept for them because they are my children, as is every human being on earth. They are mine, created by me, and I have watched them destroy themselves. I will never take their free will, but nor will I abide with debauchery and wickedness. History has shown this; as you well know."

"That was from your Word, the book of Isaiah," Dair said recognizing the reference to Babylon.

The Creator continued. "There is still a remnant left, those like Sarah Serenity Tillman, who have led a selfless life. She thinks of others before herself. And before her time comes, she will acknowledge her Creator. She still is searching. In her heart of hearts, she wonders if she is worthy of my love. She will soon realize that it is I who make her worthy. I ask you now, knowing what you do of this woman child, do you think she would ask another to die in her place to keep little Emma safe?"

"No," Dair growled out. "No, she would never ask that of anyone." And it was true. His Serenity would never ask another to make a sacrifice that was hers to give. "But, does anyone have to die? Could not they both be saved?"

"Great change requires great sacrifice. What greater sacrifice is there than to die for one another?"

"BUT WHY HER?" Dair lost his composure. His voice bellowed from his chest with the strength of the pain that was radiating through him. He didn't know how to handle the emotions that were welling up inside of him. The grief, anger, and confusion was something he had never experienced before. Everything was overwhelming him in a flood, and he felt as though a giant boulder had been tied to his ankle and then tossed into a turbulent sea, and he was sinking fast. There had to be something he could do to prevent Serenity or Emma from being harmed. Surely his existence could serve a greater purpose than giving dreams. Surely he was meant for more.

"Peace! Be still," his voice boomed and then gentled. "You weren't created for love, Brudair, and because of this you weren't created either for the pain that most assuredly always follows." The Creator's warmth and peace flowed over him and Dair was able to breathe again.

"What am I supposed to do now?" He wasn't really sure if he was just asking himself or if he was actually asking the one who brought him into existence.

"Though I created you for a purpose, I have never taken your free will and I will not take it now. I am always with you, Brudair, just as I am always with Emma and Serenity. Both of them are mine. *She* was mine long before she was yours and my love is complete, whole, and all consuming. I see the past, the present, and the future. Nothing is missed by my eyes. I am with you, no matter what you choose. But remember there are consequences for every choice made."

The warmth was gone and the darkness Dair had become so accustomed to was back. After several minutes, he raised his head to see that he was kneeling in the field just beside Serenity's home. Dair stood slowly, knowing he needed to get his bearings. He didn't want to appear in Serenity's room with the grief of her death still fresh on his face. She would know something was wrong. Dair was pretty sure that he wasn't going to be able to tell the woman he had fallen in love with that her death was coming sooner rather than later and that it would be at the end of a gun held by an evil soul.

"Okay, so thinking those thoughts is not going to help me calm down," he growled to himself. He had to step back and clear his mind. She wasn't dead, not yet, and he of all people knew that nothing was set in stone, not when humans had free will. If things were set in stone, then there would be no need for him—no need for his dreams to attempt to influence people to choose the paths laid out for them.

"She's not dead yet," he told himself again. As his

mind considered what the Creator had told him, that he had free will, he realized how he would make sure that Serenity remained *not* dead. He knew with more certainty than he had ever felt that he would take Serenity's place. She would not die. Dair had walked the earth since the beginning of time, and she had been the first light and warmth to captivate him, and he simply couldn't imagine her light being snuffed out so soon. There was so much good she could do in the world, so much she had to offer, and he would gladly sacrifice his existence for her. It would be no sacrifice, not really, if it meant that Serenity would continue on to share the light inside of her.

Dair turned and looked at the window to her room. Just beyond that thin piece of glass his love lay, sleeping peacefully lost in the dream he had made for her. And she would live to have many, many more dreams, maybe not weaved by him, but they would be beautiful nonetheless because she was beautiful.

Chapter 10

To see the grim reaper in your dream doesn't necessarily mean you or someone you love is going to die. Rather, it marks the end of something important in your life—perhaps a special relationship, a job, or the loss of a material possession you value highly.

It was Christmas Day and Glory let herself into Wayne and Darla's house as she always did when she came to visit. Glory's family celebrated Christmas on Christmas Eve. Mornings were rough on her mother and her dad like to let her sleep in. Knowing this, Serenity had invited Glory to come spend Christmas morning with her. At first Glory had tried to argue that she didn't want to impose. But when Serenity told her that Dair would be in attendance, her best friend was more than happy to show up.

"So where is the yummy immortal with the euphoric inducing voice?" she asked as she took off her coat, scarf, and hat.

"Good morning to you too," Serenity said as she wiped the sleep from her eyes. She reached her arms up over her head giving her back a good stretch. Her shirt rose up just enough to show a small amount of skin, and when Dair's fingertips glided across her back, her breath caught and her arms dropped quickly.

"Ahh, there he is," Glory grinned as Dair stepped up beside Serenity and wrapped an arm around her waist pulling her against him as if he'd done it a thousand times before.

He leaned down and pressed a kiss to her hair and whispered, "Good morning, beautiful."

Glory fanned herself dramatically and Serenity had to wonder again if her friend really was in her twenties.

"Hello, Glory," Dair said as his eyes left Serenity and turned on Glory. He held out his hand which Glory grabbed with no small amount of enthusiasm. "I've heard much about you; it's nice to finally meet you."

"She wasn't lying. You definitely have a voice that could give a girl—,"

"SOOOO," Serenity cut her friend off not even wanting to take a guess about what was about to spill from her unfiltered mouth. "How was your Christmas Eve?"

Glory let go of Dair's hand and turned a raised brow on her. "We talked about it just a little while ago when you called me. Why don't you let me and your eye candy get to know each other? I approve on the hotness level, but the rest is yet to be seen."

Serenity wanted to smack her forehead and then Glory's forehead. So began the interrogation of Brudair AKA Sandman by Glorious Day. But actually, it wasn't until Raphael walked into the room that things got really bad.

"You must be Raphael," Glory said as she held out her hand from where she sat on the couch. As he shook her hand, Glory gave him a wink. "My, my, they sure know how to grow them in heaven."

"Glory!" Serenity chastised. "He's an angel. He's doesn't…he's not," she stuttered and finished. "available."

Glory gave Raphael her signature single eyebrow raise. "You got any friends who have fallen from grace and are available?"

Serenity did smack her forehead that time.

"Kidding," Glory huffed. Then she turned her head and muttered, "Sort of."

Raphael looked from Serenity to Glory and then back to Serenity. "This is the one with no filter?"

Serenity nodded wordlessly.

Glory wasn't offended by the question. Serenity would never say anything about Glory to someone else that she wouldn't say in front of her best friend. And Glory knew it was true; her filter had been broken long ago, if it had ever existed.

"Filters are overrated," Glory said as she leaned back on the couch and got comfortable.

"And on that note, I'm going to go see if Emma is ready to join us," Serenity said as she headed for the hallway. She could feel Dair on her heels and before she could make it down the hall, he grabbed her wrist and pulled her toward her own room. He tugged her inside and turned her so her back was against the wall. Serenity looked up at him and knew he could see the question in her eyes without her even asking.

"I just wanted a moment with you," he answered the unspoken question. "I have a feeling that the rest of the day will be filled with the presence of others, and I'm a tad jealous of my time with you."

"A tad?" She smiled at him.

Dair's hands came up to cup her face as he tilted it back. She knew he was going to kiss her. Though he'd kissed her before, her breathing still quickened with anticipation, because Dair's kisses were supernatural. Well, she didn't know if that was really true, but Serenity swore that when he kissed her it was more than just their mouths connecting.

When his lips finally pressed to hers, Serenity felt the earth move beneath her feet. Her whole world shifted until Dair was all there was. For that brief moment in time, only he existed. There was no Mildred, or Rat, or the constant dread that something terrible was going to happen to Emma. It was just her, pressed close against Dair. She was almost surprised that her skin, which was growing warmer by the minute, wasn't giving off steam by now. And when he pressed even closer and his hands fisted in her hair, she was pretty sure she could hear a little crab in the background singing *Kiss the Girl*. Of all the things to pop in her head in that moment, she thought. But oddly enough it did nothing to distract Serenity from the passionate male who had her completely enraptured with his touch.

When Dair finally pulled away, he pressed his forehead to hers. Both of them were trying to catch their breaths, and Serenity wondered if her lips looked as swollen and thoroughly loved as his did.

"You test my resolve, love," Dair whispered.

"Your resolve?"

He nodded against her forehead. "My resolve to make sure you remain a pure maiden."

Serenity snorted out a laugh. "Please tell me you didn't just say pure maiden. You're showing your age when you talk like that."

Dair released his hands from her hair and smoothed it back down. He gave her a final short kiss on the lips and then stepped back, out of temptation's reach.

"I better go check on Emma." Serenity motioned over her shoulder towards her door.

"That would be a very good idea," Dair agreed. "Unless you would like Raphael to marry us and then we can pick up where we left off."

Serenity's eyes widened and her mind raced to all sorts of places at his words. "Is Raphael ordained to marry people?

Dair chuckled at her. "Go Serenity, before I decide to let you find out."

Emma blinked several times attempting to push sleep away as the morning sunlight peeked through the curtains. When she realized that there actually *were* curtains in the room she remembered that she wasn't at her aunt's house. Then her mind jumped to *why* she wasn't at her aunt's house, and she quickly pushed those memories away. She would need to deal with them eventually but that morning was not the time, not Christmas morning. Her lips spread into a wide smile as she thought about spending Christmas with Darla, Wayne, and Serenity. She didn't believe in Santa Clause. In fact, she had questioned the plausibility of his existence several years ago after she got out a map and sat down to calculate flight times from the Arctic Ocean to every other country in the world. Constrained by the laws of physics, it simply wasn't possible to visit every boy and girl in the world in one night. But that was okay with her. Christmas in her family had been about the birth of a baby given to man by God. She knew not everyone in the world believed in God, or his son, but she did. And her parents did, so that was what Christmas was to her. It was a joyful time in their home. Her heart ached with the loss and suddenly her smile was gone. This would be the first of every Christmas to come without her parents. Emma missed them beyond any words she could use to express. But if indeed there was a God, and her parents' beliefs about heaven were true, then she knew they were in a much, much better place. There were no men like Rat, or the man who had killed her parents, in heaven. There was no pain, no tears or grief, only joy and she wouldn't take that from her parents, not even to bring them back to her. She would see them again one day, of that she had no doubt.

There was a soft knock on the bedroom door and then Serenity poked her head in. She had a contagious smile on her face. Emma's own lips stretched up in response.

"Are you just going to lay in that bed all day contemplating whatever it is that geniuses contemplate?" Serenity asked.

Emma's head tilted ever so slightly. "Why do you ask? Is today something special?" Her voice was full of innocence as she stared wide-eyed at Serenity.

Serenity shrugged. "Nope, nothing special about today. You just stay in here while I go open all those presents that are under a tree that's up for no particular reason." She turned to go.

"Are there...," Emma began and then paused. Serenity turned back to face her. Emma wanted to hide the vulnerability that she knew filled her eyes but it was no use. She was worn out from trying to keep it all together. "Are there presents for me?" she finally asked.

Serenity's smile stretched even wider. "Santa doesn't forget you just because you're in a different house."

Emma shook her head at the girl who was quickly becoming like a big sister to her. She climbed out of the bed and headed toward the now wide-open door. "My mama would have liked you," Emma told Serenity as she followed her into the hall and toward the living room.

"Why's that?"

"Because you're young at heart. You definitely have an old soul, and she would have pointed that out to you as well. But, mama liked to laugh. She liked to be happy. You make people happy. You make me happy," she admitted with a sad smile.

As they stepped into the living room already filled with Wayne, Darla, Raphael, Dair, and another lady that Emma hadn't met yet, her eyes widened as they landed on the tree and the presents beneath it. She could read her name written on many of them, too many of them she decided. How was it in a world with people like Mildred and Rat, that people like Serenity and Darla could exist? Emma almost felt as if it should be an impossibility for the goodness of a family like this one to be anywhere near people like her aunt. *There is no sun without the rain, Emma Jean. There is no rejoicing if there is no sorrow.* Emma wondered if she would ever stop hearing her mother's words in her mind, and as the ones that had just popped up resonated with her soul, she hoped she would always hear them.

She was brought from her momentary stupor when Serenity gave her a small nudge in the back. She looked back at her friend, but before she could speak Serenity spoke up. "Don't argue, or say you can't accept it, or do anything else that we southerners seem to think appropriate when we don't know how to show our gratitude. A thank you is always sufficient. So go open your presents."

Emma decided that if they went to all the trouble to do this for her, she wouldn't let them down by not showing them how much she appreciated it. But instead of sitting down and immediately opening her presents, she started sifting through the pile. As she read labels she began passing them out to each recipient. When she headed toward the lady she didn't know with two bags loaded with tissue paper, Emma held out her hand. "I'm Emma Whitmore. I haven't met you before." The lady smiled and Emma could see the kindness in her eyes, though there was also a hint of mischievousness.

"Emma Whitmore," she said as she took her hand. "I'm Glory Day, and yes my parents really did do that to me." Emma grinned as Glory shrugged. "It is what it is. Anyways, I'm Serenity's friend and I'm glad to finally meet you. She's told me lots of great things about you."

After all the presents had been distributed, there was a pregnant pause before the room erupted into chaos. Emma looked around, her jaw dropping open. And when her eyes fell on Dair and Raphael, she saw that they had the same astonished look she did.

Wayne, Darla, Serenity, and Glory had all begun to tear into their presents with an exuberance that made Emma think of rabid beavers on the back of a logging truck. Paper was flying. Oohs and Ahhs bounced off the walls as they each began to get beyond the packaging to the goodies inside. It truly was a sight to behold. In Emma's home, they had always taken turns opening their presents so that everyone could appreciate and see what the gift was. She had to admit there was something so freeing and childlike about the display of eagerness.

She looked back at Dair and shrugged. "When in Rome," she muttered and began to tear into the packages before her. Emma couldn't help the grin that spread across her face, which seemed to get wider with every present she opened. Whoever had gone shopping for her had truly understood her. She loved the books.

Knowing that they were way above what she should be able to read, but also knowing that she'd have no problem with them, gave her a little bit of a confidence boost. But then, seeing the crafts reminded her that she still needed to be a kid, regardless of her IQ. All in all, it was actually one of the best Christmas's she'd ever had.

As the excitement began to die down and a sea of wrapping paper covered the floor, everyone looked around as a last ditch effort to make sure there was nothing left that could be ripped into.

"Well, I will admit that this is the first time I've ever seen rabid Christmas present opening. It's quite an experience," Emma said breaking the silence. The others laughed.

"None of us are very good at waiting on others to open their presents," Darla admitted. "We barely make it to Christmas morning most of the time. Presents under our tree often have little corners that have been torn and re-taped because of the lack of self-control."

"Darla, who happens to be the worst about this?" Wayne asked her with a knowing smirk.

Darla laughed. "I have no idea what you're talking about."

"Sure, you don't," Serenity said shaking her head.

"So what happens now?" Emma asked.

"Now we eat," Darla answered as she stood up and headed toward the kitchen where delicious smells called to the group to come partake.

Raphael placed a large but gentle hand on Emma's shoulder as she headed toward the kitchen with everyone else. She looked up at the large angel and saw so many different emotions in his eyes. She could tell he still felt responsible for what had happened. There was nothing she could say to change that. It was between Raphael and his conscience to let it go.

"After breakfast we need to return to your aunt and deal with what happened. None of us want you to return to that place, but…," he paused.

"It's where I'm supposed to be right now," Emma finished.

Raphael's jaw clenched. "You are too wise for your age, Emma Whitmore. You should not have to worry about such things."

She shrugged. "We can't see the bigger picture sometimes, big guy," she told him. "Mama used to tell me that there was a reason for everything. She'd say, *Emma Jean, there is nothing in this world that God misses. There is nothing so bad that he can't use for good in some way. We may never know what that is, but you can trust that He's got it covered.*"

"What if a person doesn't believe in this God of yours? What do they do with the horrible things of this world—the unjust, the corrupt, and evil? Where is their hope?"

She knew that he was playing the devil's advocate. Her daddy used to do the same thing with her mama. Of course, he just liked to argue more than anything. He got a kick out of seeing her mama get all riled up. "I've asked my mama that same question."

"What was her answer?"

"She told me that oftentimes it was those very things that helped them see that there was something bigger in this world than themselves. And it was our job to show those people love, acceptance, and that very hope, not judgment, hate, or ambivalence."

"And in your circumstances, with what has happened to you, you still believe there is this God who loves you?" Raphael seemed to truly want to understand. Emma wondered if, because he was an angel created for one purpose—to serve his Creator, perhaps he didn't understand free will.

"I have to believe that he has a greater purpose. Maybe I will be able to help a child one day who is going through the same thing." Emma could admit to herself and to God that she was scared, but she did believe he was with her.

"You are a rare gem, Emma," Raphael said warmly. "A rare gem in a cave of coal."

She tilted her head to the side as she looked up at him. "Even coal has a purpose."

Serenity stood next to the back passenger seat of her car as Emma climbed into the other side. Dair stood by the open driver side door looking back at her while Raphael had already sat down in the passenger seat. Dair's eyes were narrowed and his jaw tight.

"I really wish you would stay here," he told her for the third time.

She shook her head. "Not going to happen." She turned then when she heard Glory's horn honk at her as she backed out of the driveway. Serenity gave her friend a wave and then placed her hand to her ear as if it were a telephone letting her best friend know she would call her. When she turned back to look at Dair, she realized that his frustration with her wasn't going to abate anytime soon, so she gave up trying to reason with him and just climbed in next to Emma. She heard him let out a deep sigh.

"He's protective of you," Emma whispered to her.

"Which is why he shouldn't be worried. He won't let anything happen to me so I don't understand what the big deal is."

"What if I can't protect you," Dair nearly growled. "What if it is beyond my ability?"

"Brudair." Raphael's voice held a warning that Serenity didn't understand.

"What are you talking about?" she asked Dair.

"Never mind," he told her as he backed out of the driveway.

It was the first time he had ever been remotely harsh with her, and for that reason, Serenity knew that something very serious was upsetting him. What did he think he couldn't protect her from? What danger could she possibly be in? Serenity's mind conjured up scenarios ranging from her and Mildred getting into a ridiculous slapping fight to a crazy patron busting into the library brandishing a gun while yelling about the library fines he would not pay because the library was supposed to be free. Both scenarios were equally likely in her estimation. Regardless, she had no doubt that he could protect her.

The car ride into town was quiet. Serenity noted how they each seemed to be lost in their own thoughts. Was Emma thinking about how she was going to be back with her aunt and the uncertainty of her safety? Was Raphael still beating himself up about not being there to protect her? She started to wonder what thoughts might be consuming Dair when she looked up at the rearview mirror and caught his intense gaze. Their eyes connected for a brief moment before he looked back at the road. But she had felt the turmoil in those dark eyes all the way to her soul.

Her attention was taken when Mildred's house came into view. Serenity felt a churning in her gut as she stared at the house. She had never been one for violence, let alone arson, but in that moment she truly wanted to light the rotting structure up and watch it burn, and hopefully all of the evil within it.

She reached over and took Emma's hand as Dair pulled into the driveway. Emma gave it a reassuring squeeze and it wasn't lost on Serenity that it was the eight-year-old doing the comforting. In all her life, she had never met a person as brave as little Emma.

"I'll be fine, Serenity," Emma told her and the confidence in her voice almost had Serenity believing her.

"I will do what I can to protect her," Raphael promised.

They all climbed out of the car and Serenity felt as if they were walking to their doom rather than Emma's aunt's house. As the door opened and a rough looking Mildred emerged, Serenity was sure they *were* leaving Emma to her doom.

"Where you been, girl?" Mildred asked attempting to sound like she cared and failing miserably.

"Are you here alone?" Dair asked her, his stern voice and swirling eyes would have had any smart human being taking a step back. But Mildred wasn't the swiftest horse in the herd so she actually took a step toward him—toward the hunter who obviously saw her as prey.

"This is my house, boy; I don't answers to the likes of you," Mildred snarled, her true self making its appearance once again. That was the thing about a person's character; it couldn't be hidden, not for long. The truth of an individual would always come to the surface eventually, revealing what lay below.

"That is where you are wrong. Emma is under my protection."

"And mine," Raphael spoke up.

Not to be left out Serenity piped in. "And mine as well."

Dair shot her a look but quickly turned back to Mildred. "If anything happens to her while under your roof, we will hold you responsible and you will pay the consequences."

Emma started forward but Serenity grabbed her hand before she had made it two steps. She turned Emma to face her and then knelt down in front of her. "Just because you're young doesn't mean that you don't have rights. If at any moment you feel scared, you get out of there. Don't hesitate, alright? Raphael will get you out."

Emma nodded. "I know, Serenity. I will be fine. Maybe I'm here to help my aunt change her ways. Maybe I'm the only light she will see."

Serenity closed her eyes and squeezed them tightly, fighting back the tears. If only they could all be as good and hopeful as this child. But Serenity had lived longer than Emma; she knew that sometimes people didn't want to be saved. "I truly hope that that's true," she whispered to her and then let her hand go. Serenity continued to kneel there as she watched Emma walk toward her aunt. She told her good morning in a polite tone and wished her a Merry Christmas before walking past her and into the house. Mildred gave them all one more nasty look and then slammed the door behind her.

"I will watch over her," Raphael said and then disappeared.

Serenity finally stood but she didn't take her eyes off of the door that Emma had just entered. She felt as though if she looked away something bad would happen, and it would be their fault for letting her go in to that dark place.

"I'm going to call DHS," Serenity said suddenly. "This isn't right, Dair." Her heart was pounding so hard in her chest as the muscles in her stomach clenched painfully tight. "We can't let her stay here. I don't care what Emma says. This woman isn't worth saving."

Dair walked over to her and placed a gentle hand on her face. "I understand your anger and it is a righteous anger, but we cannot know the heart of another. I agree Emma should not stay here, but I do not want to see you grow bitter. Mildred's fate is in the hands of the Creator. Whether she is salvageable or not, only he knows."

"I guess I'm not as forgiving as you thought, huh?" she asked as she attempted to turn her face from his.

Dair's eyes softened. "You are human, Serenity. I never expected you to be perfect. It is the fact that you strive to be the best you that you can be that matters. You will not always succeed, but I won't hold that against you."

"Thanks," Serenity huffed.

"Are we heading back to your aunt and uncle's house for the remainder of the day?"

"Yeah, Darla's sister is supposed to be coming in this afternoon." Serenity took his hand as he guided her back to the car.

"What's she like?" Dair asked.

Serenity waited to answer him until they were both seated in the car. "Let's just say she's one of a kind. If you thought Glory didn't have a filter, well Aunt Willa is a step beyond that."

Dair grinned as his eyes glinted playfully. "Then this should be interesting."

"That's an understatement," Serenity muttered.

Emma knelt on her knees in her aunt's kitchen, scrubbing the floor with a rag that wasn't any cleaner than the filth covered linoleum. Raphael stood in the corner with his arms crossed in front of his huge chest, glowering at her aunt. Of course Mildred couldn't see him, and it was hard for Emma not to talk to him. His brooding presence was doing nothing for the gloomy atmosphere. As soon as Mildred had shut the door on Emma's friends, she'd turned her hate filled eyes on Emma. For a brief moment, she was sure that her aunt was going to hit her, and in turn Raphael was going to do something as equally distasteful to Mildred. But instead she just started barking orders: clean this, scrub that, dust this, pick up over there. Emma had decided that Mildred was trying to poison her by forcing her to wallow in this filth.

By the time she had come to the last few tiles of the kitchen floor, the sun had set and the cold dark night was draping itself over everything outside. Mildred hadn't said anything to her in a couple of hours and it didn't hurt Emma's feelings. But the reprieve wasn't to last.

"When'd you leave?" Mildred asked her as she lit a cigarette.

Emma paused her scrubbing and looked over her shoulder at the worn and wasted woman. "I left last night," she answered honestly.

"You ever think it might not be safe for an eight-year-old girl to go prancing around town in the middle of the night?"

"I think it was safer than staying here."

Mildred's eyes narrowed. The smoke from her cigarette danced eerily around her face, like a charmed snake waiting for instructions from its master. "What'd you mean by that?" she snapped.

Emma was trying to decide how much to tell her aunt and *what* exactly to tell her. She had a feeling that it didn't matter what she said. Mildred wouldn't believe her. So when in doubt, go with the truth. "That man, Rat, came into the room. He hit me and I got away from him by climbing through the window." She waited, sure that her aunt would yell at her.

Mildred flicked her cigarette ashes onto the floor Emma had just cleaned. "You probably did somethin to piss him off. He don't go hitting a girl for no reason at all."

Emma didn't say anything to that. What could she say? She knew there was no point in arguing with her aunt. Mildred wasn't reasonable and therefore could not be reasoned with. Instead, she just went back to scrubbing the floor. Emma was nearly done and she was hoping that Mildred would get caught up in one of her shows so that she could slip off to bed.

After she rinsed out the dirty rag, which really was a lost cause, she laid it on the edge of the sink. When Emma tiptoed to the edge of the kitchen floor to look into the living room, she saw that her aunt had fallen asleep in her recliner. Her mouth was opened wide and as Emma walked quietly past her and down the hall, she wondered how many spiders had found their way into her aunt's cavernous mouth. "Yuck," she whispered to herself.

When she closed the door behind her, Emma saw that Raphael was already in her room. He stood next to her window looking out into the night. Emma could see the moonlight reflecting off of the white snow making it appear bright against the darkness. It was so hard to look out into the peaceful world, blanketed in the pure snow, and know that outside of those walls was safety. Outside, away from the darkness of that house, were good people, full of light and love. But even though that was true, Emma had meant what she'd told Serenity. Emma might be the only light that her aunt would ever see. She would try to live there a little longer, in hopes that maybe Mildred would see the error of her ways and see that her life could be different.

"You should get some sleep. I will keep watch," Raphael's deep voice penetrated her thoughts.

She looked up at him, but he still was looking out the window. Emma didn't bother with sleep clothes. She was too worn out. It took all of the energy she had left to climb into bed. She was asleep before her head hit the pillow.

Raphael looked down at the sleeping child. She had worked diligently as her aunt had given her task after task and not once had Emma complained. He had to wonder who this human was that she was so important to the Creator's plan. Raphael could see that she was exceptional in her knowledge, kindness, and joy. But were those the things that set her apart for her destiny? He did not know the answer to that. He did know that even if she had been just a young child, with a simple destiny, he would still have protected her. He wished that he could protect all children from people like Mildred and Rat. Even as an angel, he did not understand the evil in the world. And after thousands of years, he was still surprised by it. Whatever her future was, wherever she went, as long as it was in his power to do so, Raphael would be her guardian. He was not human, and so it was difficult to truly say, but he figured that the way he felt about Emma was the equivalent to the way a father felt for his child. Raphael would never have children, but that did not mean that he could not offer his protection to those who might be fatherless. Perhaps, that was his purpose now, and until the Creator told him otherwise, that is what he would do.

Chapter 11

"If you dream about being a permanent marker, it means you are feeling that your situation is perpetual and stinks."

Serenity sat on the couch next to Dair with her hands twisting nervously in her lap. She didn't realize that Dair had noticed until he reached over and placed one of his larger hands over hers. She glanced up at him but he was still looking and listening intently to Aunt Willa who was bombarding him relentlessly with question after question. Willa's interrogation was actually worse than her Uncle Wayne's had been. It was another moment where Serenity felt a face palm was completely appropriate. Why hadn't she just told Dair to come see her later? Why on earth did she think it was a good idea to introduce him to Willa, who she knew was notorious for drawing information out of people? A CIA interrogator had nothing on this woman. Even after Dair had answered her as smoothly as he'd answered her uncle's questions, Serenity could see the curious gleam in her eyes. In Willa's case, pulling the wool over her eyes was not an option. Serenity knew that once Dair was gone, she would undergo her own interrogation by her aunt.

"So tell me more about this little Emma," Willa said after having finally gotten her fill of Dair's answers. "Darla's told me a little about her when we've talked on the phone."

"Did she tell you she's a genius?" Serenity asked.

Willa nodded. "And very mature for an eight-year-old. But she's living with an aunt that cares nothing for her and the girl is in danger." Her eye narrowed dangerously.

"We can't just steal her away, Willa," Darla told her sister. "Don't think we haven't considered it."

Serenity bit her lip as her eyes darted from Darla to Willa and then Uncle Wayne. "I sort of did something."

"What?" Darla and Willa asked at the same time.

"I called DHS," she admitted. The rest of her words came out in a hurried ramble. "I told them that she didn't need to be in that house and that Mildred had no business raising a child. I also told them that the house itself was not fit to be considered livable; it should be condemned. I told them about Rat and what had happened."

"What did they say?" Willa asked as she moved forward to the edge of her seat.

"They asked if she was still with us. I told them, no, that we'd taken her back to her aunt's. The lady I spoke to said that was good because it wouldn't look good to a judge no matter our intentions if we *stole* her. She asked if we felt Emma was in immediate danger when we took her home."

"Was she?" Willa interrupted.

Serenity looked over at Dair. He gave her a small nod. "I don't know, but she isn't without protection. I didn't tell the DHS lady that she had protection, but I did tell her that I didn't think Mildred was going to harm her."

"Are they going to start an investigation?" Uncle Wayne asked.

Serenity nearly growled out the words. "As soon as they can get a DHS worker out there."

"How long will that take?" Dair asked.

Willa snorted. "It's the government. They'll take as long as they damn well please, and when you call to check on it, they will say they've lost the paperwork, or the person handling the case got fired, or a sudden attack of malaria mysteriously overcame the DHS office, and they had to burn everything the sick came in contact with."

"So they aren't very efficient?" Dair reiterated.

"No." Willa shook her head. "If I had meant they weren't very efficient, I would have said that. What they are is unconcerned. Emma isn't anyone important to them. She's just another child among thousands that got put in the system and shoved in the first home they could find. I'm not saying that their jobs are easy. I am saying that someone with a brain and some common sense could come up with a better way to handle it."

"We will keep an eye on her until DHS decides to show up," Darla assured her sister. "Emma is now an honorary member of our family, and if it comes time that she needs a new home, Wayne and I are willing to take her in."

Serenity felt tears burning in her eyes. This was news to her. She hadn't known that her aunt and uncle had made such a decision but it didn't surprise her. Darla would save the world one person at a time if she could.

"Well I don't think anyone would find it suspicious if old Mildred fell down a flight of stairs because she was too drunk to see straight," Willa said dryly.

"Willa," Darla admonished, though Serenity could tell her heart wasn't in it.

Willa waved her sister off. "All I'm saying is it would leave more oxygen for the rest of us and our pets if the likes of Mildred weren't taken any in."

"I guess I forgot to mention that my aunt has homicidal tendencies," Serenity said to Dair as she blew out a breath, puffing out her cheeks.

"She wouldn't really kill Mildred."

"Um, Dair, when her dogs kill one of her ducks, she takes the dead duck and beats the dog with it and then ties the same duck to their collar and makes them drag it around for a few days. Don't underestimate Aunt Willa," Serenity warned.

"They never kill another duck that's for sure," Willa grinned wickedly.

"And on that note, I think Dair should be going and I need to get to bed. I have to be at the clinic tomorrow morning bright and early." Serenity stood and held Dair's hand as she pulled him toward the front door.

"It was nice to meet you Dair," Willa called out. "Don't be a stranger."

Dair started to turn to say something but Serenity wasn't having it. She needed to get Dair out of there before Willa started in on him again. She grabbed her coat from the rack next to the door and slipped it on as she shoved him, none too gently, out of the door.

"A less confident man would think that you were ashamed to have your family meet him," Dair said but Serenity heard the teasing note in his voice.

"Dair, any woman ashamed to be seen with you needs to have her head examined." She looked at her car and the lack of vehicle for Dair. "So I guess to make this look like you don't just pop in and out of thin air I need to drive you home." She made air quotes around the word home.

"That means I get to spend more time with

you...alone," he said waggling his eyebrows.

Serenity laughed at that. "Calm down, Sandman. I'm just going to drive to the drive-in and back. There will be no stops in between."

"A man can hope," he murmured in his deep sexy voice as he climbed into the passenger side of her car.

Serenity shook her head at him, but her lips were still turned up in a smile as she pulled out of the driveway.

The week following Christmas was blissfully peaceful. Serenity would leave in the mornings and pick up Emma, regardless of Mildred's complaints, and they would head to the clinic to take care of the animals. The owners didn't mind Emma being there and actually seemed to enjoy Emma's endless barrage of questions. In the afternoons, they would head to the library to volunteer in any way that Darla could use them, and then they would head somewhere for a quick dinner before Serenity had to take Emma back to her aunt's.

Raphael took the time to go do whatever it was that angels had to do, but he told Emma that all she had to do was say his name and he would be there. Dair was around some but Serenity had noticed that he seemed distracted and distant. Each day seemed to draw him further away from her. When she asked him what was wrong, he would tell her he was fine and then quickly change the subject. Serenity didn't want to be the nagging girlfriend, so she'd just let it slide. But by New Year's Eve, she was beginning to get frustrated with him.

"Are you coming to the restaurant tonight for the New Year's bash?" Glory's voice crackled a little from the bad reception Serenity was getting at the back of the vet clinic. She was just about done cleaning and feeding the dogs and had plans to meet Dair for lunch. Emma hadn't felt good that morning when she went to pick her up and had told her she was going to stay in bed. It had been hard for her to leave her at Mildred's, but Raphael had reminded her that he would be watching over her. Still, Serenity had called her aunt to let her know, and Darla had promised to take Emma some chicken noodle soup at lunch.

Serenity's mind had been so focused on confronting Dair once and for all over his strange behavior that she had forgotten about the New Year's Eve party at The Fireside. She had promised Glory that she'd come since Glory had to work and wouldn't get to come out to Darla and Wayne's house like she normally did.

"Yes, I'll be there. I really want to bring Emma but she said she wasn't feeling well this morning," Serenity told her.

Glory made a clicking sound with her tongue. "Do you think she needs to see a doctor? Goodness knows Mildred won't take her to see one."

"I'm not sure, but Darla is going to check on her at lunch. She'll make sure Emma gets any kind of care she needs."

"So where are you off to after you get done at the clinic?" Glory asked her.

"Dair and I are having lunch."

"Oh, like a normal couple."

Serenity laughed. "I know, right? It's almost like he

isn't an immortal being who helps shape history. He's taking me on a date, like a normal guy."

"Honey, I hate to break it to you, but there is nothing normal about Dair. Even if he wasn't immortal, men don't look like him, and if they did the world would be in trouble because women would be too busy wiping drool off of their faces to get anything done."

Serenity couldn't argue with her. Dair was a step above good looking and took sexy to a whole different level. "Alright, so I'll see you tonight."

"I'll be there with a smile on my face, after I've had a few drinks," Glory teased.

"I know better than that. You've seen firsthand what a little alcohol can make people do. And let me tell you, Glory Day, you don't need any help letting go of your inhibitions."

Glory laughed. "True enough. Later."

Serenity slipped her phone into her back pocket and gave the kennel one more look before clocking out and heading toward the front door. She waved goodbye to Dr. Little as she pushed the door open and felt the bite of winter against her face. Her eyes narrowed as the icy wind caused them to water producing a sheen of moisture to distort her vision. She reached up to wipe them as she headed to her car. Once her vision was again clear, she could see that her car was not empty.

Dair sat in the passenger seat looking at her innocently. She unlocked her door and tossed her purse into the back seat before climbing in. Serenity quickly stuck the keys in the ignition and started the engine, wanting to get the heat going as fast as possible before she looked over at Dair.

"Make yourself at home?" she asked with a single raised brow.

"I thought it would be better than just suddenly appearing in the parking lot, considering the clinic seems to be busy today. I would hate to scare some little lady and her poodle."

Serenity nodded. "Fair enough. What do you want for lunch?"

The look Dair shot her held enough heat to cause the car to warm up. It was the first time all week that he had given her one of his smoldering gazes, complete with bedroom eyes.

"I didn't say *who* do you want for lunch? I said *what*," she pointed out.

"Semantics," Dair muttered as his gaze continued to devour her.

"Okay," Serenity said, drawing out the word. "Perhaps, I better pick the cuisine this time."

As she pulled out of the parking lot, Dair reached over and laid his large hand on her thigh. Serenity tensed, having not expected the gesture. He gave it a firm squeeze before letting it relax. She didn't say anything and he didn't remove it until they had pulled into the parking lot of the drive-in. She'd decided she wanted privacy for the conversation they were about to have.

"Dair," she began, but was cut off by his words.

"Do you think it's wise for us to stay in the car, together?" He paused meaningfully. "Alone?" His voice was low and full of suggestion. Serenity felt his hand under her chin as he gently turned her face to look at him. Her breath caught in her throat as she met his swirling dark eyes. If she didn't know Dair, didn't trust that he would never try something that she wasn't comfortable with, that look might have scared her. It was intense, filled with desire and want. But she *did* know him. She knew that he cared for her deeply and because of that he would never ask for what she wasn't ready to give. If anything, she was scared of herself because if he kept looking at her like that and talking to her in that voice, she might just offer herself up on a golden platter complete with a side dish of please take me now.

Dair knew he shouldn't tempt himself or her. He was well aware of the strong desire that constantly pulled at both of them, but he needed to distract her. Serenity had noticed that he had been distant all week. What she didn't know was why. But he had gotten the feeling that her patience with him was wearing thin, and she was going to confront him about his behavior. Dair would give her anything she asked if it was in his power, but he could not give her the information she was seeking. He could not tell her what had caused him to be lost in his thoughts and drenched in grief. Even if it was allowed, how did he tell someone—not just someone, but the woman he loved—that she was going to die from a gunshot aimed at someone else? How could he tell her that she would be the reason Emma lived, but it would be at the price of her own life? And perhaps, worst of all, he didn't know what to do to prevent it from happening. If he interfered, Emma might be lost. So, he'd come up with the strategy to seduce her away from her questions. Probably not the brightest idea he had come up with in his hundreds of years. But then, he was learning that people did stupid things in the name of love.

Dair began to lean forward as Serenity got lost in his eyes. He whispered sweet words to her allowing the hypnotic quality of his voice to draw her to him. Her breath was warm against his face and her scent called to him, enticing him to get closer. As his hand slid up her neck and wrapped around the back of her head she gasped. The sound hit Dair in his gut, and he had to fight for control because in that moment, seeing her so lost to him, he wanted her—all of her.

Their lips were mere centimeters apart when she said his name. It was what she said that pulled him from the haze of lust and need and want.

"Stop," Serenity said again, only this time her voice was more than a whisper. "Dair, please, stop."

Dair closed his eyes and squeezed them tight as he pressed his forehead to hers. *Not like this,* he thought to himself. He couldn't sully any of their time together by using her desire for him as a weapon. "I'm sorry," he whispered through ragged breaths.

"What was that about?" she asked him. "I mean, I know that you're attracted to me but that was a lot more intense and intentional than you've ever been before. What's going on, Dair?"

Letting out a deep breath, he pulled away from her. He did not meet her gaze because he knew it would be full of questions and hurt. Dair didn't want to hurt her, but he couldn't tell her what she wanted to know. Not only could he not but he didn't want to. He knew Serenity, knew her heart for others, and—even if she was scared beyond reason—knew she would do whatever it took to save Emma if the young girl was in danger. He didn't want little Emma to die. Not just because of the important future that was in front of her but because she was a precious life, so young and innocent. One such as her should not have her life cut short so soon. But neither did he want his love to die. Dair felt almost as if he was having to choose between the two females who had become extremely important to him. It was a choice no man should ever have to make.

"There are some things that I can't share with anyone because it might alter the future." He attempted to choose his words carefully. Dair didn't want to make her feel like it was only her specifically that he couldn't tell, because in truth it wasn't. The knowledge the Creator had bestowed upon him had been for Dair's eyes only. It was his burden to carry and, like so many things over the centuries, he would bear it alone.

"Does it have something to do with me?" Serenity asked and her voice was less confident than it had been. "You've been. . . distant. I mean. . . not that you owe me anything. It's not like we've really established what this," she said and motioned between them, "is. I just—"

Dair reached up inhumanly fast and cupped her face, pulling her closer to him causing her words to freeze in her throat. "Listen closely, Sarah Serenity. The first time I laid eyes on you, it was as though I was seeing a sunrise for the first time. The warmth that radiated off of you penetrated through my dark world with an intensity I'd never felt before. It was like the rays of the sun breaking through a raging storm, offering hope to all that had been tormented. You say I don't owe you anything, but I would say you are very, very wrong. Before you I was just the dream maker, the Sandman. But you have made me something more, you have given me something more, and for that I am forever grateful. And perhaps, I need to establish what this," he said as he motioned with his free hand, just as she had done, "is between us so that there is no confusion. Humans would call us boyfriend and girlfriend and for the public I am fine with that. But in private, when it is just you and me, those terms do not come close to capturing what you are to me." Dair took a breath as he steadied himself. His emotions were a thrashing hurricane inside of him, raging against his desire to protect her and yet his need to obey his Creator. They had been since he had watched the woman before him die. He was unaccustomed to such feelings, and though he believed Serenity had come to care for him, he didn't want to scare her off by coming on too strong. But when the words started pouring from his lips, the censure he fought to have was completely gone. To say that the dam had broken would be a gross understatement.

"It is not fair of me to ask you for the same commitment that I am ready and willing to give to you. You are so young, your life only just beginning with a future stretched out before you with promise. I have existed for longer than your mind can fathom. So I'm asking you not to let my admission make you feel obligated to reciprocate, or even respond at all. But I feel you have a right to know since it is obvious that my feelings are unclear to you. I love you. I have never fully understood what those words meant until you. And now in all of their messy glory, I know what *I love you* means."

"What does it mean?" Serenity's words came out in a barely audible whisper.

"It means I am yours—heart, body, soul. I am yours. Whether you want me, choose to be with me, or walk away, I will always be yours. There will not be a day where the sun rises that I do not think of your safety, wellbeing, and happiness nor will there be a night that I don't make sure your dreams are peaceful and your mind rested. It means that your needs come before my own. It comes at no cost to you, and yet it will cost me everything, and it is a debt I'll gladly pay. It means there is no hell I won't walk through, no battle I won't fight, and no sacrifice I won't make to ensure that you are safe, protected, and happy."

There was silence once his voice no longer filled the small space. The only noise came from the muffled music that was playing from the drive-in's speakers and the muted voices of the other people ordering their food. Serenity sat still as stone. Her eyes held his but she gave nothing away. He didn't know if she was in shock, scared, happy, or angry about what he'd just told her. Dair was trying to be patient but he was close to growling like an animal, needing to know her thoughts. To be fair, he had told her that she didn't have to respond. He wanted to kick himself for that. He wanted her to respond even if it was to laugh at him; he needed to know where he stood with her.

"Is that all?" she said suddenly breaking the silence.

"Is that all what?" Dair asked his forehead scrunching up in confusion.

"Is that all it means?" Had Dair not seen the slight quirk of her lips and the wicked gleam in her eyes, he would have thought she was serious.

"I suppose it is rather a letdown," he told her, playing along. "I should have added in some jewels or castles."

"Definitely would have been more impressive," she agreed with a nod. His hand was still against her warm cheek. He left it there a moment longer before finally pulling it away. Silence once again filled the car but thankfully it didn't last long.

"I know you said I didn't have to respond or

whatever," Serenity began, "but do you mind if I do?"

Dair loved the way she bit her bottom lip as she looked up at him through lowered lashes. "Of course not." He gave a casual nod encouraging her to proceed.

She let out a breath blowing the wisps of hair that framed her face. She seemed hesitant, yet there was a determined tightness to her mouth. Dair waited. He waited to see if she was trying to let him down easy. He waited to hear the words that would either throw him back into a world of darkness or words that would keep him wrapped in her light.

"The only love I have received or given was that of a child to a parent or other family member," Serenity said as she leaned back in her seat. "So I admit that I don't have any experience with other types of love. But I do know that what I feel for you is like nothing I've felt before. It's strong, intense, wild, and—at times—a little scary."

Dair's eyes were riveted to her face as Serenity spoke. His chest rose and fell with every breath that felt hinged on what she would say next.

"I'll be honest; I'm afraid to say that I love you because it seems like we should know each other longer before such a strong sentiment is given, but I don't know what else to call what I feel for you." Her head lifted and turned, finally looking at him. "I'm also afraid to feel these things because I don't know what kind of future we really have together. I lost my parents and the pain of that has never gone away. I don't know if I can stand losing someone else I care deeply for. But even to keep from having a broken heart, I can't ask you to leave. The idea of you not being here is. . . well. . . it's horrible. It leaves an emptiness inside of me that takes my breath away."

"Don't ask me to leave." His plea came out in a hoarse whisper as his hand reached for hers. "I can't, not even if I wanted to."

Emma stared up at the ceiling in her room. She was tired. That had been the real reason she'd told Serenity that she didn't want to go with her to the clinic that morning. Raphael had stayed with her as he did every night, but he couldn't stop the yelling match that carried on most of the night between Mildred and her guests. Emma had needed to pee since early that morning but hadn't dared to leave her room until Mildred and the others had fallen asleep. They had all collapsed into drunken stupors, so thankfully they were out cold, at least for a while. She had hoped she would be able to go to sleep but so far all she'd managed was a short nap. Raphael had been quiet, though that wasn't anything new. She could tell he was trying to let her rest.

After another few minutes, Emma finally gave up. She sat up and pushed herself back until she was leaning against the cold wall behind her. Raphael didn't turn toward her even when she spoke.

"Do you ever wish you were human?" Emma asked him. It had been a question that had bounced around her head several times over the weeks that she'd gotten to know the angel. He watched everything around him with such intensity, and she couldn't help but wonder if he ever got tired of being on the outside looking in. He didn't seem surprised by her question, but then it seemed very little could surprise Raphael.

"I cannot miss what I have never had." His voice held its usual coolness and there was no inflection.

"That doesn't mean you aren't affected by the things you see in this world. Families, couples, children—things you will never have. Does it bother you?" After the question was already out, Emma realized that it might have sounded a little cruel. She sometimes spoke before she thought because her mind was always curious, always wanting to learn more. Her questions were most often just a need to know the facts, not to be intrusive. She supposed that for all of her intelligence and maturity she still was just an eight-year-old after all. Instead of apologizing, she simply waited to see if he would answer.

"I was not created for any of those things. The drive that lives inside of me is the need to protect the Creator's creation and to fight evil, the enemies of the Creator. I find that when I see humans living out their purpose, happy and content, then I find pleasure in that, but I do not wish for it. Besides, if I hadn't been created for protection, then who would do it?"

Emma's forehead wrinkled as she looked at him trying to understand what he was saying. "You mean that if you weren't there to do your job, then maybe it might not get done?"

The angel shook his head. "Not at all. The Creator always accomplishes his purposes. But I am privileged that He created me to aid in those purposes."

Emma thought about that and decided she could understand someone feeling satisfaction by doing what he was created to do. She still wasn't sure what she had been created for, but she felt like it was important. Why else would God give her such intelligence? Her need to focus on something other than the stirring she heard happening in the other room had her asking more questions.

"When you say enemies, what are you talking about?"

Raphael turned to face her. His large arms were folded across his chest as he leaned back against the wall. She could tell he was deciding how much to tell her. His shoulders seemed to relax as he came to a decision.

"In your time, in your church, have you ever heard of the angel Lucifer?"

She nodded. "He desired to be like God and was cast from heaven."

"Correct," he confirmed as his eyes glazed over and memories pulled him from the room. "The biggest rebellion to ever stand against the Creator happened that day. Lucifer and those he had convinced to follow him were thrown into the depths. He was given the earth as his domain and the fallen angels that slowly withered until there was nothing good left in them. Their bitterness at the Creator ate away at them until all that was left were grotesque creatures that reflected the darkness they held inside." He paused and Emma found herself leaning forward with her arms on her knees and her hands on her face supporting her head as she watched and waited for Raphael to continue.

"But Lucifer's heart was full of greed and malice. He wanted more than just the earth. He wanted all that inhabited it as well. His goal has been to inflict as much pain on the Creator as he can by corrupting and destroying all that the Creator has fashioned."

"My mama used to say that Lucifer and his demons only had as much power as we were willing to give them. She told me that if he knocks on my door and I open it to him while offering him cookies and lemonade then I shouldn't be surprised if he kicked back and stayed a while."

Raphael gave her one of his rare smiles. "Your mother said a lot of interesting things."

Emma laughed. "I think I could write a book just based on her sayings."

"That is good that you have those memories of her. She left a piece of herself inside of you through her wisdom. Treasure that, because wisdom is rare commodity in this world."

"People are always so surprised when things around them seem to fall apart. But why should they expect anything different if they build their house from twigs and spit based on a blueprint of stupid?" Emma grinned.

"Mama?" Raphael asked with a raised brow.

She nodded. "Will you tell me more?"

His answer was to continue his story. "The mistake many humans make is believing that because Lucifer is fallen that he must not be too bright. The truth is he is the most cunning of beings. His mind is a calculating labyrinth of ways to draw people into darkness. He is patient, relentless, and thoughtful in his attacks. There is a reason that at one time when he was still in heaven he stood at the Creator's right hand side. He was beautiful, a bright shining beacon of heaven's glory, but it was not enough.

"After all the time he has roamed the earth, he has learned who to prey upon and has succeeded in taking many with him. He is always trying to find out the

Creator's plans and thwart them, and he will use any weapon he has at his disposal. One such weapon is the demons that serve him. They roam the world unseen, wreaking havoc on unsuspecting humans. Myself and other angels have been tasked with destroying them, but we can only attack if they are attempting to cause physical harm to a human by their direct actions. If they influence another vessel to cause the harm we cannot intercede. We cannot interfere with free will. It has to be the human's choice to turn away from the evil. The demons can whisper all they want into the minds of those who are willing to listen and we can do nothing, but if they raise a hand to harm them, then we can act."

"All that is going on around us and we don't even know it," Emma said softly.

"Some can feel it," Raphael corrected her, "like those who are very attuned to the spiritual. They feel evil when it comes near and can even feel my presence without me making myself known. They are rare, but they are out there."

Emma didn't have time to sift through this new information because her door was suddenly flung open so hard that it bounced off the wall nearly returning closed. Her aunt stood in the doorway looking very annoyed, which Emma didn't understand because she hadn't done anything to annoy her—other than breathe that is.

"You got someone here to see you," Mildred told her as the cigarette she hadn't bothered to remove bounced against her lips as she spoke.

Emma slid from the bed glancing back at Raphael. She knew her aunt couldn't see him, but it still seemed odd to Emma because he was just so big and his presence so profound. She didn't know how Mildred couldn't feel it. She walked past her aunt and into the living room to find Darla standing just inside the doorway holding a covered bowl and a box of crackers. Her smile was like a brilliant star lighting the dark sky.

"I heard you were under the weather and wanted to see if you needed anything. I also brought you food."

"Of course you did," Emma said as she smiled at the woman she'd grown to love like a mother. She took the bowl and crackers from her and carried them to the table in the kitchen. Darla followed, taking no notice of Mildred who stood at the hallway entrance.

"Are you alright?" Darla asked, her eyes taking on a serious glint.

"Yeah, I'm fine. It's probably just a little virus."

Darla's smiled returned. "The fact that you even know what virus is is a little scary."

Emma shrugged. "Actually the fact that I know how to assemble a bomb is what should scare you."

Darla's mouth dropped open. "Why on earth would you know how to do something like that?"

"Curiosity, and the need to see if I could actually do it. Don't worry, when I was building it, my dad made me substitute the explosive parts with foam. Then he made me disassemble them since all someone would have to do to make them active was exchange out the foam for C4."

Darla just shook her head. "Okay, I have to get back to work. Please promise me that there will be no bomb building."

Emma nodded. "I promise. I'll do something normal like make friendship bracelets or something."

After Darla left, Emma was suddenly aware that Mildred was still watching her. She looked over at her aunt and for the first time saw a glimmer of longing in her eyes. It was gone as quickly as it had come. Mildred continued to stand there and stare, but it was as though she were looking through Emma, seeing something no one else could. Emma decided to see if maybe she could get some answers out of her aunt while she seemed to be reflective. Mildred's friends had all left. Emma figured that must have been the rummaging about she'd heard earlier.

"Aunt Mildred, can I ask you a question?" Emma asked gently.

Mildred's eyes regained their focus and the pinched expression she always wore came back. "I have a feeling you gonna ask no matter what I say." She shuffled over to her chair and sat down, but she didn't turn the television on. Emma took that as a yes.

"How did you and my mom end up so separated? Aren't sisters supposed to be close?" Emma tried to sound nonjudgmental.

A few moments of silence passed and Emma didn't think her aunt was going to answer but then, to the young girl's surprise, she began to speak. "We weren't full blooded, only half-sisters. We had the same mama, but different daddies. I was older, and when mama left my daddy, she left me too. She went on and found her an educated man, and suddenly she was better than the rest of her kin. My daddy wasn't exactly thrilled to be stuck raising a snotty nosed brat. That's what his nickname fer me was. Our upbringings weren't nothing the same. She got what I never had."

"Why would grandma leave you with a man who didn't treat you right?" Emma asked, unable to imagine her grandmother doing such a thing. She knew there had to be more to the story.

"She was just a kid herself when she had me. My

daddy was a mean SOB and he threatened to kill her if she took me. She believed him. He didn't want me, not really, but he didn't want her to have me neither. She tried to get me back after she married her fancy man, but by that time I didn't want nothing to do with her or my so-called sister. I did the best I could with what I had."

Emma could see the sadness and pain in Mildred's eyes. It was with those things that she fed the alcohol and drugs, or perhaps, it was the other way around. It was the holes left inside of her from her mother's abandonment and her father's abuse that she had been trying to fill her entire life. Emma didn't know what to say. It was obvious that Mildred had never considered a different path than the one her father had taken. She probably had believed she wasn't worthy of something better. It was a painful realization for her. It didn't make the way her aunt acted excusable, but Emma understood it a little better now.

They were both silent. Emma ate the soup that Darla had brought her and then washed the bowl. Just as she was heading back to her room Mildred looked back at her.

"I don't want you goin out tonight. It's New Years and a lot of no good heathens will be about. It ain't no place for an eight-year-old."

Emma was shocked by her words. It sounded as if she actually cared. Okay, so it wasn't exactly a profession of love, but for Mildred it might as well have been. Emma nodded. "Yes ma'am." She closed the door behind her as she entered her room. Raphael was still there. She figured he must have known she wasn't in danger when she'd left earlier and that was why he hadn't followed.

Emma's head turned when she saw the cat peek out from under her bed and make a swipe for the mouse that continued to elude it. "I guess it's just us tonight, guys," she told them. The cat gave her an annoyed look like it was Emma's fault that it couldn't catch the sneaky mouse. "Hey, it's not my fault that you're too lazy to stand up when you try to catch your dinner. Sliding on your belly is really pretty pitiful." It yawned as though bored and then slid back into the shadows under the bed.

Emma looked at Raphael as she climbed up on the bed and sat with her legs crossed. She wondered what angels did on New Year's or if it was something they even acknowledged at all. She figured not since they seemed to see time differently than humans. She kind of felt bad that he would be stuck, bored, with a little girl to watch over—not a lot of excitement there. She thought for a few minutes before a mischievous smile stretched across her face.

"So Raph, want to build a bomb? We can bring in the new year with a bang." She smiled. "Pun intended."

Raphael gave her a dry look. "You told Darla you would not."

"Yes, but I didn't say anything about instructing and supervising while *you* did."

Raphael shook his head but a smile tugged at his lips. "You really are too clever for your own good."

Chapter 12

"If you dream you are a lion tamer in a circus, your subconscious mind is expressing your need to conquer the beasts in your life, or your need for danger to feel alive."

The Fireside was packed by nine o'clock and already a few rowdy men (and some women) who'd taken their libation very seriously had had to be tossed out. Serenity sat at one of the makeshift bars that had been set up along the outer walls of the restaurant. The center tables had been removed creating an open space for dancing, and a raised platform had been assembled on the far right wall where a local band was playing. Serenity tapped her hand absentmindedly to the beat as she watched Glory flit about the room with a tray of drinks. She laughed as her friend danced with different customers as she passed out the orders. Serenity would never have attempted to dance with a tray of drinks above her head. Knowing her luck, she'd end up wearing the beverages instead of delivering them.

She resisted the urge to check the time on her phone, considering it probably hadn't been three minutes since she'd looked the last time. Dair had told her it might be a little later before he would arrive, but that it would be sometime before midnight. Despite their new relationship, he still had a job to do that took him to all corners of the world. But it seemed to Serenity that his assignments had been increasing lately. Given this, she was actually quite surprised with the amount of time he was able to devote to spending with her. After all, there were a lot of people in this world. Didn't it stand to reason that there would be a lot of destinies that needed influencing? When her mind wasn't drifting to thoughts of Dair, it was continually jumping back to Emma.

Darla had tried to reassure her by telling her that Emma was fine when she had brought her the soup, but it still didn't put her mind at ease. Even knowing that Raphael was with her didn't seem to be enough to calm her worries. She could only imagine what Mildred and her minions had planned for the night's festivities. She really hoped that maybe Mildred had decided to go to one of her friend's houses instead of having her usual gathering at her home. She'd rather Emma be home alone than with those cretins.

"Why do you look like someone just ran over your dog, stuffed it, and then gave it to you as a Christmas present?" Willa asked, taking one of the empty bar stools, asked as she saddled up next to Serenity..

Serenity laughed. "You and Glory have to be related."

Willa looked over at the long legged, blonde who continued to dance around. She snorted. "If we're related then I want to slap her for taking all the good genes. My entire leg is as long as her calf. If she wasn't so nice, I'd probably slash her tires."

Serenity slapped the bar as laughter bubbled up at Willa's comment. Leave it to the snarky woman to hand out a backhanded compliment with such irritation. "Hey, at least you're athletic. I'm about as graceful as a hobbled cow being dragged by a mule."

Willa glanced at her from the corner of her eye. "True. You best be glad you've got nice boobs; they make up for just about any flaw—at least in the eyes of the opposite gender."

"I'm not sure whether to thank you for the compliment, or be weirded out that you think I have nice boobs."

"Oh, please, don't even act like you don't notice when another female has nice assets. If chicks didn't notice other chicks being attractive then there would be no need for Spanks, push up bras, or the amazing back fat reducers. Because, let's be honest, women don't wear that crap for men; they wear it to keep from being judged by other bitches."

"While I might actually agree with that statement, I'm wondering if Glory needs to cut you off." Serenity eyed the other woman speculatively.

"Naw," Willa waved her off. "I haven't had anything other than Orange Crush to drink. I just don't have a problem telling it like it is."

Serenity considered her words. "Is that because of what you've been through?" She knew that Willa wasn't shy to talk about her experience with breast cancer, but she still hoped that her question wouldn't offend her.

Willa shrugged. "Maybe I'm a little worse since surviving it. I've always said what I thought, but perhaps, now that I've been faced with the reality of my own mortality, I definitely hesitate less." Willa stood and straightened her shirt. "This is too serious talk for a night of celebrating. But since we are on the topic, I'll give you some advice. It's free this time. Don't wait to have death staring you in the face, taunting you with the reality that you aren't as invincible as you thought, before you start living every minute as though it would be your last. I can promise you something; when you do finally face the reaper, the life that flashes before your eyes needs to be one that you can be proud of. I'm not saying live with no regrets, because hell, regrets are what help us grow to be better than we were. What I'm saying is be able to die knowing that what you're leaving behind is worth something. Your influence doesn't die with you. That's something I realized when I learned that my life might be coming to its conclusion. I wouldn't be physically here anymore, but my actions, words, and beliefs would continue to impact others—whether I wanted them to or not—long after I was gone." Willa smiled at her as she patted her leg. "I better go check on your aunt before I get onto any more soapboxes."

Before she could walk away, Serenity grabbed her sleeve. "Willa."

The other woman turned and met her eyes.

"Thank you." Serenity wasn't sure what she was thanking the woman for—maybe for occupying some time while she waited for Dair and worried about Emma, or perhaps, for the advice that she didn't know she needed. Whatever it was, she wanted Willa to know she appreciated it. "I'm glad you kicked cancer's ass."

Willa laughed. "Apparently, I still had important conversations to have at New Year's Eve parties surrounded by drunk, stupid people and bad dancers."

Serenity watched Willa as she was swallowed by the crowd as she walked away. That had definitely been a strange conversation to have at a party. But, then again, it was New Year's Eve. And what was New Year's if not the time for making changes, whether they be changes in behavior or thoughts. So perhaps, it wasn't such a strange conversation after all.

"You look entirely too contemplative for this crowd." A warm breath caressed her ear causing

Serenity to shutter.

She turned around abruptly on the stool to find Dair standing there leaning against the bar looking like a dark, mysterious character straight from the paranormal romance novels that had become so popular. She could only imagine the description an author would use to create the image of him in the minds of the reader. Serenity didn't think there was any way words could adequately portray his otherworldly beauty—chiseled features, a solid form, and dark eyes that would cause even the most saintly female to be tempted—which he had no qualms about using on her.

His lips tilted up in a knowing smile and Serenity's heart sped up. Nope, she was pretty sure there was no way words could capture what that smile did to her. "Just had an interesting talk with Willa," she finally answered after pushing away the strong desire to throw herself in his arms. Yah, that wouldn't be pathetic at all.

"I have a feeling most talks with Willa would be categorized as interesting," Dair said as he leaned closer to her so she could hear him above the music. Her brow rose in surprise when he grabbed the seat of her stool and pulled her closer until he was standing in between her legs. Dair reached up and tucked her hair behind her ear as he stared into her eyes. "How are you tonight?"

What could she say? *I'm better because you're here.* Or maybe something like, *Well a few minutes ago I could barely breathe because you're my air and without you I might suffocate.* Okay, so maybe that was a little much, but Serenity made it a point to attempt to be honest with herself, and honestly there were so many answers to that question. She could try to be sexy and flirty but his touch was doing weird things to her brain and its ability to cause her mouth to form words. So the only thing she was able to squeak out was, "Fine."

Dair bit his bottom lip as humor danced across his features. He knew what he did to her and he was shameless about it.

"Well, I for one am much better now that I'm with you," he told her as his hand rested on her hip giving her a gentle squeeze.

Serenity had to remind herself to breathe. *In and out, Sarah,* she told herself as she held his mesmerizing gaze. They sat silently staring at each other for several minutes. The music suddenly changed to a slower pop song with a sensual beat. Serenity turned to look at the band, thinking there was no way they were playing it, and she saw that the band was taking a break and a DJ had taken over.

"Would you like to dance?" Dair asked, drawing her attention back to him.

Serenity smiled. "The Sandman knows how to dance?" She knew he heard the challenge in her voice, and by the look in his eyes he was more than up to it. Dair took her hand as he stepped away from the bar and pulled her from her perch. He led her through the throng of dancing people, some with partners and others just in groups. Serenity couldn't help but notice there were quite a few that had some pretty good moves. Her hand grew sweaty as she watched several couples moving so sensually with one another that for a brief instance she felt as though she had walked onto the set of *Dirty Dancing*.

Dair turned around once he had found a clear piece of floor. He pulled her close, taking her hands in his and lifting them to wrap around his neck. Serenity's eyes widened when those hands then slid across her arms to her shoulders and then down her rib cage to her hips. It was more intimate than any kiss they had shared. She wasn't sure if it had anything to do with the way he was looking at her or if maybe the coolness of his skin against her warm skin caused the heightened effect. Dair pulled her closer and she had to tilt her head back further in order to look at his face. Serenity couldn't take her eyes away from his.

"Are you doing something to me?" she whispered. She'd intended it to be louder but she couldn't seem to get her breathing under control and so her words were much softer.

Dair leaned down closer, his gaze continuing to penetrate into her soul. "Not yet." The whispered promise was enough to cause a churning in her gut. To hell with butterflies, she had a hoard of dragons dive bombing each other in her stomach.

She knew he could see the anxiety that had suddenly risen up in her.

"Relax, Sarah." Dair's deep voice rumbled in his chest. "Just dance with me. I'm not asking for anything more."

She felt his hands begin to guide her hips to the beat of the music and, to her surprise, as Dair continued to lead her, she discovered there on that dance floor that the Sandman had some wicked moves. Serenity wouldn't say that she was a great dancer, but she could move to a beat. Glory loved to dance and they had spent many nights dancing in Darla and Wayne's living room. Glory insisted that since there was nothing to do in their little bitty town then they'd to make something to do. Serenity figured they could be doing a lot worse than watching YouTube videos to learn new moves. Glory had even tried to teach Darla.

Now that was a night to remember.

"Are you with me?" Dair's breath against her ear brought her attention back to the present. She looked up at him and smiled. Movement directly behind him drew her attention. Glory leaned around him and grinned.

"I'm on break," she yelled. "How about you and I put all those moves we learned for no reason to good use?"

Serenity groaned inwardly. Well, if she was going to embarrass herself, at least she wouldn't be alone. She stepped back out of his hands and gave Glory a nod. "Let's do this," she said as she looked up at Dair, hoping that the look in her eyes was every bit as alluring as his was. She figured she did something right because his eyes began to swirl like obsidian liquid and he reached for her. She slapped his hands away and shook her head at him. Glory came around to his side, her body moving perfectly with the music. Serenity moved to his other side and began to mimic Glory's moves. She knew she wasn't as smooth as her best friend, but she held her own.

Dair's breath was stuck in his throat as he watched Serenity dance. He knew that Glory was next to him as well, but he only had eyes for his girl. There was something so primal about dancing, if done right it was almost like a claiming, and as Serenity moved around him getting close enough to touch and then backing away, Dair laid claim to her, to her heart, her mind, her body and her soul. They were his and he would care for them as no other could. There was nothing physical about it, though one day he hoped to be the one claiming her in that way as well. This was a claim on her as what he could only describe as his soul mate. As the tempo of the music changed again, he vaguely heard Glory tell Serenity that she had to get back to work. The music was no longer a sensual beat and the atmosphere of the dance floor changed accordingly. Couples embraced and swayed as the slower tune began to fill the room. Serenity slowed her movements and was looking at him in a way no one ever had. He stepped closer to her, placing both hands on her hips and pulled her into his body.

Dair heard the quick intake of her breath as he settled her tightly against him. He leaned down until his mouth was next to her ear. He briefly took a breath, momentarily enraptured by her scent. "Put your arms around my neck, Princess," he whispered, letting his lips brush up against her skin as he spoke. Dair loved the way she responded to him. It let him know that he wasn't the only one affected. She was just as lost as he was.

He recognized the song that was playing and began to sing it softly to her. The words were so incredibly perfect for how he felt, it was as though the writer had plucked Dair's thoughts from his mind as he crafted the song.

"You are beautiful, baby undeniable.
You are warmth, completely sunshinable.
And you've captured me.
You are my weakness, baby temptation,
You are completeness, utter salvation.
And you've saved me.
I won't deny it; I can no longer breathe,
Without you beside me,
This world I would rather leave.

I need you baby, like crops need the rain,
My existence was dark,
But since you there's been no pain.
You are desire, baby irrevocable
You are sensation, totally strokeable,
And you've ensnared me.
You are mine, baby unsharable
You are splendor, wholly stareable.
And you've humbled me."

The words poured out of Dair as though he had written them himself and he meant them with every fiber of his being. Serenity was everything the song described and more. To him, she was it. No other existed to him. She pulled herself closer to him and his stomach tightened as he thought about her fate. Dair didn't want to think about that. He wanted to be here in the moment with his love. He wanted to build memories with her that they could carry with them from this life into the next.

Dair felt her lips on his neck and he fought the urge to pull back and claim her lips with his own. Serenity tested every ounce of control that he never thought he could lose. He would give her whatever was in his power to do so, and he'd even try to give her what was not in his to give. As the song ended, he pressed a tender kiss to her jaw before whispering, "I love you."

Serenity wished she had more control over her emotions when it came to Dair, but when he spoke those words with such conviction, she was lost. Pulling back to look up at him, her eyes were slightly blurry with unshed tears. His hands came up to cup her face and his eyes held hers. They didn't say anything. There were no words in that moment. Dair leaned down until his lips were pressed to hers. The music played around them and other bodies moved as they were still in the current. For Serenity, in that moment with his large hands holding her and his full lips holding hers captive, there was only Dair. He crowded every thought pushing out any distractions. The kiss lasted longer than was probably socially acceptable but she couldn't bring herself to care.

When he finally pulled away, she saw the sly smile on his sensual mouth. He knew what he did to her. She knew he could feel it, the way her world suddenly zeroed in on him, and he loved it.

"Your voice is beautiful," she said, finally breaking the intense moment.

"I have a slight advantage; being immortal leaves a lot of time for practice," he told her with a wink.

Okay, so the wink was just about her undoing. Nothing should be that sexy. Truly Dair should be kept out of close proximity from any female because if he went around flashing that lust-worthy smile and winking, he would create a mob of women desperate to have just a few seconds of his attention. He took her hand and led her from the dance floor to an empty space at one of the makeshift bars. Serenity took the water he had ordered from the bartender and downed the whole glass. She couldn't help it. Her throat was dry and she needed to occupy her mouth with something before she lost control and occupied it with Dair.

"You alright?" he asked her as he brushed her hair back away from her face. His fingertips grazed her neck causing her to shiver.

She needed to take a breather for just a few

minutes and clear the lust induced fog that was clouding her brain. She nodded. "I'm good, just need to run to the ladies room real quick."

As she started to walk away, Dair caught her hand and she looked back at him. His eyelashes swept down as he gave her a hooded look. "Don't be long; I've missed you today."

Serenity was pretty sure she whimpered at his words and the emotion his voice held. From anyone else it would have been cheesy, but from Dair it was as smooth and effortless as breathing. The only thing she could give him was a nod. That's the only thing her scrambled brain could manage. She turned back, letting her hand slip from his, and headed to the ladies' room.

Serenity stood at the bathroom sink staring at the person who looked back at her. Her hands were sweaty and her heart was pounding out a rhythm that she was pretty sure was to the tune of *I love Dair*. It was on the tip of her tongue when he had been holding her and singing to her on the dance floor. Why hadn't she said it? The only thing she could come up with was fear. She was afraid to care so deeply for him, knowing that she might lose him. As she turned on the cold water, Serenity let out a steadying breath and then stuck her hands under the cool stream. She cupped her hands to gather the water and then splashed it onto her face. Serenity was surprised no steam rose off of her heated skin. It helped, a little. She at least was beginning to feel like she could breathe again, and she might not combust if Dair winked at her again. But there was no guarantee.

Serenity was drying her hands when she felt her cell phone vibrate in her back pocket. She pulled it out and looked at the screen. It was a local number but not one that she recognized. Normally she might not have answered it, but for some reason, she felt compelled to.

"Hello?"

"Serenity," Emma's voice came through the phone but Serenity could tell immediately that something was wrong.

"Emma, are you okay? Are you sicker? Do you need to go to the hospital?" Her mind was running a million miles an hour as she considered the possibilities of why the girl would have called her. Serenity immediately thought it had to do with the fact that she hadn't been feeling well. She hadn't even considered that it could be worse—much, much worse.

"I hate to ask this of you, but could you please come to my aunt's house?" Emma's voice shook as she spoke and the tears she was crying were evident in the quick intake of breaths that she took in between words.

"Of course, I'm on my way. Are you okay?" Serenity asked again because she needed to know that Emma wasn't hurt.

"I'm not really sure how to answer that."

Emma's words were drowned out by a slurred voice. "Quit your chit chatten, little girl, and tell yer friend to hurry up and git here."

Serenity's stomach dropped to her feet as she heard the voice was Rat's. At that point, she was no longer thinking. She was simply on auto pilot. In hindsight she would realize that she should have taken a few minutes to go and tell her aunt and uncle and Dair, but her only thought was get to Emma. She flew out of the bathroom. Instead of going back out through the large room full of people, she raced toward the other direction, down the hall, and out the back door. The cold air rushed into her lungs as she slammed through the door and into the night. Serenity hadn't bothered to stop and grab her coat, and as she reached her car she was thankful that she'd taken her car key off the key chain and stuffed it in her front pocket. She hadn't wanted to carry a purse with her and all her keys were too big to fit comfortably in her pockets.

Her hands were shaking as she reached into her pocket to get the key. The ridges got caught on the fabric and she heard it rip when she forced the key out. The lock was frozen so Serenity had to be careful not to break the key off attempting to unlock the door. Her mind was filling up with horrible scenarios as she leaned down and breathed warm breath over the key hole, all the while praying that she would get there in time. In time for what, she didn't know. She just knew she needed to hurry. Mercifully, she felt the key finally slip into the lock after her fifth attempt. Serenity was pretty sure something or someone was helping her along because she had never moved as fast as she did in those few minutes. She threw herself into the seat, closing the door and starting the car at the same time. She had it in reverse and was flooring the small car through the ice-covered parking lot faster than she could sing the first ten presidents of the song she'd learned in the fifth grade. For whatever reason, when she was extremely stressed, that song popped into her head and she would sing it in her mind. Weird, she knew.

Her car was on the road to Mildred's house in a flash, slipping and sliding, but somehow, miraculously, she didn't end up in a ditch. There were no other cars on the street, which was a massive blessing. Something about the dark night seemed so sinister in that moment. The emptiness of all the parking lots and the lack of people loitering around the stores was eerie. Considering everything within the city limits was practically in walking distance of each other, Serenity was sure that Mildred's house had somehow jumped up and walked clear across the county as long as it was taking her to get there. Her fingers tapped a beat to the worry that was bouncing around in her head. She wanted to kick herself for not going and getting Emma. Serenity should have known that Mildred would be throwing some sort of sick soiree with the vermin she called friends.

Her hand slammed down against the steering wheel as she shouted, "DAMMIT." How could she have been so foolish? And now because Serenity had talked herself out of picking the little girl up, Emma was stuck in the hands of those monsters. Where the hell was Raphael she wondered? She couldn't imagine that he would leave Emma, especially if Mildred's friends were around.

Serenity's foot pressed harder on the gas pedal as her destination came into view. She hit the driveway at a speed that caused her low front end to bounce off the uneven concrete. Serenity didn't care. All she could think about was getting to Emma. She threw the car in park and was out the door without even realizing that she hadn't shut the engine off. Her feet pounded against the unforgiving frozen ground, causing a jarring pain to shoot up her legs. She ignored it. She also ignored the pain of her shoulder slamming into the front door as she turned the knob and shoved her way into the house.

With all of the scenarios she had built up in her mind, she hadn't come close to hitting the mark. The scene before her was like something out of a horror movie. The room was dark with only a small lamp casting a low light. Serenity quickly found Emma standing against the far wall with her eyes wide and her body stiff. Raphael stood behind her but she could tell no one else could see him. In that moment she wanted to yell and scream at the angel. What the hell was he doing just standing there? How could he not be getting Emma out of the house while a drunk, high—and who knew what else—mad man waved a gun around muttering under his breath. Rat didn't even seem to register that Serenity had entered the room. Mildred sat slightly dazed on the couch, her eyes shifting from person to person. She truly didn't seemed bothered by Rat or his gun. Serenity wondered why people like this were allowed to live. They only existed to hurt others. Their lives seemed like a serious waste of space, and she knew those thoughts were utterly hateful, but she couldn't bring herself to care as she watched tears stream down Emma's face.

"Mildred," Serenity practically growled. "What have you done?" She pointed at Rat and her lips curled up like a vicious predator ready to devour its prey. "Why would you let that man in here with a gun while your niece is in the house?"

Her voice finally jarred Rat from his demented rambling as he stopped his pacing and turned his head slowly towards her. It reminded Serenity of a scary movie she had once watched where a demon had crawled across the ceiling and then stopped to turn its horrible face on its victim just as slowly. She battled with herself to stand her ground, to not step back away from the evil that stood before her. And that's what he was—pure evil. There was something in his eyes that hadn't been there the first time she'd met him. Almost as if Rat wasn't the only one home, something else had taken up residency in his body and was influencing his actions.

"Pretty, pretty, pretty." His voice was slightly higher than last time, and Serenity hadn't thought she could be any more freaked out. She was wrong. "Pretty." His body turned towards hers as he whispered the word that would now be forever burned in her mind, in that voice. Serenity was sure that if anyone ever called her pretty again she would vomit on them.

Serenity was frozen under the sinister glare. Everyone in the room seemed to be holding their breath as they waited for the puppet before them to say something more. The fear rolling off of Emma was palpable, and Serenity just wanted to cross the room and gather her up in her arms, shielding her from Rat and his gun. But she couldn't move so she did the only thing she could in that moment, she prayed, *God help us.* The thought repeated itself over and over as she waited for Rat to make his next move.

Chapter 13

"If you dream that you are in a circus, tied to a spinning board, and the knife thrower is flinging his blades at you, it means something painful is about to happen in your life."

Emma was like stone against the wall staring at Serenity who looked as shocked as she felt. *How had this happened,* she kept asking herself? Her mind sifted through the events of the evening, trying to determine where her situation went from 'kind of bad' to 'category five hurricane bad'. She and Raphael had been sitting in her room, attempting to entertain themselves by drawing up the plans for a large scale incendiary device, or BKB, as Emma had called it. When Raphael had asked her why she called it a BKB, she just rolled her eyes and said, "*Big Kablooey Bomb,* duh." Raphael had refused to get her the material but he at least agreed to let her sketch it out on paper. There had been a wall jarring bang and then the sound of Rat's voice filled the house. Emma recalled the look on Raphael's face when he'd heard Rat's voice.

"Raphael, what's wrong?" Emma asked him. She knew that he was worried about Rat hurting her, but the look on Raphael's face went far beyond worry. Fear, then anger, then resolve, flashed in the angel's eyes.

Raphael didn't answer her as he stood and went to the bedroom door. She watched as he did something to the door knob, working his angel mojo she decided. He didn't move from that spot. Emma sat still, trying not to hear the things Rat was yelling and cringing when she did. He sounded frantic, almost out of control. She wondered what drug could bring out such a reaction, because the only effects she'd seen so far on her aunt and the others were the sluggish kind. Rat was anything but sluggish.

The sound of shattering glass filled the hall, and for a brief moment, she imagined the glass was her own life breaking into a thousand tiny little pieces. She knew that all her efforts to keep it together had been futile. The cracks were too many and too deep. How had she thought she could handle living here? How did she think she could possibly survive in the care of one such as Mildred, who wouldn't care if people hurt her? Emma felt like an optimistic fool. She was eight years old for goodness sakes. Who was she that such ugliness couldn't touch her?

"Emma," Raphael's voice was sharp.

She looked up at him and saw the stern glare that pierced her.

"Do not let it taint you."

"What?" she asked, her voice sounding hoarse.

"The evil that has entered this house; it is not just the evil of a man's flesh. Something supernatural is happening and it is affecting you. I can see it in your face; do not let it crush you. The lies it is whispering to you are just that—lies. Fight back with truth."

She was trying to catch up with what the angel was saying, but negative thoughts swirled in her head clouding her mind. Raphael had said something about supernatural. Her eyes narrowed and she sucked in a breath. "Do you mean a demon, like what you were talking about earlier? Is it because you told me about them—sort of like that saying, speak of the devil and he will…," her words trailed off as she watched his reaction.

Raphael's shoulders tensed. He was so rigid that Emma thought if she pushed him he would fall stiffly to the ground like a statue being toppled on its side. His jaw flexed as he ground his teeth together. "Rat is a weak man," he finally said. "I told you that the minions find people who are weak and influence them. They gain their power off of those like Rat who have no willpower to fight back. Rat has practically rolled out the red carpet for the beast."

"Cookies and lemonade," Emma said with a sad shake of her head. "Like mama said, 'What do you expect if you offer the devil a recliner and hand feed him grapes?' "

Raphael's lips twitched. Emma thought it was funny that the angel got such a kick out of her mama's sayings. She was glad someone appreciated them as much as she did. Another crash had her attention snapping back to the present. It was quiet suddenly but Emma didn't think the chaos was over. No, it was more like the calm before the storm. She couldn't have been more right. Her door smashed inward under the force of someone either kicking it or ramming their shoulder into it. Emma stood quickly and backed away, looking from Raphael to the door. The look in the angel's eyes was one of complete helplessness. Finally, the door crashed in and Rat stood in its place.

"Time to come out and play," he said as a sinister smile stretched across his wild-eyed face.

Something was wrong with him and it wasn't just the drugs. Raphael didn't need to tell her that. She could see the man. It was clear Rat was under the influence of something so twisted and evil that it made it difficult for anyone in the room to breathe. She took a tentative step toward the doorway. She'd much prefer to exit on her own rather than being man handled by Rat. As she walked past Raphael, she felt the brief warmth of his touch on her shoulder and heard him speak in a language that she didn't understand. Rat's head snapped up as though he had heard the angel. Emma looked from one to the other, waiting with baited breath. All of a sudden she was quite certain, judging from the look of utter hatred stretched across the gaunt man's face, that Rat could see Raphael.

Raphael's eyes met Rat's. But it wasn't a man's eyes that stared back at the angel. It was an ancient evil, one he had contended with many times before. This demon was extremely cunning. He knew with exacting certainty the rules that would keep him from being cast into the fire, and he was careful not to cross them. Raphael could see humor in the beast's eyes. He was laughing at Raphael. The demon knew that the angel couldn't touch him. Free will of the humans prevented the angels from interfering. Unless given a direct order by the Creator, Raphael could not intervene when the rules had not been broken. Raphael had received no such order.

"Why are you even here, light bearer?" The demon's voice was a hiss and sounded odd coming out of Rat's mouth. "You know you can do nothing. You have no purpose."

Raphael's muscles flexed with the urge to do battle. He had served in the Creator's army and fought many foes, and still the demons of hell paraded across the earth wreaking havoc. Of course, the only power these foul creatures wielded was whatever the humans allowed them.

"I serve a greater purpose than you can imagine, ancient one. It is you who truly has no place in this world. You are nothing but a parasite, weak without your host." Raphael could see that his words had hit a nerve. Demons were extremely prideful beings and hated to be insulted. This demon in particular was one that specialized in violence. These types of creatures seemed to be especially prickly. Raphael was surprised that Rat didn't carry the demon of addiction, considering his recreational habits. A demon which, though no less dangerous, was much more subtle.

"You know what must take place and what is ordained," the demon taunted. "I have been given permission."

"Not to harm the human!" Raphael growled. "You may influence your host, but he must choose. It must be by his hand." Raphael moved faster than a human could track and had Rat's arm in his hand before the man could back away. He felt the demon squirm inside of the man as Raphael searched Rat's mind. He had to know if there was anything salvageable left in the man. Could he be reasoned with so that he could fight off the evil that was attempting to coerce him to act? He could see Emma out of the corner of his eye. She stood, watching and barely breathing. He imagined she was attempting to keep from drawing Rat's attention to her. Smart girl, Raphael thought.

Raphael searched the man's mind and found that it was depraved beyond his worst imagining. He fought the urge to crush him, to prevent him from playing his part in what was to come, but it was not his place. He would not be like Lucifer so many millennia ago who decided that he should be equal to the Creator. He would trust and obey, as he always had. Raphael released the man's arm and stepped back. "I will be watching," he warned the beast.

A sick giggle bubbled up out of Rat's throat. He motioned for Emma to move forward. She hesitated at first, but one hiss from the demon had the girl's feet moving quickly across the stained and worn carpet. Raphael followed them both into the living room. Mildred was sitting on the couch with her eyes glazed over. As soon as Raphael entered the room, her eyes snapped up to meet his, and she let out a high squeal that should never have come from a human's mouth. The demon staring back at him from her face was weaker than the one that occupied Rat. Raphael held its gaze, trying to get a read on what type of entity he was dealing with. He watched Mildred fidget as the beast inside her grew uncomfortable under the angel's scrutiny.

"Leave us be, light bearer," the demon said softly. "She invited me in; it was her choice."

Raphael knew that the demon hadn't been in the woman long. Mildred did not have the signs of one that had been possessed for a significant amount of time. She was gaunt looking, but not from supernatural evil. Her broken appearance was her own doing. It saddened him anytime he came across a human that had given into the lies that were whispered to them by hell's minions. It meant one more of the Creator's children had wandered too far.

"You will call the girl that was here with you the other day," Rat's voice was his own again but Raphael could still feel the demon's presence. "You might not be old enough for what I want, but she is. Call her, or I will kill your aunt and make you watch. Then you will join her." He stared at Emma as he pulled the gun from where it had been hidden under his shirt.

Emma's hands shook as she picked up the phone that sat on the edge of the worn out couch. Her eyes stayed on Rat as she spoke. "I'll call her; just give me a second to think of her number."

Rat growled. "Hurry up!"

Raphael took a step toward the man but forced himself to stop. All he could yet do was be present for Emma so she would not be alone. He felt useless and angry. He did not understand why it had to happen this way.

Emma hadn't been trying to stall when she told Rat that she needed to remember the number. Her mind was a jumbled mess and her hands were shaking from the adrenaline that was racing through her body. Her heart was pounding so hard in her chest that Emma was sure she was going to be one of the few eight-year-olds in history that had died from a heart attack. Deciding she was pretty sure that she had the number figured out, she pushed the on button of the old, wireless phone. Emma hadn't been around when these phones had been in almost every household in America, but she was pretty sure that this one had been dragged out of the garbage long after those days had passed. The years of grime that coated it made her want to wipe it down with those Clorox wipes her mama loved so much, spray it with Lysol, and then wipe it down again. Emma's fingers stuck to the buttons as she pushed them, and she tried not to think about the myriad of substances that might be causing the tackiness.

As she pushed the last number, she thought it was funny that though there was a man holding a gun on her, in that moment she was thinking about not wanting to hold that disgusting phone near her face. That right there proved that she must be going into shock. The phone began to ring and she tried not to hold her breath while she waited for Serenity to answer.

"Hello?" Finally, Serenity's voice crackled over the line. It was both the most precious and most devastating thing Emma had ever heard. She knew she was dragging Serenity into her mess and she hated it. But she couldn't stop herself because she didn't want to die alone in that house.

Serenity wanted to look at Emma again to make sure that she was alright but she didn't want to take her eyes off of Rat. He was the threat in the room and she would be stupid to think he wouldn't use the weapon in his hand.

"You're gonna come with me," Rat finally spoke. His crazed and lust-filled eyes roamed over her, causing Serenity to feel as though she needed a bath and perhaps to be dowsed in bleach as well.

"Let Emma leave first," Serenity countered and was surprised that her voice didn't shake. She wasn't feeling nearly as confident as she sounded but she couldn't show him weakness. "Let Emma leave and then I will go with you. You have my word."

Rat let out a disgusted snort. "The word of a woman, what good is that?"

Serenity tried not to roll her eyes. *Great, he's got mommy issues,* she thought. *If he hates women there's no telling what his sick mind has planned.* She knew that she couldn't let her mind wander down that road or she'd vomit right there in front of him.

"I can't speak for others, but my word is good. If I say I'm going to do it then I'm going to do it," she told him and then looked over at Emma. "Come here, Emma." She motioned with her hand. Emma started to move forward but Rat pointed the gun at her and she froze.

"Stop!" Serenity yelled. "If you shoot her then you might as well shoot me too because you will not take me alive from this house if you don't let her go." Rat looked at her, back to Emma, and then back to Serenity again. She could tell that he was trying to figure out if she was bluffing. She hoped that he chose correctly.

"Fine," he huffed like a petulant child. "But if she goes for help and someone shows up here, I'll kill you."

Serenity ignored his threat as she again motioned for Emma to come to her. Emma moved cautiously across the living room and, though it was only around twenty five feet, it felt as though miles separated the two as she waited for the girl to reach her. When Emma was less than a foot away from Serenity's outstretched hand, Rat suddenly lifted the gun and, from that moment on, everything seemed for Serenity to move in slow motion.

Her eyes widened as she looked over at Rat and saw something else staring out of the man's eyes. It was an evil so vile and dark that the already meager lights in the room seemed to dim.

"She must die," Rat howled, but it wasn't Rat's voice, and even that statement seemed to come out in a slow motion scream.

Serenity simultaneously pushed Emma behind her while moving toward Rat and the gun that was now aimed at her. Rat pulled the trigger and the bullet flew from the barrel. Serenity felt as though she could see it slicing through the air moving directly toward her.

Somehow, from somewhere far away it seemed, she heard Dair's voice. It was a primal roar, and she could feel pain in the sound. But despite that awareness, she was at total peace. For so long she had wondered what her destiny was. She never knew what she wanted to do or where she wanted to go. Since her parents' death, she had felt as though she was just going through the motions of life until…until Dair. Flashes of his handsome face flew threw her mind. Then she saw the future she could have had with Dair shatter along with her rib cage as the bullet sliced into her body. The projectile hit with such force that it knocked her back against the wall behind her, and her head made a resounding thud but her body never hit the floor. Dair's arms were around her, lowering her gently to the ground. His dark eyes bore into her, swirling with emotions. She wanted to reach up and smooth away the crease in his brow but her arm would not obey her command. She shivered as the cold crept inside, enfolding her in death's embrace.

Serenity was dying. She knew that with utter certainty and yet she was not afraid. There was a part of her that was sad. The part of her that belonged to Dair wanted her to fight. It wanted a life with him and it refused to leave this life behind. But another part of her, somewhere deep inside, knew that this had been her path all along. This part of her knew that it was her destiny all along to be here to save Emma, and it was resigned and at peace with what had happened.

"Don't leave me," Dair whispered against her ear. She felt the darkness surround them and knew that Dair was using his disappearing act to take them somewhere else but she was quickly growing tired. She wasn't able to concentrate on the sounds that now filled the air. Dair laid her down on a firm surface and suddenly there was a flurry of people surrounding her but none of them were Dair. He was pushed back away from her and she wanted to cry out for him to come back. If she was going to die, she wanted his face to be the last thing she saw and his voice to be the last sound she heard. But instead, as her eyes slipped closed, the last thing she saw were green scrubs leaning over her, and the last sound she heard was the voice of some random person saying, "We're losing her." And then there was nothing.

Dair fought the urge to push the medical staff out of the way to get back to where he belonged, back to her side. He had no idea if she could be saved, but he had to try. He couldn't just let her go without a fight. His footsteps echoed against the tile floor as he paced outside the room where the doctors and nurses were attempting to save his love's life. The harsh florescent lights seemed even brighter as fear and anger filled him. Dair couldn't get the image out of his mind. He had appeared in Mildred's house to the scene of his darkest nightmare.

He had waited for Serenity to return from the ladies' room, and after fifteen minutes he had gone back to check on her. When he realized she wasn't in the restroom, he had searched the restaurant, and the longer he went without finding her the more frantic he had become. Just as he was walking out to the parking lot to see if her car was still there, he heard Raphael's voice in his mind. "Come to Mildred's. Now." The angel's voice had been so filled with rage that Dair had begun to shake with his own.

Then he was there watching Rat pull the trigger, the bullet rushing through the air, and then hitting its target—his Serenity. Dair hadn't been able to move. As though his feet were encased in cement, deep in the ground, he was trapped in the spot where he had appeared. As he watched her body fly back with the impact and crash into the wall, he saw her begin to crumble to the floor. That brought him out of his stupor and he caught her before she could hit the ground. Her body was limp, lifeless, and broken. Dair looked into her eyes, searching for her, imploring her to fight. Serenity's breathing was labored and he could hear her heartbeat stutter as it fought to keep pumping. He could see the light fading from her, pulling further and further away from him, and he panicked. Dair knew what the Creator had shown him. He knew that this was her destiny but he could not accept it. So he vanished with her in his arms and reappeared at the hospital not caring if he scared some poor soul to death when he suddenly materialized in the ER doorway.

The hours ticked by as he continued to pace. He was vaguely aware of Serenity's aunt and uncle arriving with Raphael, Glory and Emma. They didn't approach him and he imagined that had something to do with Raphael, and he would be forever grateful to the angel for interfering. Although the looks Glory was shooting him made it clear she was not happy about not being able to speak with him. He wasn't sure that he could be polite and maintain the correct social etiquette that the situation warranted. Dair didn't want to hurt Darla or Glory or be rude so it was better if he just stayed separate from them for now. Raphael, however, didn't seem to be worried about Dair's temperament.

"Are you alright?" the angel asked, his voice flat,

betraying no emotion.

Dair shook his head unsure of how to answer. He didn't know if he was alright and he wouldn't know until Serenity's fate was made clear. If she died, then the answer to that question would be a huge resounding hell no.

"I killed the human who shot her." He told Dair this as if he went around killing humans every day, which was not the case.

Dair's head snapped up as his furrowed brow deepened. "You broke the law?"

Raphael shook his head. "No. The demon that the man housed took matters into his own hands. He made the human raise the gun and pull the trigger. He took the man's free will away and so I destroyed him. But it cost the human his life."

"It's no less than he deserved," Dair growled through clenched teeth. He finally stopped his pacing and stood in front of his long time comrade. "I have something I have to do. Will you stay here with her?" The last thing Dair wanted to do was leave Serenity, but there was one who could save her, one who had that power, and he would try anything to save her. Even begging.

"Of course."

Dair nodded his thanks and then stepped around the corner of the hallway, making himself invisible to all but two. He came back around the corner and passed Raphael without a word, heading straight for the young girl who sat quietly in one of the dingy waiting room chairs. Dair knelt down in front of Emma and gave her a sad smile. "How are you doing?" he asked with more gentleness than he realized he was capable of in that moment. Glory sat next to the young girl holding her smaller hand tightly in hers. Her face also was streaked with tears but Dair could tell she was trying to keep it together for Emma's sake.

A single tear slid down Emma's cheek as she looked up at him. Her eyes darted away to check and see if anyone was watching her he assumed. If anyone was watching, it would appear that she was talking to herself. She apparently wasn't worried about what Glory would think, probably because Glory knew all about him. When her eyes were back on him she let out a shuddering breath. "I didn't want to call her. I did this to her. If I'd told Rat no then—,"

"Then you would be dead, Emma," Dair interrupted. He wouldn't sugarcoat it, not for her. Such patronizing would be insulting to her intelligence. "Rat did this, not you. Nobody blames you, and you know Serenity doesn't either."

"She's going to die, isn't she?" Emma asked, her words shaking out of her.

"I don't know," he answered honestly. "I hope not."

"I'm praying that she doesn't. It's not her time, Dair. She's too young; I mean she's older than me but mama would still call her a barely blossomed flower. She'd say Serenity hadn't reached her full bloom and that the sun was still rising in her life. She used to say that to me all the time. She'd say my mind bloomed way before the rest of me. Serenity shouldn't be picked before her season is over. Think of how many people will miss out on knowing her. She saved me, Dair, not just my life but my spirit. She and Darla and Wayne took me in and loved me, and now Serenity will pay the price for knowing me and being a part of my messed up life."

Dair placed his finger under her chin and raised her head once again so she would look at him. She was so wise for one so young, and yet she was still just a child in so many other ways. The grief she had already experienced in her few short years was more than most would experience in an entire lifetime. The fact that she wasn't a complete mess was a miracle, and yet she truly had no clue just how special she was. "First of all, even if Serenity had known the outcome, even if she could have seen into the future, and had known what happened today, she would not have changed anything. She would still have latched onto you and taken you as her little sister. She would have still loved you fiercely and she would have given her life knowing that yours was one worthy of saving. Whatever the outcome of this, I hope that you will not let it make you bitter. You've lost so much, Emma Jean, and yet you remain a beacon of light in a dark world. Don't change, not for anything or anyone."

Emma wiped the tears from her eyes as she attempted to give him a reassuring smile. "What about you?" she asked. "You love her."

He nodded.

"If she dies, what will become of you?"

Dair attempted to let out a slow breath but it felt tight in his chest and threatened to choke him. He didn't want to think about Serenity dying. He didn't want to give a second's thought to a world without her. "I do not know. I have never experienced loss. The emotions that I've recently begun to feel are new to me, and I will admit that I don't know what I will do if I lose her."

"You deserve her, you know," Emma said gently. "I know you don't think you're worthy of her. My daddy used to tell my mom that all the time. My mama would look at him and say, *stupid man, it is the love we choose to give each other that makes us worthy.* Don't sell yourself short, Sandman. Sure, you have terrible taste in clothes and your job is pretty weird, but you chose to love an imperfect human and she chose to love you. I think that proves that you both are worthy too."

Dair patted her softly on the knee and then stood. Emma truly baffled him at times with her wisdom and knowledge and it left him speechless. "I have to go for a little while. Raphael will stay."

"I'm asking Him too."

Dair's head tilted to the side.

She nodded up toward the ceiling. "The Creator. That's where you're going, right? Well, I'm talking to Him too and asking Him to leave her here with us."

Dair didn't know what to say. Again he was speechless. So he only nodded and then disappeared. Emma was right; he was going to the Creator. He had no clue what he was going to say. But he knew he had to petition Him, to intercede on Serenity's behalf. Dair wasn't sure if he was about to face the wrath of the Creator for his interference, but he would risk it. For her sake, he would risk anything.

Chapter 14

"Dreaming that you are moving toward a bright light does not necessarily mean your time on earth is coming to an end. It could perhaps mean that you have a brilliant idea brewing and don't even know it."

Serenity opened her eyes and felt the warmth of the sun on her skin. She took in a deep, painless breath and smiled as a gentle breeze blew across her face. As she looked around her, she realized she was standing in a large field surrounded by green grass, full trees, and blooming flowers; the landscape around her was nearly too perfect. Perhaps, this was what it was like to be dead. She was surprised to find that the idea that she was indeed dead didn't upset her. She had peace about it, just like when she had decided to move in with her Aunt Darla and Uncle Wayne. She just knew it was the path she was supposed to take.

"Do you think that there is but one path for a person to follow?" A deep voice surrounded her, and though she probably should have been frightened, Serenity found that she couldn't be. Her spirit recognized the one who created her, and she could feel her Creator's love radiating in the very rays of the sun beaming down on her. Serenity hadn't always 'believed' in the Creator, and yet somehow she had always known he was real. Feeling his love now, she suddenly wished she had searched more while she'd been alive. She couldn't see anyone around her, but she could feel him.

"I don't know," Serenity answered honestly. "I've heard people talk about destiny and fate, and I have wondered if someone could stray from the path destined for them. Would there be no opportunity to get back on it? Would there be a plan B?"

"Do you have an answer to your questions?" the Creator asked.

Serenity thought about it. Even though she couldn't feel any physical 'arms,' she felt as though she were being wrapped in a warm embrace—one that was full of love, peace, and comfort. She knew that, as the one that created her, he would want her to fulfill her purpose. After all, her parents had created her physical body, and they cheered her on every step of the way. They held her when she cried, they instructed when she failed, and they believed in her when she doubted herself. If her parents felt that way about her, how much more would the Creator, who created her spirit and ordained every day of her life, care about her. Surely he would give second chances, and third and fourth and fifth for that matter. He knew his children better than anyone, and he certainly knew their propensities to wander. So there had to be more than one way to fulfill her destiny.

"Yes, I think that there must be more than one path, more than one option." She felt his approval. When he said nothing more, she asked her own question. "Is my life over? Was that my path?"

"You fulfilled one purpose in the life given to you," he told her. "There has been an outcry on your behalf by those who love you. I created humans in my image, and therefore their emotions are strong, though they are only a fraction of what I feel. Death is a very difficult truth for them to process, and they see it only as a negative result. They do not consider that in death you are truly being born into a life that will go on forever, spent with me as you were designed to in the beginning. There is no grief, no pain, or disease. There is no anger, hatred, wars, or natural disasters. With me there is only ever peace. That is what death is—simply a new birth into a new life." There was a pause and Serenity thought he might not say anything else. But then his voice rumbled across the field once more.

"I can hear the cries of my people. They desire you to stay with them. But I want to hear from you. Daughter of mine, what is it that you want? What resides in your heart of hearts? Do you feel that there is still a purpose left for you on earth?"

Serenity plopped down ungracefully on the soft grass under the weight of his questions. Those were doozies. He wasn't asking her favorite color or food; he was asking whether she wanted to live or die.

"Does my answer affect the outcome?" she asked.

"It is how it was always to be."

Serenity wasn't sure what that meant. Did that mean that her choice was already decided and had been before he ever asked her, and therefore, the outcome could never have been changed regardless of the cries of her family and friends? She supposed that that was a question she could wrestle with for eternity and never find the answer. Her little brain couldn't even scratch the surface of understanding the Creator, much less form a working knowledge of predestination.

Serenity thought about His words—about how in death she wouldn't experience all the painful things of life. She thought about eternal peace and everlasting joy, but she still couldn't really grasp them. All she had known her eighteen years was the struggles of life on earth. Did she want to go back to that? And if she decided she did, did that make her ungrateful for the gift that the Creator offered in the afterlife? Because if she was truly honest with herself, though she loved the peace she felt now, there was a big part of her that wasn't done living.

"You gave your creations life, right?"

"Yes, child, I created them and blew breath into them."

"So you must have wanted them to live and experience the world that you created. I'm not talking about all the messed up stuff; I don't even want to get into that. I just mean the things that make life worth living—the love of good parents, the miracle of birth, birthday cakes, and dancing with friends. There is such an abundance of life that I still haven't experienced—being proposed to, a wedding, children, and all that comes with them. There is joy in the life you created that I haven't felt and I want to."

"What if those things aren't yours to have in life? If there were no children in your future or no wedding?" He asked and it was a difficult question.

Serenity swallowed down the disappointment and looked past the sorrow of never having those things. There was more to life, wasn't there? It wasn't all about the love of a man and woman or raising children. There had to be more.

"Then I will find joy in the other things. Humans aren't the only thing you created. I mean, you created this huge round ball of water and land and beauty and mystery. There is plenty for me to find purpose in even if I am not to have a husband or children."

"So you have made your choice then?" the Creator asked her.

"I have. I want to live. If there is more for me to do then I want to do it."

Emma's tears had finally stopped. Her tears had flowed until her head hurt as much as her heart. She had rung in the New Year with her aunt being arrested, Rat dying, and Serenity saving Emma's life and fighting for her own. Now as she sat in the dim hospital waiting room with Darla holding her hand and Wayne pacing the already worn path from one end of the room to the other, there were no tears left. What was the point in crying? Tears didn't solve a problem. They didn't bring someone back to life or undo a horrible event. Tears simply left her with an ugly headache and puffy eyes. Just as those thoughts crossed Emma's mind, a memory surfaced of her mother.

"I hate crying. It doesn't fix anything. Mama, why do we have tears?" Emma had once asked.

"God wanted us to be able to wash away the things in this life that bring us pain. He gave us tears because crying is like cleaning the slate. You're right child; tears don't fix whatever it is that might be wrong, but they do cleanse us and help make us ready to move forward."

Emma didn't feel cleansed. Even after all those tears, she didn't feel ready to move forward. She understood what her mama had been saying, but right in that moment the only thing she could see was a friend who had sacrificed herself for her.

"Darla, why is there so much ugly in this world?" Emma asked, her voice raspy from crying.

Emma's small hand was in Darla's and the older woman squeezed it gently. "So that we could appreciate beauty."

"There was nothing beautiful to appreciate tonight."

Darla shook her head. "I have to kindly disagree."

Emma's head turned as she looked up at her. Darla had her full attention because she couldn't imagine, after all the horrible events of the night, anything could possibly be beautiful.

"Serenity loves you like a sister. She loves you so much that she was willing to die so that you wouldn't have to. That is beautiful, Emma Jean. And you are here in this waiting room. Though you're tired, scared, and have no clue what the future holds, you are here waiting because you care about Serenity. That, too, is beautiful. Painful? Definitely, but that doesn't make it any less beautiful."

Glory, who had been quiet most of the time let out a sigh. "Leave it to Darla to find the beauty in this and damn it if she isn't right." She looked at Emma. "Serenity loves you, and it's not hard to see why. You Emma, are beautiful too."

"I don't want her to die," Emma said suddenly and the tears that she thought she couldn't possibly cry anymore welled up again.

"Oh, baby," Darla soothed as she wrapped her arms around Emma. "I know you don't. None of us do. Serenity is like you. She's unique—special—and everyone who meets her knows it. She's also strong and a fighter."

Emma shuddered. "But what if fighting isn't

298

enough? Mama said that we all have a time we're appointed to go. She said that we can't expect to live forever, and when it's time there is no amount of medicine or man's wisdom that can stop it."

Darla pulled back and looked down at her. "I wish I could have known your mama." She smiled and Emma couldn't help the small smile that pulled on her lips. Darla had that effect on people; she was contagious.

"She would have liked you too," Emma agreed.

Darla's face grew serious then as she looked into Emma's eyes. "If this is Serenity's time you have to make peace with that. You have to accept that she lived her life caring about others and died the same way. There is a reason that bullet hit her tonight and not you, Emma. So you grieve and you be angry and you mourn, but then you dry your tears and you figure out what it is that you're supposed to do and you do it."

"What if I can't?" Emma's lip quivered as she tried so desperately to hold herself together.

"You can't, not on your own," Darla's eyes sparkled. "But you aren't alone. You have me and Wayne, Glory and Dair and your very own guardian angel, not to mention all the ladies at the library." She winked at her. "You are surrounded by people who love you and want to see you succeed. Never forget that."

Emma said thank you because she didn't know what else to say, and even that felt so very inadequate for the gratitude she felt. She, Darla and Glory sat in silence after their talk. There was nothing left to say or do but to wait. Finally the doors to the room where Serenity had been taken opened and a very tired looking doctor walked out. Glory and Darla stood and pulled

Emma up with them. They, Wayne, and Raphael all converged on the doctor but none of them said anything.

"You are Ms. Tillman's family?" the doctor asked.

Darla nodded. "She's our niece and she lives with us."

The doctor let out a slow breath. "The bullet that struck your niece was the kind that shatters on impact. So instead of a clean entry and exit, it destroys more than just where it hits. We had to do a transfusion and fix some major arteries. She's stable, but not conscious. As far as we can figure, she must have hit her head when she fell after being shot because she has quite a lot of swelling around her brain."

"When will she wake up?" Wayne asked.

"We don't know if she will."

"Is she going to live?" Darla's voice was tight with emotion.

"Honestly, that remains to be seen. Head injuries are unpredictable. Right now all we can do is wait. The nurses are getting her set up in the ICU. Visiting hours are over, but I've told them to let one of you go back and see her for a few minutes."

The doctor gave his condolences for not having better news before heading back in the direction from which he came. Things were quiet after that as they waited for the nurse. Emma hadn't given much thought to what would happen after that night. The police had allowed Darla and Wayne to take Emma into their custody while they tried to get in touch with DHS, and so she had just assumed that she wouldn't have to deal with those worries for a few days at least. You know what they say about assuming.

The clickity clacking of high heeled shoes echoing

off the quiet hospital walls drew all of their attention. The short, dumpy woman dressed in business attire before them was not the nurse they were expecting.

"Emma Jean?" she asked as she stepped onto the carpeted area of the waiting room.

Darla stood and stepped in front of Emma. "Emma's been placed in our custody for the time being," she said boldly to the short woman.

The woman nodded impatiently and started flipping through a folder. "Yes, yes, the police told me but it seems you won't have to take on the burden; we've found a place for her to go."

"I assure you," Darla said as her voice dropped and Emma heard Wayne mumble *uh-oh* under his breath, "that she is *not* a burden."

The woman, who Emma had figured out was from DHS, simply waved Darla's obvious ire off. "Of course not, of course not. I just mean that you don't have to worry about her. She can come with me." She held out her hand fully expecting Emma to take it.

"Where are you planning on taking her exactly?" Darla asked in clipped tones.

"That's not something I have to discuss with you. Emma is a ward of the state and the state decides what's best for her."

Emma could tell that the woman was getting frustrated that Darla wasn't just hopping on her bandwagon.

"Emma was put into our care by the police, and we plan to pursue to have her placed permanently with us. Why is it necessary for her to go somewhere else if she has a safe place to stay?"

The woman huffed. "There are protocols and rules in place for a reason Mrs.—" She paused.

"Darla, you can call me Darla."

"Mrs. Darla. We can't just give you a child when we don't know anything about you. There are classes you have to take and background checks and—"

"If you took her from us tonight, where would you be taking her?" Darla interrupted.

The woman paused and sifted through the folder again and then tapped something on one of the pieces of paper. "Ah-ha, here it is. It says that her grandfather will be taking custody of her until her next hearing."

"What grandfather?" Darla asked.

The woman continued to read on and then answered. "The father of one Mildred Jones."

Emma's insides tightened as she remembered the conversation she'd had with her aunt about her father. She didn't remember Mildred saying whether or not he was still alive, but regardless of that, he wasn't Emma's grandfather.

"Mildred's father isn't my grandfather," Emma spoke up as she stepped around Darla. "My mom and her sister had the same mama but different daddies."

The woman nodded as though she was listening, but Emma could tell she wasn't. "Blood doesn't really matter at this point. He's the closest thing to a relative we could find, and the state likes to see kids placed with relatives as often as possible."

After several minutes of a silent stare off, the DHS woman rolled her eyes. "Look, I understand that you care about her but I'm doing my job. I was told to come get her and so I am. If I have to call the police to arrest you for interfering in a DHS investigation, then I will, but I'd rather not have to."

Emma looked up at Darla and Wayne and she could see it in their eyes. They would fight for her.

They would stand there facing off with the DHS lady and make her call the police before they would turn her over to the woman. But then they would be arrested and Serenity would be at the hospital alone. Emma couldn't let them sacrifice anymore for her.

She stepped forward and looked the woman in the eyes. "You don't have to call the police. I'll go with you."

"Emma!" Darla's voice was desperate.

She turned and looked up at the woman who had become a mother to her and pasted a smile on her face. "I'll be alright."

"You don't have to go with her," Darla pleaded.

"Yes I do. You guys don't need any more trouble. Serenity needs you."

"She needs you too," Darla told her. "We need you. Don't you want to live with us?"

Emma nodded. "Of course. But we can get it all figured out once Serenity's better." The eight-year-old in her wanted to cry and beg the DHS lady to let her stay. But that wasn't how her mama raised her to act, and she would feel like a fool if she ever did behave that way. So instead she put on a brave face and did what she had to do. She reached up and hugged Darla. She felt Wayne's arms come around them both, and for a few minutes they just stood there holding each other as though the world would fall apart if they let go. The clearing of a throat had them finally releasing each other.

"We will get you back," Darla told her as she squeezed Emma's shoulders. "You belong with us; don't you forget it."

Emma nodded and bit the inside of her cheek to keep from crying.

Glory stepped up then and knelt down so she was face to face with her. Her eyes were full of understanding as she took Emma's hands. "You're strong little one. Don't let anyone kick you down. You keep yourself safe until Darla and Wayne can get you back, okay?"

Emma nodded and gave her a hug. She hadn't known Glory long, but she already loved what she did know.

She turned and looked at Raphael who had been silent throughout the whole exchange. She realized, when the DHS lady turned to look at what Emma was staring at and looked confused, that he had taken on his invisible form. Only she could see him.

"Hope there's room in her car," he told her in his deep voice.

Emma smiled. She knew she probably looked crazy to everyone else, well, except Darla. She was pretty sure Darla knew that Raphael was the real deal.

"What?" he asked. "Surely you did not think that you could get rid of me that easily?"

Emma shook her head at the angel and then turned back to the dumpy lady. "I don't have my clothes with me."

"Don't worry about that, we will get your things. You don't need to go back to your aunt's house." She gave Darla a curt nod. "Thank you for taking care of Emma during this difficult time."

Emma nearly laughed as Darla gave the woman a look that could only be interrupted as one thing—*Go jump in a lake, lady.*

"No need to thank us for taking care of one of our own," Wayne answered before Darla could say something that might get her in trouble.

"Come along then, Emma, we have a long drive and you've already had a long night." The woman turned and began walking away, her shoes once again clacking on the hard floor.

Emma looked back at the people who had become her family. "Give Serenity a hug for me, okay? And you'll let me know when she wakes up, right?" she asked Darla.

Darla nodded as she wiped tears from her eyes. "Of course."

Emma didn't look at her long because she would start crying too. "Raphael is coming with me, Darla," Emma told her, hoping that would help ease some of the strain she could see lining her face. "I'll be fine. I promise." She gave them one last wave before turning to go, with Raphael by her side.

Emma followed the DHS lady and she thought about her words and wondered who she was trying to convince—Darla and Wayne or herself. She had just traded a life with Mildred and all of her mess for a life with the man who had created Mildred and helped make her the mess she was. *Any words of wisdom now, mama?* She thought to herself. The only thing that came to mind wasn't something her mama had said. It was something her daddy had told her. *"People will underestimate you, Emma Jean. Like bringing a tooth pick to a sword fight, they will come unprepared for how to engage someone like you. Your job is to always make sure your weapon is prepared for battle. Your weapon is your mind. Keep it sharp by never doing drugs or drinking. Keep it healthy by feeding it wholesome things. Keep it intact by not allowing in the lies of others."* Emma shook her head at her father's words. "Why couldn't my parents ever just talk like normal parents?" she muttered under her breath.

"Because that would have meant they had a normal child," Raphael answered unexpectedly. They had finally made it out of the hospital and were now walking through the cold parking lot. The DHS lady hadn't stopped typing away on her phone since they got in the elevator.

"So you're saying I'm not normal?" she asked him.

"I'm saying you're extraordinary."

"Who are you talking to, Emma?" The woman asked as she turned back to look at her.

Emma glanced at Raphael from the corner of her eye before looking up at the woman innocently. "My guardian angel."

The woman paused in mid step and tilted her head, examining Emma as if she were a bug under a microscope. After several seconds she shrugged. "Well that's sweet, dear. It's always nice to think someone is watching over us." Her voice was patronizing, as though she were speaking to a little child. Then again—Emma thought—she supposed to the DHS lady, she was just a little child. She didn't realize that Emma had more knowledge in her pinky than the woman had acquired in her entire life. Just as her father had said, the woman had underestimated her.

"Well," Emma began, attempting to hold back the smile. "My mama said that we all *had* to have guardian angels watching over us."

"Oh, why did she think we *had* to?" the DHS lady asked.

"She said we had to have guardian angels because it wasn't a coincidence that God calls us sheep."

The woman paused again and gave her a questioning look, before finally smashing the button on her key fob to a red Honda Accord. "I still don't understand," she said as she motioned for Emma to get in the back seat. "What does being called sheep have anything to do with needing someone watching over us?"

"Sheep are the dumbest animal ever created. They literally cannot survive without a shepherd. In fact sheep are so stupid that they will walk right off the end of a cliff unless something or someone guides them away from it." Emma paused while the woman started the car and fastened her seatbelt. She could tell that the DHS lady was thinking about her words. And because Emma had had a rough night, she couldn't help but mess with the lady just a little more. "So really, if my mama's logic is correct, perhaps, it isn't nice to have someone watching over us. Perhaps, it's actually rather insulting."

Raphael was sitting next to her in the back seat. Of course, the DHS lady had no clue. He looked at Emma and then back to the lady who looked to be in pain as she tried to reason out what Emma had said.

They drove in silence for quite a while before the lady who had mentioned briefly that her name was Frieda, which Emma found odd because she thought she looked more like a Jennifer, finally spoke up. "So what is your answer to the question? Is it nice or is it insulting?"

Emma waited until Frieda's eyes met hers in the rearview mirror and then answered in her best sheep voice. "Baaaaah."

Raphael was shaking his head at her as he laughed. "You know she does not understand what you just did?"

Emma shrugged. "That only adds further proof that my mama was right." Frieda didn't say anything more the rest of the drive.

About an hour later, Raphael turned and looked at Emma. His eyes were somber and his lips tight. "There are more than just sheep in this world, Emma." He paused. "You saw that tonight with Rat and your aunt."

"Wolves in sheep's clothing," Emma muttered as she remembered the inhuman look that had been in Rat's eyes and in her aunt's. Raphael had said they had been possessed by demons, and Emma had no doubt in her mind that they had been.

"I do not understand all that is going on, but I will tell you that the demon I destroyed tonight had a mission, and it was to destroy you. He did not complete that mission."

She looked up at him; her eyes narrowed. "You think the demons want me dead?"

"The evil one wants you dead, for whatever reason, and he will use whatever resources he can to make that happen."

Emma saw Frieda's eyes widen as she glanced in her rear view mirror. Emma tried to give her a sweet, *I'm not crazy*, reassuring smile. The woman shivered and Emma was pretty sure she hadn't succeeded.

"I want you to be aware, Emma. Mildred did not seem to think highly of her father. What did I tell you about the types of people that draw evil to themselves? They are weak minded, easily influenced. That is where the minions go."

Emma understood what the angel was saying, but she didn't understand what made her a target for a bunch of demons.

"We need to get you back in Darla and Wayne's custody as quickly as possible," he continued. "I may have to enlist a friend to help keep an eye on you while

I speak with Darla. Her spirit is open and she believes in the supernatural. She is a good ally to have."

Emma perked up a little. "I get two guardian angels?" Silly? Maybe. She was an eight-year-old genius in DHS custody; she'd take her kicks where she could get them.

Raphael's eye twinkled as he looked down at her. "I told you; you're extraordinary."

Emma rolled her eyes. "One could also argue that a sheep that needs two shepherds is just twice as stupid."

Raphael shook his head at her logic. Emma was one of those rare humans with which he could debate for hours the various angles from which a situation could be viewed. She truly was extraordinary. She settled back in the seat and closed her eyes. There was more he could tell her, more that might help prepare her for whatever it was that was brewing, but she had already been through so much. After having a gun pointed at her and watching her friend be shot, then having to endure being told that she was being taken away from the people she'd come to love as family, she needed a break. She was resilient, and strong, but everyone had a limit. So for now, in the quiet of the car of a woman Emma didn't know, going to a place she'd never been, Raphael would give her the small amount of peace that he could. He laid his hand on her forehead and whispered something in a language only his kind understood and then watched as the sleeping child relaxed. He didn't know what her future held, but he knew that whatever it was he would be by her side. She had lost her mother and her father, and Raphael could not bring them back to her, but he could offer the support and protection that they should have been able to give her.

His attention was drawn away from her when the human female's phone started playing some hideous song. She answered it in the voice Raphael had come to recognize as her own. But after several minutes, her voice changed. He watched the woman called Frieda in the rearview mirror and listened as she spoke.

"I have her. No, there were no problems." There was a pause and then she spoke again. "She mentioned a guardian angel." Pause. "Well then how *was* he destroyed?" She growled in a deep voice.

Raphael tensed. He could not sense a demon in the woman, but he knew something was very wrong.

"It will be taken care of," Frieda huffed. She tossed the phone onto the seat and then glanced back in the mirror at the sleeping form of Emma. Her eyes narrowed before finally looking back at the road. She let out a slow breath as she spoke. "Who are you little one and what have you done?"

Raphael looked down at Emma and then back to Frieda who couldn't hear him. "The better question, human, is what *will* she do?"

"Sometimes your dreams don't mean anything. They are just dreams. It is not wise to put meaning where it does not belong."

Dair knelt, his head bowed low as he approached his Creator. He felt the warmth from his light and the peace that only came in his presence. But that wasn't what he'd come for.

"You know why I've come." His voice was steady, but there was no mistaking the pain in his words.

"I know that you love her," the Creator spoke. "I created her. Think how much more she means to me, Brudair."

"You do not lose her either way. If she lives or she dies, she will still be yours." Dair's words came out in heavy breaths as emotions he was still learning how to control swamped him. "I've only just met her. Her life has just begun."

"What do you want, Brudair?"

"I WANT HER TO LIVE," Dair roared as his shoulders shook. He kept his head bowed though it was an effort to remain kneeling when he wanted to rant and rave over the loss he was feeling.

"Then go tell her that."

Dair's head nearly snapped up.

"You can make each other stronger or weaker," the Creator continued. "She will now be a consideration in every aspect of your life, your choices, and your purpose. She will be a part of you. That is what a mate is. Is she your choice?"

"She is," he answered without pause.

"Then go and find out if you are hers."

When Dair raised his head, he realized that he was no longer in the throne room but now in the quiet hall of the hospital. The clock hanging on the stark white wall said that it was three in the morning, and the sign next to it told him he was in the ICU. He didn't have to ask the nurse at the station where she was, he could feel her. As though they were connected by a rubber band that had been stretch apart and was now rebounding back, she pulled him to her. Dair closed his eyes and when he opened them again, he was standing beside her bed.

The lights on the machines around her blinked on and off like blaring hazard lights warning him to be careful. She was fragile, nearly broken, and he had been unable to save her. Dair reached out a hand and gently brushed some stray hair from her face. She looked peaceful. The pain and fear that had been on her face the last time he'd seen her were gone, replaced by her namesake—serenity. She was his princess of peace and yet she had gone to battle.

"I know it's not fair to ask you to stay. I've seen how dark this world can be. But I've also seen how amazing it can be, and I want to experience those things with you." Dair closed his eyes and pushed his mind into hers, seeking her out in her dreams. He found her sitting by a stream surrounded by trees and a night sky lit up by thousands of stars.

"Why are you still here?" Dair asked her as he sat down beside her.

"I've been waiting on you."

This surprised him. "You couldn't wake up to wait

for me?"

"It's peaceful here," Serenity said as she pointed to the rippling water. "Nobody is pointing guns or threatening innocent little girls." Though she said the words lightly, they were heavy with the weight of her fear and pain.

"And I'm going to ask you to come back to that world." Dair lifted her chin so her eyes would meet his. "But before I do, let me ask you this. What do you want, Sarah Serenity?"

A smile pulled at her lips. "Someone else asked me that today."

"Oh?" Dair tilted his head slightly. "What was your answer?"

She laughed. "You can't possibly ask a girl what she wants and expect her to have only one answer."

Dair shrugged. "I'm still learning." He shuttered as her fingers ran up his arm and across his collar bone to his lips. Her eyes held his and he wouldn't have been able to turn away if he wanted to. She captivated him.

"I want to live, Dair. Whatever that entails, I want it." She paused and suddenly the confidence she had just worn like a comfortable pair of jeans wavered. "And I want you."

Dair would like to say that he remained composed and didn't kiss her senseless in her dream, but he tried not to lie if he could help it. He placed both hands on her face and pulled her close to him. Their lips were nearly touching; both their breaths were coming out in rapid succession as he whispered, "Then you have me." He didn't give her time to respond before pressing his lips to hers. The kiss was fierce, but quick. Dair pulled back and smiled down at her. "Now wake up so I can do that for real."

Dair slipped out of her mind and watched as her eyes blinked. Gradually, they opened. The room was dim and yet she still had to squint against what little light there was. When her eyes finally found his face, her lips spread into a smile so bright that it lit every dark place in his soul.

"Hey," she said.

"Hey." Dair sat on the edge of her bed and traced her jaw with the tips of his fingers. He didn't want to stop touching her, assuring himself that she was alive and with him.

"How is Emma?" Serenity asked as she studied him just as intently as he did her.

"She's safe," Dair assured her, unaware of all that had taken place while he'd been gone.

Serenity smiled. "She deserves to be more than just safe."

"You're right; she does. I have a feeling your aunt and Uncle Wayne make sure that happens. And we will be there every step of the way."

She was quiet, just watching him watch her.

"So what happens now?" She finally asked.

"Well, right now," Dair's voice dropped as he leaned closer. "I'm going to pick up where your dream left off. Everything else can wait."

Just before his lips touched hers, she stopped him with a hand to his chest. "This isn't going to be easy is it?"

He understood that she was talking about a relationship between him, the Sandman, and her, a mortal human. He wouldn't lie to her. "No, beautiful, it isn't going to be easy." Dair leaned in and stole a kiss lingering for just a moment as he let her taste and scent saturate him before whispering, "But I promise it will be worth it." He kissed her again but pulled back when she would have taken it deeper. She was tired and needed rest and that was something he could give her.

"You need to sleep. You will have a room full of people tomorrow all wanting your attention."

"Will you stay? I mean, tonight, stay with me."

"Always," he told her gently.

She smiled up at him and settled back into the pillows of the hospital bed. "Then weave me a dream, Sandman."

He chuckled. "Close your eyes, Princess."

Serenity closed them but one eye snapped open as she said, "And make it a good one."

From the Author

Thank you so very much for taking your time to read Dream of Me! I truly hope that you enjoyed it. I've always found the subject of the Sandman fascinating and though my twist on him was a little different, I hope I did him justice. If you are new to my work, thank you so much for taking a chance on my book! There is so much more to come in this series and the other series that I have written and I hope you will continue on the journey with me! God bless you and yours!

Quinn

Books by Quinn Loftis
Grey Wolves Series
Prince of Wolves
Blood Rites
Just One Drop
Out of the Dark
Beyond the Veil
Fate and Fury
Sacrifice of Love
Luna of Mine

Gypsy Healers Series
Into the Fae
Wolf of Stone

The Elfin Series
Elfin

Rapture
Iniquity (coming soon)

Dream Makers Series
Dream of Me

Stand Alone Works
Call Me Crazy

Stalk Quinn:
www.quinnloftisbooks.com
@AuthQuinnLoftis
Facebook: Quinn Loftis Books

CPSIA information can be obtained at www.ICGtesting.com
Printed in the USA
LVOW08s0231280616

494384LV00005B/161/P